MADRIGALS
AND
MAYHEM

MADRIGALS
AND
MAYHEM

ELIZABETH PENNEY

St. Martin's Paperbacks

This is a work of fiction. All of the characters, organizations, and events portrayed in this novel are either products of the author's imagination or are used fictitiously.

First published in the United States by St. Martin's Paperbacks, an imprint of St. Martin's Publishing Group.

MADRIGALS AND MAYHEM

For information, address St. Martin's Publishing Group, 120 Broadway, New York, NY 10271.

www.stmartins.com

ISBN: 978-1-250-34413-7

Our books may be purchased in bulk for promotional, educational, or business use. Please contact your local bookseller or the Macmillan Corporate and Premium Sales Department at 1-800-221-7945, ext. 5442, or by email at MacmillanSpecialMarkets@macmillan.com.

Printed in the United States of America

St. Martin's Paperbacks edition / December 2024

10 9 8 7 6 5 4 3 2 1

Dedicated to the late Keith Mansfield and Bob Anstee from the Cambridge Memories UK Facebook group. Gentlemen, your help and insights will never be forgotten by this grateful author.

CHAPTER 1

Bells jingled as I slipped out of the bookshop into a frosty December morning. Located in the heart of Cambridge, England, Magpie Lane was quiet at this hour except for Tea & Crumpets, my destination across the cobblestones. Customers were coming and going, travel mugs in hand, or sitting behind the steamy windows, tapping on phones and laptops.

The lane was dressed for the holiday season, and I took in the enchanting sight with a sigh of pleasure. Strings of white lights were wound around trees and lampposts, where kissing balls with red bows hung. Wooden tubs sported trimmed evergreen trees, and decorated shop windows framed piles of enticing gifts.

Christmas in England was a new experience for me, and I was resolved to enjoy every moment. Last spring, my British mother and I had moved from Vermont to help my great-aunt run my family's ancestral four-hundred-year-old bookstore, Thomas Marlowe—Manuscripts & Folios.

A bumping sound turned my attention to our shop window. Puck, a black stray cat who had adopted me, was batting the glass while Clarence, Aunt Violet's tabby, sprawled across a plush snowman as if it were his kill. Laughing, I waved at the cats. "I'll be back soon." Puck's glare said *I doubt it.*

Halfway across the lane, I stopped dead. There were lights on in the toy shop across the street.

Pemberly's Emporium, with its mullioned bow window and extravagant gilded sign, had been closed for over a year, heavy black curtains blocking any view inside, even through the glass front door. Those curtains were now finally open.

Drawn as if by a magnet, I went down the lane to check it out. The shop was in the building past Tea & Crumpets, a Tudor-style timbered structure similar to the bookshop, which had been built in the 1600s.

The window featured toys both vintage and new, and although I was almost thirty years old, my heart skipped a beat. I scanned the display eagerly, taking in dolls of all kinds, miniature trains and wooden trucks, teddy bears and building blocks.

Then I caught my breath. A Victorian dollhouse sat at the back of the window, its three floors with four bays open to view. I bent closer, squinting, studying the furnishings and the dolls dressed in period clothing. This was a far cry from the basic yet beloved dollhouse I'd owned as a child. The furnishings were so incredibly detailed and complete that if I suddenly shrank to a few inches tall, I could walk right in and live there.

Dollhouse books. The idea for a perfect holiday display at the bookshop came to me in a flash. I adored books about dollhouses, and as a librarian, I'd made sure our small-town Vermont library kept classics on the shelves. My absolute favorite, *Charlotte's Dollhouse*, was rather obscure, published in London in the early 1920s, and I'd been lucky to snag the discard copy from the library.

When I got back to the bookshop, I'd scour our shelves and the dealer sites and put together a great assortment. Maybe I'd even find another copy of *Charlotte's Dollhouse*.

Excited about the day ahead, I returned to Tea & Crumpets, definitely ready for a cup of coffee. Daisy Watson, the owner and my best friend, also offered incredible baked goods. I was in the mood for one of her signature scones.

Daisy was behind the counter, talking to a customer, and she waved me over when I walked in. "I was hoping you'd be in this morning," she said. "Molly Kimball, meet Charlotte Pemberly. Molly is the one I was telling you about, Charlotte."

I would have asked what she'd been saying but I was stuck on Charlotte's name. "Pemberly as in the toy shop?"

Charlotte, a striking redhead with green eyes, patted her chest. "That's me. What do you think of the window? I've been working on it for weeks."

Daisy, who knew my standing order, started making a pour-over dark roast coffee. Charlotte already had a to-go cup in hand.

"It's amazing," I said. "I love the mix of toys, and that dollhouse is incredible."

"Isn't it?" Charlotte took a sip from her cup. "It belonged to my great-great-grandmother. My grandfather, who owned the shop, got offers for it all the time. He made me promise never to sell it."

"I wouldn't." The way she'd phrased things, I guessed that her grandfather had died. "So you're taking over for your grandfather?"

The brightness in her gaze dimmed. "I am. Grandad was too ill to run it last year and had to close the shop. Then he died and . . . well, I really shouldn't talk about it."

Shouldn't or couldn't? "I'm sorry for your loss," I murmured, thinking of the recent death of my father. The partnership offer from Aunt Violet had allowed Mum and me to make a new start. Perhaps that was why Charlotte was here now, for a new beginning of her own.

"Thank you." Charlotte's forehead creased. "I should have quit my job and come home sooner. He kept telling me he was going to be fine. He was so proud of me, you see, and my important position at the BBC." Her lips twisted. "I was a production assistant."

"That must have been so interesting." Daisy put my tall coffee on the counter. "Do you want anything from the case, Molly?"

"I do." I stood back and surveyed the offerings. "One cranberry white chocolate scone, please."

"Great choice," Daisy said, her standard remark. She pulled a paper leaf from the box and grabbed the biggest scone. "For here or to-go?"

Seeing me waver, Charlotte said, "If you'd like, Molly, I'll give you a tour of the toy shop after your breakfast."

How could I refuse? "Fantastic. The bookshop doesn't open until ten so I have plenty of time."

"I'll take a scone, too, Daisy," Charlotte said. "Since I'm staying."

We settled at a nearby table to eat. "I love Thomas Marlowe," Charlotte said. "I've been going there since I was a child." She broke off a piece of scone and nibbled.

"That's awesome." I wished I could say the same for myself. "I've only been here since May."

"Oh, I've heard about you, Vermont lovely." Her tone was teasing.

I put a hand to my face. "I do get around, don't I?" Tabloid journalists had coined the nickname when I started dating Kieran Scott, the son of Lord and Lady Scott. As the younger son, Kieran was title-adjacent, which was fine with me. I'd never been a royalty groupie but I have to admit that the situation thrilled me. It was ridiculously fun.

Kieran's bike shop, Spinning Your Wheels, was next door to the bookstore and that's how we met. Daisy was dating his business partner, Tim Ellis, and the four of us often hung out together.

"How did you decide to move to Cambridge?" Charlotte asked.

I gave her the short version, how Aunt Violet had sought our help a few months after my father died. "To be honest, the whole thing was a huge surprise. I didn't even know I still had any English relatives," I found myself saying. "Mum was . . . um, estranged from her parents after she married an American and left England. They're gone now. She does have a brother, though. He's halfway through a divorce from an awful woman. They have one son. He's pretty cool." Which was amazing, considering his mother.

Any mention of such sticky family situations seemed to either push people's buttons or rock their secure little world, so I rarely brought them up. To my relief, Charlotte took my revelations in stride. "Families can be difficult." She rolled her eyes. "Believe me, I know."

"Aunt Violet is amazing, though." I paused for a sip of coffee. "I'm learning so much from working with her. My role includes updating the shop's web presence and social media plus building the children's section. My late uncle Tom, Aunt Violet's brother, specialized in juvenile literature so I'm carrying that tradition on."

"I adore children's books," Charlotte said. "When I was little, I thought I was named after one."

I smiled. "Let me guess: *Charlotte's Dollhouse*?"

Charlotte nodded. "My great-great-grandmother, who owned the dollhouse, was called Charlotte and I was named after her. I thought my name came from the book." She shrugged. "Not such a stretch. The dollhouse in the book looks exactly like ours."

I thought back to the dollhouse in the toy shop. "You're right. It does." After another bite of scone, I asked, "Do your parents live in Cambridge?"

Charlotte shook her head. Not meeting my gaze, she said, "They died when I was nine. A car accident. My grandfather was my only blood relative left."

"I'm sorry," I said softly. And here I sometimes felt sorry for myself for losing one parent. She'd lost both— and at such a young age.

"Yeah." Charlotte breathed out a sigh. "I'm an orphan now." Her lips twisted. "Well, sort of." She cast her eyes up, thinking, then nodded. "Yeah, I definitely am. Kind of like Cinderella, actually."

It took me a second. "Bad step-relatives?"

Charlotte looked both ways before leaning across the table. "Heinous is the word. They're an absolute nightmare."

Before she could elaborate, Daisy came up to the table. "How's it going? My helper is here so I can go next door anytime you're ready."

I glanced at the counter, where a student with lavender-striped hair was now waiting on people. "I'm almost done." I took the last couple of bites and washed them down with coffee, then cleared our dishes while Daisy wiped the table.

Charlotte fished through her handbag and pulled out a set of keys. "Let's go."

As we walked to the toy shop, Charlotte gestured toward the building's second floor. "I'm planning to live upstairs. I've almost got it cleaned up." She inserted a key in the front door lock. "No one has lived there for ages. Grandad had a house here in the city."

"Have you been staying there?" Daisy asked.

"I couldn't." Charlotte unlocked the door and pushed it open. "Go ahead."

Again, I wondered at her choice of words. Had she been too upset to stay at her grandfather's house? Or were some of the relatives she'd alluded to staying there?

The toy shop was nice and warm from the hot air gusting out of floor vents. We stood for a moment near the door, taking in the displays. The space was more long than wide and almost every inch was filled with fully stocked shelves or rotating racks. Toys were even hanging from the ceiling.

"I could spend days in here," I said. "Was it left like this or have you been adding inventory?"

"Most of it was here." Charlotte went to the wooden front counter and tucked her handbag underneath. "A lot of what we sell is vintage so fortunately it didn't need to be updated. I only had to add some of this year's popular toys."

"Cute shop clerk you have there." Daisy nodded toward the three-foot-tall stuffed bear sitting on a stool behind the counter. He wore a bow tie and a Santa hat.

Charlotte turned with a laugh. "That's Griffin. He's the shop mascot. See?" She held up a brown paper bag printed with the store logo, which included a sketch of Griffin. "We dress him up for each season."

"What fun." Although dying to take a closer look at the dollhouse, I politely followed as Charlotte gave us a tour through the store.

As we reached the rear, Charlotte said, "We have a stockroom back here as well as a break room and loo." She stepped through a dark doorway and flipped on a switch.

Then she jumped backward with a scream. "What are *you* doing here?"

CHAPTER 2

Daisy and I crowded through the doorway to see a young man wearing jeans and a sweater sprawled on an orange vinyl sofa, his eyes at half-mast. Empty plastic drink bottles lay scattered on the floor and a bakery box sat on the coffee table. Party for one?

The young man groaned, clutching his stomach, and a whiff of vomit drifted to my nose. *Ugh.* I bumped into Daisy, who was also backing away.

"Who is he?" I asked. "Is he drunk?" I couldn't think why else he would be so sick.

"Maybe." Watching where she stepped, Charlotte made her way to the sofa. "Barnaby." She pushed at his shoulder. "Barnaby. You need to leave."

"Is he your boyfriend?" Daisy asked.

"No. My grandfather's step-grandson." Charlotte peered closely at Barnaby's face. "He doesn't look right. His face is *green*."

With a sigh, Daisy edged past me and went over to the sofa. "It could be alcohol poisoning. We'd better call an ambulance."

"If so, where is the alcohol?" Charlotte pointed out. "I only see energy drinks." Bravely, she bent close and inhaled. "I don't smell any booze."

I took a few steps into the room. "Is it something he ate? Maybe he's allergic."

Daisy turned and flipped the bakery box open. "Tea cakes. Most of them are gone." She picked up a card lying next to the box. "Huh. This card is from my shop. It says, 'Enjoy.'"

I took the card, recognizing the Tea & Crumpets logo. "Those cakes came from your shop?"

Daisy wrinkled her nose as she studied the confections. "Nope. I never use blue frosting. It doesn't appeal to me."

So someone had deliberately tried to give the wrong impression regarding the cakes and where they had come from. Very strange. Nefarious? Maybe. I took a picture of the card with my phone.

Charlotte pulled a phone out of her jeans pocket. "I'm calling nine-nine-nine. He's not breathing that great." The front door bells jingled. "Molly, can you tell whoever it is that we're closed?"

"Sure thing." I hurried out into the main room, weaving through the displays and trying to locate the customer.

A thin young woman with short black hair was standing in front of the dolls. She glanced at me with curiosity. "Is Charlotte here?"

"She is, but she's busy right now," I said. "The store isn't open yet," I added when she took a baby doll off the shelf. Not to mention we had a backroom emergency.

"I know." She put it back. "I want to talk to Charlotte. She's my, um, step-cousin. Who are you?"

Another step-relative? "Are you related to Barnaby?"

Her brows rose. "Yeah. He's my brother. Well, adopted—"

I gestured. "Come with me. He's in the back room and really sick. We're calling an ambulance."

She started running, leaving me to follow at a more normal pace. By the time I arrived at the back room, she and Charlotte were facing off.

"What are you doing here, Tori?" Charlotte asked.

Tori pointed at her brother. "Looking for him. He wasn't home last night." She leaned over him and touched his face. "He's all clammy. Is he going to be okay?"

Charlotte sighed. "I sure hope so. The ambulance will be here any minute." As Tori continued to fuss over Barnaby, she tilted her head toward the main room. "Let's give them some space."

Once out of earshot, Charlotte clenched her fists and said through gritted teeth, "What is he doing here? I knew I should have changed the locks."

"He broke in?" I asked. That put a whole new spin on the circumstances.

"Well, he used a key, I'm sure," Charlotte said. "There's a whole lot more to the story." She glanced toward the open doorway. "Now is not the time to talk about it."

Flashing lights outside the front window caught my eye. An ambulance was easing down the alley.

"I'd better go meet them," Charlotte said, striding away.

Daisy and I looked at each other. "Should we leave?" I asked.

She shook her head. "Not yet. After the medics examine him." Frowning, she chewed at her lower lip.

"What are you thinking?" I could tell something was weighing on my friend's mind. She shook her head again, turning as the front door opened and two medics came in, with medical bags and a gurney.

"He's back here," Charlotte said, leading the way.

"This place is cool," the male medic said. "I haven't been in here for years."

"Thanks," Charlotte said. "I'm reopening this week."

Charlotte showed them into the back room, and Tori moved aside so they could work. "We came in, what?" Charlotte glanced at us. "Fifteen, twenty minutes ago? We didn't find him right away. Only when we came back here, to this part of the store."

Daisy and I nodded to confirm this. "We found him lying on the sofa, obviously ill," I said. "He had even thrown up."

"I had no idea he was in the store," Charlotte told them. "I didn't stop in before I met Molly and Daisy at the tea shop this morning."

"When was the last time you were in the shop?" the female medic asked.

"Yesterday evening around five or six. He wasn't here when I locked up and went home."

Had he been hiding upstairs, perhaps? If so, why? What possible business could he have in the toy shop?

The medics were now taking Barnaby's vital signs and although they were careful not to say much, I caught their concerned glances. The male medic spoke into his chest radio. "Preparing for transport."

"You're taking him to the hospital?" Tori burst out. She'd been standing to one side and watching, her eyes wide with fear.

"We are," the female medic said. "And you are . . . ?"

"His sister," Tori said. "Tori Winters. Can I meet you there?"

"Of course," the medic said.

Working together, the medics rolled Barnaby out of the break room and through the store. Charlotte and Tori accompanied them.

"Should we leave now?" I asked Daisy.

She was still staring at the box of cakes. "Go ahead, if you want. I need to talk to Charlotte first."

"I'll stay, then," I decided. "Want to go out front?"

We stood near the windows, watching as the medics loaded Barnaby into the back of the ambulance while Tori and Charlotte looked on. I was close to the doll-house so I took a peek inside, marveling at the intricate detail. A cook doll stood in the kitchen, pots and pans on the stove. In the dining room, a man sat at the table holding a miniature newspaper; a cake and a tea set were on the table.

The ambulance doors shut and lights whirled as the ambulance began to amble up the alley. Charlotte came back inside and we all stared at each other for a moment. Charlotte shook her head. "I didn't expect that this morning."

"I hope he'll be okay," I said.

Charlotte checked her phone. "Tori promised to call me as soon as they know what's going on." She put the phone down with a sigh. "What a mess."

"What *is* going on?" I asked tentatively. Although it was none of my business, I had so many questions.

She gestured toward stools near the counter. "If you have a few minutes, I'll tell you."

Daisy and I sat. Charlotte paced behind the counter, organizing papers and small toys. "Sorry. I think better when I move." She offered us a mug holding small candy canes and we each took one.

"To really understand, we have to step back five

years," Charlotte said. "My grandfather married a horrible woman."

"I'm sorry." I could definitely relate to this situation. The horrible woman part, I meant, thinking of Aunt Janice.

"I mean, she's impressive. Not only is she scary smart and attractive, she's a professor of Renaissance music, an expert in the field. Consults for films and plays. By the way, my grandfather was her third husband." She paused. "The other two died."

Naturally my suspicious mind jumped to conclusions. Could she be a black widow? Losing one husband was bad enough, but three?

Charlotte continued to pace, a sign that her emotions were churned up. "She came with some baggage, namely her daughter-in-law Dorcas, also a professor, and Dorcas's kids, Barnaby and Tori. All of them are *awful*." She shook her head.

"Then, about a year ago, my grandfather came to his senses. He kicked his wife out and changed his will back to me as sole beneficiary."

"They fought it," I guessed. What a messy situation it must have been.

"Uh-huh. You see, he got sick right after that happened. So Althea moved back in to 'take care of him.' She would only let me visit once in a while. And when I did, she or one of the others was always in the room with us." Charlotte's eyes filled with tears. She pulled a few tissues from a box. "So, after he died," she croaked, "they found out about the will, of course." She paused to blow her nose. "It was so awful. Althea demanded a share, as his wife. The others . . . well, Dorcas is deeply in debt and her kids had 'expectations,' you might say."

I could easily imagine the situation. Not only was Charlotte dealing with a terrible loss, she had people fighting her for the inheritance. "What happened?"

"We all got lawyers, of course." A wry smile twisted her lips. "I won. So they started looking for the doll, a plan B of sorts. That's why Barnaby was here, I'm sure of it."

Daisy's brows rose in inquiry. "Because of a doll?"

Charlotte nodded. Picking up her phone, she scrolled to a picture of a beautiful blond doll dressed in furs, with a little dog also wearing a coat. "This is a rare handmade Madame Alexander doll. Only half a dozen exist." Taking the phone back, she studied the picture. "Grandad invested a lot in the doll, before it skyrocketed in value. He told me he wanted me to have it. Now they're trying to steal it."

I glanced around the shop, asking the obvious question. "Where is it?" At the bookshop, we locked the most valuable books in a case.

She shrugged. "I don't know. He hid it somewhere, probably realizing it would disappear otherwise."

"He didn't put it in a safe deposit box?" Daisy asked, frowning.

"Nope, even though I suggested it. He was worried Althea would get to it somehow." Charlotte's expression was haunted. "I even thought at times that his mind was going. Maybe not, right?" She moved a stack of manila folders to reveal a copy of *Charlotte's Dollhouse*, which she held up. "The last time I saw him, he gave this to me and said, 'Remember how we used to read this together? Read it again and think of me.'"

A thought struck me. "I might be reading too much

into it," I said. "Pun intended. What if there is a message for you in the book? About the doll, I mean." It wouldn't be the first time I'd found clues to mysteries between the lines of a story.

Charlotte stared at the book. "Really? You think so?"

"Molly could be right," Daisy said with enthusiasm. "If they wouldn't let you be alone with him so he could tell you where the doll was, he might have come up with a different way to get the message across."

My thoughts returned to Barnaby. I had two questions—what was wrong with him and how had he gotten inside the shop?

"If Barnaby had a key, you ought to change the locks." I glanced up at the ceiling. "Put in some cameras and an alarm system, too."

Charlotte nodded. "Yeah. It's time. I didn't think he'd go that far, to actually trespass." She put on a snooty accent. "They're so respectable, you know." Returning to her normal voice, she said, "He could lose his place at St. Aelred if I pressed charges. He really is an idiot."

So Barnaby was a student. I was familiar with St. Aelred due to a murder case I'd found myself involved with. "Does Tori go there, too?"

"No, she's at St. Hildegard's. Under the wing of her mother and grandmother."

"My great-aunt went to St. Hildegard's," I said. Maybe she knew Althea. Besides the college connection, she might have met her through the bookshop. Academics were among our best customers. Not a surprise since Cambridge had more than thirty colleges.

Flashing lights up the alley caught my attention, and

I moved to the window to see what was going on. A police car was easing down the cobblestones.

I really wasn't surprised when it rolled to a stop in front of the toy store. Barnaby's illness was definitely out of the ordinary. "We have company."

CHAPTER 3

Charlotte and Daisy hurried to join me at the window. Fear flashed over Charlotte's face when she saw the officers getting out of the car. "What are they doing here?" She grabbed my arm. "Do you think Barnaby *died*?"

"I hope not." I recognized one of the officers, which only made me more nervous. Sergeant Gita Adhikari usually worked with Detective Inspector Sean Ryan on murder investigations. Constable Derby was with her, not Sean Ryan, which eased my concerns somewhat.

Constable Derby, burly with a shaved head, rapped at the door. He noticed us through the window, a smirk sliding across his beefy face. Charlotte hurried to answer.

"Can I help you?" By her composure and the coolness of her tone, no one would guess how upset she was.

Gita displayed her warrant card. "Cambridge police. May we come in?"

Charlotte eyed the identification but didn't move. "What is this in regard to?"

The sergeant narrowed her large brown eyes in annoyance. As on the other times I'd seen her, she was immaculately put together, from her glossy French twist to polished court shoes. She glanced beyond Charlotte and noticed me and Daisy. The frown deepened. "What are you two doing here?"

Charlotte whirled around. "You know her?"

"We've met," I said. "During a case . . . or three." Speaking to Gita, I said, "Daisy and I were getting a tour of the shop when we found Barnaby on the couch in the break room."

Gita nodded. "Miss Pemberly? I need to speak to you about Barnaby Winters. May we come in?"

Charlotte sagged against the doorway. "Is he . . . dead?"

"Why do you ask?" Gita gave no quarter. She was even tougher than Ryan, who was no picnic to deal with.

"Well"—Charlotte waved her arm—"because you're here. I'm guessing you're not here to tell me he's all better. Right?" She moved back from the doorway with a gesture, indicating they could enter.

The officers entered, glancing around at the shop. Despite their being on duty, I saw a glimmer of delight in their eyes. No one could resist a toy shop, not even a hardened police officer.

Gita looked pointedly at me and Daisy. "Don't you two have somewhere to be?"

"No," Daisy said, surprising me and the officers. I'm usually the obstinate and outspoken one. "I have something I need to discuss with you."

"I want them to stay," Charlotte said. "They have a right to hear the update, whatever it is."

Constable Derby looked at his superior for a cue. Finally, she sighed. "All right. Derby, can you take notes? I want to see where you found him."

We all trooped through the store to the back room.

Once we got there, Charlotte gave them the play-by-play while we chimed in with details.

The pair nosed around the room, examining the cakes and the drink bottles, even the pool of sickness. "Derby, evidence bags." Gita pulled out a pair of gloves and put them on, then examined the cake box. She picked up the card, read it, and threw Daisy a look.

"That's what I wanted to talk to you about," Daisy said. "The card obviously came from my shop. Those cakes did not."

Gita glanced down at the cakes. "How do you know? You sell tea cakes, don't you?"

Daisy gave her a closed-lip smile. "I don't use blue frosting. Ever."

"That's odd," Derby said. "It's my favorite."

My friend shuddered. "Tell me a food that's naturally blue. Besides a blueberry and they're much darker than that." She jabbed a finger at the pale blue frosting.

Gita made a slicing movement. "Derby, the kit." The constable hurried from the room. "Miss Watson, I'll take a statement from you, noting that you deny making the cakes."

Daisy lifted her chin. "I certainly do."

Charlotte waved. "Hold on, everyone. Why are the cakes so important? Won't you please give me an update on Barnaby?"

Gita huffed a little, her nostrils flaring. "Barnaby was poisoned and he's lucky to be alive. It's very possible that the poison was in the cakes."

"Poisoned?" Charlotte's mouth opened and closed a couple of times. "Why would he bring poisoned food here and eat it?"

A very good question, and as I pondered it, an appalling realization dawned. No other scenario made any sense. "Charlotte, whoever poisoned the cakes wasn't trying to kill Barnaby. They were hoping *you* would eat them."

A dead silence fell over the room. Then the officers and Charlotte began to talk over each other, protesting and exclaiming.

The sergeant clapped her hands. "Quiet!" she bellowed. Once the other two shut up, she said, "Mo— Miss Kimball, what makes you say that?"

"Think about it," I said. "Charlotte has been busy getting ready to open up the store. Someone leaves a treat, pretty little cakes, with a nice card. Thinking they're from Daisy, she eats them. There is no reason on earth, as Charlotte said, for Barnaby to break in here and bring refreshments. He must have—"

"Hold it," Gita said. "He broke in?"

Charlotte answered. "Yes, he did. He's not supposed to be in here. He knows that." Her cheeks flamed with heat. "I told the whole family to stay out. To stay away from me. In fact, I'm ready to file a protective order."

Constable Derby chose that moment to return. "Oh, my. That's a serious matter. Protective order against your own family."

Gita didn't look pleased at his comment but before she could say anything, Charlotte turned on him. "They're not my family. They're my grandfather's step-relatives. They tried to take my inheritance and now they're trying to steal from me."

"What do you mean?" Gita asked. "Do you keep money here?"

Charlotte huffed a sigh. "No. I'm not even open yet and when I am, I certainly won't keep cash here. My grandfather left me a valuable doll and they're after it." Constable Derby looked highly amused by the idea of a doll with value. His eyes bugged out with amazement when she went on. "It's worth hundreds of thousands of pounds. And before you ask, I have no idea where it is. My grandfather hid it."

Gita blinked. "If they trespass again, call us and we'll arrest them. If you really want to go that route."

"I might have to," Charlotte mumbled. After a moment, she asked, "Is Barnaby going to be all right? I mean, I certainly don't wish him ill."

"That's not for me to say." Gita's tone was repressive. "Now, if you'd step out, Miss Pemberly, we need to get to work."

Charlotte's response was to bolt from the room. A moment later, I heard her talking on the phone. To Tori, judging from what I overheard.

Daisy and I followed. "I suppose I should get back to the tearoom," Daisy said. She put a hand to her forehead. "I can scarcely wrap my mind around all this."

"Neither can I." To think we'd only wanted to look around the toy shop. Maybe take a close look at the dollhouse and even play with it. Now we were embroiled in a possible attempted murder.

Charlotte hung up as we approached. "Barnaby is holding his own," she said, relief evident in her voice. "Tori thinks he'll make it."

Daisy and I exchanged smiles. "That's really good news," I said. "Can you keep us posted?"

"Definitely." Charlotte turned back to her phone. "Daisy, I have your number. Can I get yours, Molly? I am so glad you two were here with me this morning. I honestly didn't expect to find Barnaby lying deathly ill in my back room." Her expression grew grim. "What if I hadn't come in today?"

He might well have died, alone and in pain. I provided my digits and when she texted me back, I added her to my contacts. "Listen, Charlotte," I said tentatively. "Don't take this the wrong way, but I think you need to get an attorney. It's possible that charges will be brought."

Her brows drew together. "Won't that make me look guilty?"

"Not at all," Daisy said crisply. "It's the smart thing to do under the circumstances. Even if you didn't poison the cakes, which of course you didn't, it still happened in your shop."

Charlotte put a hand to her mouth. "I might be found liable? Oh no." Her face crumbled.

"You have business insurance, right?" At Charlotte's nod, Daisy went on. "You might also need an attorney to help you navigate a serious insurance claim."

Anger snapped in Charlotte's eyes. "I suppose you're right. Will it ever end? That family is going to be the death of me."

"Not while we're around." Daisy gave her a hug. "Talk later?"

Charlotte gave her a squeeze, then turned to me. "Thank you, Molly."

"I'm not sure I did much," I said, returning the hug. I guess moral support counted for a lot at times, though.

Charlotte went over the counter and picked up her copy of *Charlotte's Dollhouse*. "You said there might be clues in here. Do you mind looking through for me? Maybe a fresh set of eyes will spot something."

I didn't have my faith in my ability to figure anything out but I took the book anyway. "I'll do my best."

"Molly has solved lots of mysteries," Daisy said. "She's amazing."

I really wished she hadn't said that. Nothing like setting up expectations. "I'll look through it tonight."

Outside the store, we gave each other a hug of solidarity and promised to touch base later before going our separate ways.

Magpie Lane was coming to life now. Lights were on at Spinning Your Wheels and a delivery truck was parked near the pub, which opened for lunch. There was also a work vehicle parked in the alley between the bookshop and the next building, and as I got closer, I recognized my uncle's van. He was a roof thatcher, an intriguing profession that was going strong. I still found it hard to believe that straw or bundles of river reeds could form an adequate layer.

The cats were gone from the window, which meant action elsewhere. "Hello," I called as I stepped inside the bookshop. "I'm home."

"We're in the kitchen," Aunt Violet called back.

The kitchen was in the back of the store, so I wound through the warren of shelves to the door, which was propped open.

My petite great-aunt, who had high-piled white hair usually hiding a pencil or two, was standing near the AGA, watching as my mother, Nina, and Uncle Chris hovered over a metal trunk. Uncle Chris was wielding a bolt cutter, attempting to remove the padlock securing the lid. If you didn't know they were siblings, you might guess. Both were lean and wiry, with dark hair shot with threads of gray. Clarence and Puck were sitting nearby as well, keeping a close eye on the proceedings.

"What's up?" I asked. Aunt Violet mimed gestures asking if I wanted tea and I nodded. My coffee had worn off long ago and I needed the boost.

Uncle Chris glanced up. "Hello, Molly. Finally got

around to bringing over your mum's trunk. Been in the attic for years."

"Things from your childhood?" I guessed. This was interesting. Uncle Chris now lived in my grandparents' house, which my mother had left over thirty years ago. She'd gone off to college and never returned home. Instead, she'd married an American and moved overseas.

"Yes," Mum said, her tone terse. Any reminder of my grandparents or her childhood still upset her. She and my uncle hadn't exactly been close until he'd apologized for how he'd treated her over the years, if mostly by default. He'd been the favorite, content to bask in family approval and support.

"Why was it locked?" I asked. "Did you do that, Mum?"

She shook her head. "Not I. That trunk used to be in my bedroom. I was pretty sure all my stuff was gone. Either thrown away or sold in a rummage sale."

Uncle Chris had a funny look on his face and I wondered if he knew something about Mum's belongings. With a snap of the cutters, the padlock hasp broke. "Ah. There we go." He put the cutters down and removed the rest of the lock. With a creak of his knees, he got to his feet. "It's all yours."

"Tea?" Aunt Violet asked him as Mum took his place.

"Don't mind if I do." Uncle Chris pulled out a chair at the long kitchen table. "Be a nice warm-up before I head out into the cold."

"Are you thatching today?" I asked, thinking it would be a chilly job.

"I am." He added milk to his cup and stirred. "North of the city."

Mum was leafing through the trunk and I went to stand beside, curious about its contents. "My favorite books," she crowed, holding up copies of *The Wind in the Willows* and *James and the Giant Peach*. "Can you put these on the table, please?"

I did as she asked, stacking them. A set of C. S. Lewis Narnia books and *The Doll's House* by Rumer Godden followed. "Oh, this reminds me," I said, holding up Godden's book. "I want to do a special display of books featuring dollhouses for Christmas. You should see the dollhouse across the street, at the toy store. That's what inspired me."

"I have seen it," Aunt Violet said. "Many times. It's delightful. The store is opening again? I wondered if it would after Arthur died."

"Charlotte Pemberly, his granddaughter, is taking over." Seeing that Mum didn't have any more books to give me, I sat down.

"Saw an ambulance over there when I came down the alley," Uncle Chris said. "Everything okay?"

I groaned to myself. I'd been hoping to wait until he was gone to hash everything over with Mum and Aunt Violet. I didn't know my uncle well enough to do that with him.

"I think so," I said. "Charlotte's, um, cousin was taken ill. She gave me and Daisy a tour of the shop this morning." *And an earful.*

Mum was sorting through clothing now, everything she flapped in the air releasing the fragrance of mothballs. "Where is it?" she muttered.

"It's the perfect time of year to open a toy shop," Aunt Violet said. "Pemberly's has always been the best one in Cambridge. The mix of vintage and new toys is brilliant."

"Totally is," I said. "I could spend days in there."

Down at our feet, Mum made a sound of disgust. "It's not here." Her tone sharpened. "Chris."

Brows raised, he turned in his chair. "Yes, Nina?"

"My Sasha doll is missing." My mother's chin wobbled. "Where did she go? Mum knew she was my favorite."

CHAPTER 4

"I have no idea," my uncle said. "Honestly. I never even looked through that trunk."

"Did someone else?" Mum asked. "Someone must have taken her." She stabbed a finger at the trunk. "I know she was in there when I left."

Uncle Chris spread his hands. "No idea. It's been thirty years, Nina. It's only because I decided to scope out the attic that I even found your trunk."

If it was locked, how did he know it was hers? I was about to ask when I saw the stenciled letters on the lid: NINA.

Mum grunted in disbelief and annoyance but dropped the subject. She closed the lid and washed her hands at the sink. "Any more tea in the pot?"

As an answer, Aunt Violet filled a mug for her. Mum pulled out a chair and sat, moodily staring into her cup.

Uncle Chris finished his and stood. "Well, I'd best be off." He nodded at Aunt Violet. "Thanks for the cuppa." He clapped a cap on his head and shrugged on a canvas jacket.

"Hold on, Chris," Mum said. He braced himself as though expecting a further scolding about the doll. His shoulders visibly lowered when she said, "Christmas. I do hope you and Charlie can join us for dinner."

"That's so nice of you," he said. "We'd love to come. Let me bring the Pimm's, okay? And whatever else you'd like us to contribute." Pimm's No. 3 brandy combined with apple juice and spices was a classic winter hot drink.

"I'll text you," Mum said. "We're still working on the menu."

Uncle Chris shifted his feet, indicating there was more. "Er, I do have a question." Mum made a go on gesture. "Janice . . . well, we're talking again. If—if things work out, is she invited to dinner?"

What could we say? None of us liked Janice but she was family.

"Of course," Mum said through tense lips. "Keep us posted."

"I will." He nodded at us. "Good day, all."

He went out through the French door to the garden, to access the alley that way. In the fraught silence after his exit, my belly rumbled. Loudly.

Aunt Violet bit her lip, sending me an amused look. Mum didn't even react. She was staring into space, frowning. "Didn't you have any breakfast?" Aunt Violet asked.

"A scone, that's all." I thought about scrambling an egg and eating it on buttered toast. Yes, that's what I wanted right now. Comfort food. "You will not believe what happened at the toy shop today," I said conversationally as I got up and went to the fridge. Cheddar would be a great addition to my egg, I decided. Plus a couple of mushrooms.

"What happened at the toy shop?" Aunt Violet prompted me.

"Attempted murder." I cracked the egg into a bowl, waiting for the reaction. I wasn't disappointed.

"What on earth?" My announcement had startled Mum out of her funk. "Can't let you go anywhere."

"Ain't that the truth?" As I continued to make my breakfast, I filled them in, blow-by-blow, from our arrival at the toy shop to being dismissed by the police. I also told them about the fight for the inheritance and the bad blood between Charlotte and Althea's clan.

"Is Barnaby going to be all right?" Mum looked worried.

"I don't know. I sure hope so." Butter sizzled and I added sliced mushrooms to the pan. "I really don't like the fact that they used one of Daisy's cards."

"They were trying to hurt Charlotte," Aunt Violet said in a decisive tone. "It's plain as the nose on your face."

"I think so, too." I gave the mushrooms a stir. "Poor Charlotte would have thought the cakes were a shop-warming gift." Would the police see it that way, or were they going to blame Charlotte for poisoning Barnaby?

"His greed got the best of him," Aunt Violet said. "Unfortunately, the apple doesn't fall far from the tree."

Mum's brows rose. "Tell us what you really think."

Aunt Violet gave a rueful chuckle. "Chalk it up to experience. Althea has always had her eye on the main chance, long as I've known her. I also heard that her son left a lot of debts when he died unexpectedly. His wife has been struggling ever since. I'm sure they were counting on Arthur's money."

"So you do know Althea," I concluded, pouring a golden stream of eggs into the pan. "I thought you might."

The response was a snort. "She was a year ahead of me, the queen bee of that cohort." Aunt Violet stood abruptly. "Hold on. I'll get the photo album."

"Awesome." I was glad that Aunt Violet had kept photographs from her college days. During a prior murder case, they had helped us research the people involved.

By the time she returned, I was seated at the table, digging into the scrambled eggs. "Sorry," she said. "I forgot where I put this." She set a large black album on the table between Mum and me and began flipping pages.

"The cast of *Madrigals and Mayhem*. There I am." Aunt Violet chuckled as she pointed to her younger self, dressed in a medieval gown and a hat that resembled a folded towel.

"Love the outfit." I studied the other actors. "Where's Althea?" Aunt Violet tapped the picture right in the center. "So she literally was the queen," I joked.

"Of course. She wrote the play, you see. And selected the music. She's made a fine career as an expert in Renaissance music."

"That's what Charlotte said. That she's not only a professor but has consulted for movies and plays." I took a closer look at Althea, who had impeccable posture and a proud, almost haughty expression on her bold features. Looking so aloof and intimidating might have been due to her role . . . or not.

"*Madrigals and Mayhem*?" Mum said. "I just saw that mentioned somewhere." She picked up her phone and began scrolling. "Here it is. They're looking for volunteers to round out the cast. Dorcas Winters is the contact."

Aunt Violet nodded. "That's the daughter-in-law I

mentioned. Barnaby's mum. I saw in the alumni news that they were bringing the madrigals back to St. Hildegard's. Dorcas has dusted off the play with a rewrite and Althea is directing, of course. She's even got the BBC interested in filming it as part of *A Christmas in Cambridge*."

"That's amazing," Mum said. "Maybe we should go."

"If we can get tickets," Aunt Violet sounded doubtful. "With the Beeb involved, all the college bigwigs will be attending."

"I've heard of madrigals," I said, "but I'm not quite sure what they are."

"Madrigals are part-songs for groups of a cappella singers," Aunt Violet explained. "They originated in Italy and later became popular in England. Althea's production featured a Renaissance royal court, starring the Lord of Misrule as master of ceremonies."

"The Lord of Misrule." I looked at the photos again. As I thought, a certain young man had played that role back in the day, belled cap and all. I grinned. "How perfect."

"What?" Then she recognized the student. "Oh, of course. Sir Jon." Sir Jonathon Yeats, MI6 agent turned bookseller and, Mum and I thought, in love with Aunt Violet.

"He brought the house down," Aunt Violet said. "Now *there's* someone who can stand up to Althea. The rest of the cast were afraid of her." She considered. "Except me. I abhor bullies."

"So do I." The picture Charlotte had sketched of family dynamics was becoming clearer: Althea had tried to bully Charlotte into giving up her inheritance. Would Althea escalate to murder? It was possible.

"Too bad she's so awful. Otherwise it might be fun

participating in the madrigal dinner." In Vermont, I'd been in a caroling group that performed during our town's holiday celebrations.

"You have the voice for it, Molly," Mum said. Her smile was teasing. "If you change your mind."

"Probably not." I'd find other ways to enjoy the season. Pushing back from the table, I carried my empty plate to the sink.

"Can you please snap on the kettle?" Aunt Violet asked. "We'll make a fresh pot."

I did as she asked, then rinsed my plate and put it in the dishwasher. I was washing my frying pan by hand when Aunt Violet asked, "When did Barnaby go into the shop?"

"We're not exactly sure. Charlotte said she left around five or six last night. So sometime between then and this morning." I rinsed and dried the pan and hung it on the rack.

She brought the teapot over to the sink to rinse out the leaves and add fresh ones. "When I got up in the middle of the night for the loo, there were a couple of people in the alley near the toy shop."

My pulse gave a leap. "What did they look like?"

Measuring tea leaves, Aunt Violet shrugged. "I couldn't see much. They were about the same height, wearing trousers and those jackets with hoods. I thought they were coming from the pub." There was an alley at the end of the lane that cut through to an adjacent street.

"They might have been." Or it had been Barnaby with a friend—or Tori. It made sense they'd waited until after most people were asleep to go inside the shop. It probably also meant that Barnaby had been lying deathly ill on that sofa for hours. It was fortunate that we'd found him when we did. I shuddered at the thought of Charlotte finding him deceased.

I wondered if Aunt Violet should tell the police what she'd seen. Unfortunately, since she couldn't identify Barnaby or the other person for sure, they probably couldn't do much. A possible missing witness was frustrating, though. They might shed light on what had happened and where the cakes had come from.

Otherwise, Charlotte was sure to be blamed.

"Time to open," Mum said, eyeing the wall clock.

Carrying our mugs of tea, we went into the shop. I put my tea on the counter and went to unlock the door and put out the flag, taking the opportunity to check out the action. Of which there was none. The cruiser was gone and the lights in the toy shop were off. I made a mental note to check in on Charlotte later.

Customers began to filter in, and between directing them or checking them out, I searched our shelves for books about dollhouses. We had one copy of *Big Susan* by Elizabeth Orton Jones, published in 1947. I loved the illustrations, which were delightfully old-fashioned. I think it was in this book I first read the word *celluloid*. The dolls were made of that material so they couldn't bend their arms or legs. Somehow that didn't hamper them from coming alive.

I put *Big Susan* aside and moved along. Next, I found the two-book series by Marjorie Filley Stover, *Midnight in the Dollhouse* and *When the Dolls Woke*. Both featured the same dollhouse one hundred years apart, with secrets galore.

A special find was Tasha Tudor's *The Dolls' Christmas*, with its lovely color illustrations. I carried this book and the others to the counter, trying to decide how to design the display. Too bad Mum's doll was missing. We could include it, as way to draw attention.

"What does a Sasha doll look like?" I asked as I set the books down.

Mum glanced up from the computer, where she was updating inventory. "You've never seen one?"

"Before my time," I said, cracking a smile. "They're antiques now, right?"

She swiped at my arm. "I'm not that old. Look them up online. I'm sure you'll find plenty."

That gave me an idea. What if I could find a replacement for her missing doll? When it came to favorite childhood toys, it wasn't about the actual toy. It was all the memories it invoked. The anticipation leading up to Christmas, followed by the joy and gratification of unwrapping a special gift. The fun of playing with the toy, maybe with friends.

I took out my phone and searched. A ton of information immediately came up. Sasha dolls were created by a Swedish artist named Sasha Morgenthaler. The dolls had solemn, elegant faces, the heads large in proportion to their bodies.

"What did yours look like?" I held the phone so my mother could view the screen.

She moved her reading glasses down her nose and studied the pictures. "That one. Long dark hair, wearing a sundress with a straw hat similar to that."

I saved the picture to my phone. Maybe Charlotte had the right doll in stock. If not, I would scour auction sites and other toy shops.

Mum was going to get her favorite doll this Christmas.

Moving on, I looked for book display inspiration. I wanted something small and eye-catching that I

could put near the door. One idea was really cute: a
wooden stepladder with boards through the shelves. If I
put little dolls and furniture throughout, it would look
like an A-frame dollhouse. I could probably find the
accessories at the toy store.

"Oh, this is great!" I exclaimed, grabbing a piece of
paper to make a list.

"What'd you come up with?" Mum asked. I drew a
sketch, showing her my idea. "We have a small stepladder in the basement. It's pretty old but you could
clean it up."

"I'll go look." I'd prefer to use what we had around
rather than buy one.

The door to the basement was next to the loo, in the
short hall that also included the stairs to the second
floor and an exit to the garden. I pulled the string for
the hanging bulb and slowly made my way down the
narrow, uneven steps. The basement was gruesome
with its stone walls; damp, musty smell; and cobwebs.
Pretty standard for a building that was over four hundred years old, I supposed.

Using my phone as a backup light in the dim space,
I hunted for the ladder. Sagging shelves along the
walls held all kinds of junk: paint cans, ancient canned
goods, tools, and building repair supplies. And a cardboard box long and wide enough to be a coffin.

What a ridiculous analogy, I scolded myself as I
moved closer to the box. Then I saw what was written
on the long side: *Tom.*

This was bizarre. Surely Aunt Violet didn't . . .

Laughing at the ridiculous direction my thoughts
were heading, I tentatively pushed the box. It moved
readily, meaning whatever it contained was light.

Were bones light? Probably so. But wasn't it illegal

to bury people at home? Even more so to keep their non-cremated remains above ground? Definitely illegal.

Setting my phone to record, I said, "Hello, I'm Molly Kimball and I'm in the four-hundred-year-old basement at Thomas Marlowe. I've just discovered a mysterious box. Should I open it?" I panned the box, which definitely looked creepy in the shadows.

I sometimes made reels for the bookshop's social media, where I also posted photos of books, often in interesting settings around the city. Our fans were going to love this. If I didn't find anything good, I wouldn't post it, that's all. My friends would get a kick out of it, though.

I set my phone on a shelf, camera still recording, and grabbed the box, pulling it out onto the floor. "The top has flaps," I said. "A vote for *not a body*. Wouldn't a cardboard coffin have a lid?"

Adjusting the camera so viewers could see inside, I opened the flaps in a hasty gesture and folded them back.

"And we have . . . Santa." A life-size plastic St. Nicholas lay inside, his bulbous red cheeks and twinkling eyes radiating good cheer. I was definitely taking him upstairs.

I grabbed the phone and panned his whole body before shutting off the recording and tucking the phone into my back pocket. I tried to pick up the box but it was just too big and bulky. So instead, I picked *him* up. Barely able to see around his rotund body, I had to keep my eyes on my feet as I navigated up the stairs and through the store.

"Molly. What on earth . . . ?" Mum stood up behind the counter as I set Santa down near the front window.

"Isn't he gorgeous?" I balanced him on his feet before standing back in admiration.

In the window, Clarence rolled over with a glare. Puck slunk toward us as though stalking this strange new creature. I found the cord and plugged it in, hoping the internal bulbs still worked.

Santa lit up like a Christmas tree, glowing red and white. He and I were about the same height. What a hoot.

"You found Santa." Aunt Violet emerged from the depths of the shop, a customer in tow. "I forgot all about him. Tom used to put him out every year, with a grab bag of little gifts at his feet for children."

"That's a great idea." Another way to bring holiday cheer to the bookshop.

The door opened and a customer entered, visibly taken aback when she spotted Santa. We all laughed, including her. "Excuse me," she said to the statue, hamming it up. "I wasn't expecting to see you there."

I moved him over a couple of feet to the left. The book display could go just past him, so people would notice it. Speaking of which, I hadn't located the stepladder yet, so I headed back into the basement.

Painted pale green, the ladder was leaning against a shelf and draped in cobwebs. Ugh. I decided to clean it before dragging it upstairs. Which mean grabbing a dust cloth.

By the time I returned with the cloth, Puck was in the cellar, prowling around the shelves. "What are you doing?" I said in a cajoling voice. "Looking for mice?"

I brushed off the ladder before touching it, dragged it out, and set it up in the middle of the floor for a more thorough dusting. Once I got it upstairs, I'd sponge it off before bringing it into the shop.

A box thumped to the floor behind me. Turning, I saw a wide-eyed Puck standing frozen in place. *Oops.* He wasn't a huge cat so the box must have been precariously placed for him to budge it. Something had rattled inside, but at least I hadn't heard glass breaking.

Before putting the box back, I opened the flaps to make sure there wasn't any damage. Stuffed inside were a number of artificial candles, the kind people put in windows. I was definitely putting these on display, upstairs and down.

"Thanks, Puck." I put the candles aside and folded the stepladder for easy carrying. His response was to jump down and walk slowly in front of me. *Cats.*

I was wiping down the ladder with a damp cloth when Aunt Violet trotted into the kitchen. "Molly. The police are back. Two cars this time."

My heart immediately gave a painful thump. Had Barnaby died? Were they about to arrest Charlotte? "They went to the toy shop?"

Aunt Violet shook her head. "No. They stopped in front of Tea and Crumpets."

CHAPTER 5

"Tea and Crumpets?" The rag went flying and landed in the sink, where I'd aimed it. "Why would they go there?" I grabbed my coat from the peg and threw it on. "I'm going to find out what's going on."

By some terrible twist of fate, were they blaming Daisy for the poisoning? She'd already told them that the tea cakes weren't from her shop. Though of course she would say that, right? Then again, why use her own card? I growled in frustration. The chatter of contradictory thoughts was maddening.

"I'll be back quick as I can," I said, rushing out of the kitchen and through the shop.

Halfway across the cobbles, I heard a whistle followed by, "Molly. Hold up."

I whirled around to see my boyfriend, Kieran Scott, striding toward me. Brown curls blowing in the wind, he looked hip yet casual in faded jeans and a navy peacoat. Not to mention devastatingly handsome.

"Kieran. Hi." I pointed toward the tea shop. "We need to go help Daisy."

Alarm flashed over his features. "I saw the cruisers but I didn't think—is she okay?"

I started walking again. "Physically, yes. I think

they're searching her shop." I hoped that was all they were doing. "Did you see the ambulance this morning?" I wondered how much he already knew. Magpie Lane was a small, close-knit community.

"I did. A customer said someone was sick and went to the hospital."

Bless Kieran's incurious heart. He and Tim, Daisy's boyfriend, were so absorbed by their business that they didn't spend much time gossiping. They were too busy making sure people bought or rented the right-sized bicycle and had all the accessories they needed.

"You could put it that way. Barnaby Winters was poisoned and I'm sure they suspect his step-cousin, Charlotte Pemberly. From the toy shop. Have you met her? Or maybe they've moved on to Daisy now. The tea cakes had her card with them."

"Tea cakes? Card?" He put a hand on my arm to stop me. "Please. Fill me in so I'm not flying blind in there."

Taking a deep breath, I organized my thoughts. Then I gave him the gist, promising we'd have more in-depth discussion later. "There's a ton of family drama," I concluded. "We don't have time to talk about it now."

"Got it." He fell into step with me. "Daisy would never leave her card with poisoned cakes. That right there proves she's innocent."

"Totally agree. The thing is, will the police believe it? They don't make judgment calls. They go by evidence."

Kieran's smile was wry. "Oh, that pesky evidence."

The tea shop door opened and several customers emerged, looking disgruntled. "You think it's drugs?" an older man with wiry gray hair asked. "Darn. I'd hate to lose this place. I'm in there two or three times a week working on my novel."

"Drugs?" a young woman shrilled, tossing her hair. "I'm going to kill Becka. She told me this place was the bomb." She pulled out her phone and began tapping.

I had to nip this in the bud. But how? The truth wasn't much more palatable: *She's being investigated for attempted murder.* Finally, I just went for it.

"Hey, folks," I said. "I couldn't help but overhear. Let me assure you, Daisy Watson does not use or deal drugs." I glared at the phone. "Please do not post rumors on social media. Daisy is a lovely person, a hard worker, and the best baker in Cambridge. You could ruin her life."

Kieran stepped forward, bestowing his famous smile on our little audience. "Molly is right. In fact, my mother is a huge fan. Lady Asha Scott. Maybe you've heard of her?"

He never—and I mean never, ever—pulled rank or used his family name to gain advantage. Which is one of the many reasons why I admired and respected him so much. However, at this moment, I grabbed the lifeline his connections offered.

"Lady Asha?" the older man looked impressed. "She's your mother?"

Kieran nodded. "Uh-huh. Last time I checked."

The young woman was tapping away again and now she gave a squeal. "You're Kieran Scott." She turned to me. "And you're his rustic beauty." Another of the many monikers bestowed by the tabloids.

"That's me," I said. "Rustic all the way."

Kieran gestured toward the tea shop. "Now, if you'll excuse us." Without waiting for a reaction, he opened the door for me.

"Molly. Kieran." Daisy was seated near the window and she jumped to her feet. "Do you believe this?" She pointed her chin toward the officers searching behind the counter and in the kitchen.

"What are they looking for?" Kieran asked. "Did they provide a warrant?"

"Oh, yes." Daisy scooped a document off the table and handed it to him.

I read over his shoulder. "'Formulations containing aconite. Blue food coloring.'" That list told me two things: Barnaby had ingested aconite, and they hadn't believed Daisy when she said the cakes weren't from her shop.

Standing with her arms folded, Daisy gave me a crooked smile. "I've never been a murder suspect before. Guess what? It isn't that much fun."

I threw my arms around her. "Hang in there. It's bogus and we'll prove it."

"Prove what, Miss Kimball?" a woman said behind me.

Gritting my teeth, I turned to face Sergeant Gita Adhikari. "Hello, Sergeant. You know Daisy didn't have anything to do with Barnaby's poisoning."

Her gaze was cool. "Kindly allow us to do our jobs, Miss Kimball." She took Kieran in with a flicking glance. "Mr. Scott. What brings you here today?"

Disconcerted, Kieran ran a hand through his hair. "We're here to support Daisy. It's very upsetting to have your premises searched by the police."

She nodded, giving him that much. "Support given. Now please leave."

Kieran and I stared at each other. We really had no choice. At least we'd found out what they were after. "All right, we'll go," I said. "Daisy, please call me as soon as they're gone."

"Definitely. Since they're making a mess, I'll have

to close for the day. Shall we have lunch? I can bring sandwiches over."

"Come to the bike shop," Kieran said. He pulled out his phone. "Tim is asking me what's going on. He thinks I came over here for crumpets."

Daisy eyed the bakery case. "I'd give you some but they won't let me." She sighed. "Tell Tim I'll see him soon. I didn't want to bother him . . . any of you. Not while the shops were open and you were busy."

"Bother us any time," I said. "I mean that." If it had been me having my shop searched, an SOS would have gone out immediately. Daisy had that famous British reticence about making a fuss.

We reluctantly left the shop, Daisy staring forlornly out the window behind us.

"What a cock-up," Kieran exclaimed. "They can't seriously suspect Daisy of trying to murder . . . who was it again?"

"Barnaby Winters. Charlotte's step-cousin? Not sure exactly how you define the relationship. He's the grandson of Charlotte's grandfather's second wife."

He raised one brow. "Maybe you can draw a family tree for me. Does Daisy even know him?"

"Don't think so. Charlotte just took over the shop recently. She's the sole owner so Barnaby shouldn't have been in there." I thought of a key point. "Besides, Charlotte must have been the intended victim. Look." I showed him the snapshot of the gift card. "I think someone left the cakes in hopes that Charlotte would think they came from Daisy. Then she'd be the one in the hospital with aconite poisoning."

"Aconite," Kieran mused. "Where does that come from?"

I had already looked it up. "It's derived from the

monkshood plant, which is also called wolfsbane or devil's helmet." The picture showed a plant with pretty purple flowers shaped like hoods. "Used in hunting and warfare by poisoning the tips of arrows. All parts of the plant are poisonous." The symptoms were gruesome. "Barnaby is lucky to be alive."

"So is Charlotte," Kieran said. "If your theory is right."

And if it was, then the killer, having failed once, might try again.

◆◆

At lunchtime, I went over to the bike shop to join my friends. The police had left and Daisy had managed to put together sandwiches despite the disorder in her kitchen. Proof of which she sent through photos.

We gathered around the counter, the two men standing while Daisy and I sat in folding camp chairs. As I unwrapped a delicious-looking chicken salad loaded with vegetables and pickles, Tim said, "I'm really ticked off about this whole thing." He didn't need to elaborate. Athletic and good-looking, Tim had a blond fade and kind blue eyes.

Daisy sighed. "Me, too. And guess what? They aren't going to find anything." Her smile deepened into a smirk. "They're barking up the wrong tree, for sure."

I hoped someone hadn't managed to plant evidence in the tearoom. Rather than voice that obviously paranoid thought, I said, "I'm worried about Charlotte. I think they'll try again."

Kieran put his sandwich down and fished around in a packet of crisps. "Who is *they*?"

"Well, unless Charlotte has other enemies we don't

know about, it's got to be someone in her family. Meaning, her late grandfather's wife, Althea; her daughter-in-law, Dorcas; and Dorcas's two kids, Barnaby and Tori." I told the guys about Charlotte's ordeal with the family after her grandfather died and left everything to her. "There's also the matter of a missing doll that's worth a ridiculous amount of money. That's probably why Barnaby was in the store, looking for it."

"How did the grandfather die?" Tim asked.

The question dropped like a bomb into the room and we all looked at each other.

"That's a very good question," Daisy said. "I got the impression it was natural causes. Charlotte said he was sick for a while."

"Arthur Pemberly," Kieran mused, scrolling on his phone. He cleared his throat. "Here we go." He read the obituary to us, which said that Arthur had died after "a period of declining health." Family members were listed as Althea, Dorcas, Barnaby, and Victoria Winters and Charlotte Pemberly.

"Charlotte must have loved being named last," Daisy said. "Obviously Althea wrote the obit. According to Charlotte, Arthur was planning to divorce Althea before he got sick."

Tim nodded. "Definitely foul play involved."

"You could be right." I took a sip of water to wash down the last of my sandwich. "Talk about a nightmare family. According to Charlotte, Althea's first two husbands died, too. One is unfortunate, two is awful, three is a trend, don't you think?"

"Finding number four will be tough, I'm guessing," Kieran said. We shared a laugh.

I had a question. "Have you heard about *Madrigals*

and Mayhem, the show Althea is putting on this year? Aunt Violet and Sir Jon were in the debut performance during their college years. She showed me photographs, which were a hoot."

"Sir Jon," Daisy said with a sigh. "If I was forty years older . . ." We laughed.

"He's my role model," Tim said wistfully. "Maybe in forty years, I'll be half as cool."

Daisy got up and put her arms around him. "You'll get there," she teased. He pretended to be offended and they mock-tussled, which made me smile.

"Actually, I have heard about this year's show," Kieran said. "My mum is helping with a fundraising raffle. First prize is two front-row seats."

I wasn't surprised. Lady Asha was involved in a lot of charitable organizations.

"But wait," Tim said. "There's more." His arms still around Daisy, he grinned at Kieran, who rolled his eyes.

"I've been asked to join the cast," Kieran admitted. "Althea cornered me at one of Mum's teas. I'm going to be Lord Nightingale." Tim snickered.

"Really?" I said, surprised. "I didn't know you could sing." He was certainly handsome and outgoing enough to be a presence on stage.

"Want to do it with me, Molly?" There was a tinge of desperation in Kieran's voice. "Want to be my Lady Nightingale? Otherwise, who knows who she'll stick me with." Kieran sang a few bars of the Jefferson Starship song "Be My Lady." What a voice.

Tim and Daisy exchanged amazed looks. "Britain's Got Talent," Tim quipped, referencing the star search show.

I waved a hand in front of my face, crushing even harder after that performance. "Wow, Kieran. You're amazing."

He shrugged, looking both pleased and modest. "Anyway, give it some thought, okay?"

"Okay," I said, although the idea of getting up on stage wasn't especially appealing. Especially not such a high-profile event. I'd never done more than a few plays and church choirs.

The door opened and several customers came in, signaling the end of our lunch. After picking up the wrappers and water bottles, Daisy and I put on our coats and left together. "I'll come help you after the shop closes," I offered, hating to think of Daisy toiling away alone.

"How about I let you know?" she said. "I might be done by then. Cleaning is helping me discharge my aggression over the whole thing."

"I don't blame you for being upset," I said. "Anyone would be."

She sighed. "Well, it's over, right? I hope. Once I'm finished cleaning, I'm going to take a hot bath and get ready for dinner with Tim." A sparkle lit her eyes. "Can I tell you something?" This last was said in a whisper.

"Of course." I leaned closer to listen.

Daisy glanced over her shoulder at the bike shop then, smiling, she whispered, "I think Tim is going to propose this Christmas."

"What?" I shouted. Then I cringed. "Sorry. That's awesome news, Daisy. You two are the best couple." I gave her a hug. "I'm so happy for you."

Daisy blushed, flustered. "Yes. Well. It hasn't happened yet."

I had a feeling it would. Daisy wasn't someone who exaggerated things or made something out of nothing.

Early afternoon was busy but during a lull, I grabbed a cup of tea and carried the borrowed copy of *Charlotte's Dollhouse* to my favorite red velvet chair. Tucked in a nook, the seat allowed privacy while letting me keep an eye on the front door for customers. Puck followed, as he often did, today lying along the back of the chair. If I moved too much, he'd hook a paw in my hair, but otherwise it was nice how he kept my head warm.

After placing the tea on a handy side table, I held the book to my nose, inhaling very old paper and ink. That alone told me it was probably a first edition. My heart warmed with anticipation and joy as I opened the cover, which depicted a dollhouse much like the one in the toy shop.

Charlotte's Dollhouse, written and illustrated by Emilie Dunbarton. Published in 1920, by Madison, Jeffers, and Kline, London. The typesetting had charming flourishes, which fit the book perfectly, and the illustrations were marvelous.

Charlotte's Dollhouse

The dollhouse was magnificent, three stories high with a tower and a roof garden, and twelve rooms furnished to the last perfect detail. There were even cabbage-rose painted chamber pots under the beds.

Charlotte hated it. She despised the chamber pots. Sneered at the tiny plates on the penny-sized dining table. Turned her nose up at the fitted velvet wallpaper and the lights that actually worked. As for the dolls, they'd been met with a scornful, scoffing laugh and tossed onto the floor, where they still lay.

Poor dolls. And poor Charlotte.

"What are we going to do with her?" Mrs. Morton asked. She lay on the carpet, skirts splayed in a most unbecoming manner, she was quite sure. In addition, her apron was flipped up over her face. She reached up and pulled it down. That was better. If only she could get up.

"I don't know," Mr. Bear said. "But we'd better do it fast." He rolled toward Mrs. Morton and then sprang to his feet, extending a paw. "Let me help you, madam." Mr. Bear, with his red bow tie and waistcoat, had the most beautiful manners. "A bear isn't always a boar," he often said.

Once on her feet, Mrs. Morton took stock of the situation. Polly, the bisque doll, was patting her hair, making little fretting noises. She was obviously back in fine form.

The soldier doll, the Lieutenant, peered out from behind a shoe, gun at the ready. "Any sign of the enemy?"

"What a thing to say." Mr. Bear's button eyes glared behind his eyeglasses. "She's only a little girl."

"With a ferocious throw," the soldier said, slinking out from behind the shoe. "I thought I was done for. My rifle barrel stuck into the carpet and sent me into a somersault."

"Buck up, old man," Mr. Bear said. "Where is Jingles?"

The muffled ringing of bells answered him. "I'm under here," the jester called.

"Where?" Mrs. Morton scanned the shadowy corners of the room, looking for a glimpse of red and green. "There he is, behind the bureau."

Mr. Bear headed in that direction to rescue their friend.

The dolls could only move and speak between sunset and sunrise, which often annoyed Mrs. Morton no end. Outside those hours, they were dependent upon the whims of their owner. If spending the day lying on the floor was a portent of things to come, well, they were in deep trouble.

I smiled at the dolls' antics. When I was a child, I'd often pondered the idea of my dolls coming to life as well as the possibility of shrinking and entering their world. Turning the page, I noticed a slip of paper tucked into the spine: a receipt. Nothing special, it contained only a list of items purchased at a drugstore.

Then I turned it over. "The Little Drummer Boy" was handwritten on the back. I put it aside and flipped through the rest of the book. No more pieces of paper, no handwritten clues in the margins. Nothing.

If a receipt with a song title written on the back was our clue to the missing doll, well, I was definitely stumped. I hoped Charlotte would be able to help decipher it.

CHAPTER 6

Late Sunday morning, Daisy and I headed to the nearby village of Hazelhurst to buy Christmas trees at a place Charlotte had suggested. Daisy was driving because her blue-and-white Mini Cooper had a roof rack. Our plan was to meet Charlotte at the farm and then go out to lunch.

"How was your night?" I asked.

Daisy wiggled her bare left ring finger at me. "No news yet. We did have a very nice—and expensive—dinner at the Holly and Ivy." The Holly & Ivy Inn was an elegant boutique hotel located at the intersection of Magpie Lane and Trinity Street.

"Sounds wonderful." I smiled at the contrast between our dates. "We were at the pub. Burgers and chips, followed by a rousing game of darts."

"That's a bit more my speed, to be honest," Daisy said. "Tim did look a treat in his suit, though. Yum."

"I bet." The low-key evening spent in a hubbub of chatter and laughter had actually been perfect after Friday's upsetting events. Barnaby had pulled through, we'd heard, but was still in the hospital. Charlotte hadn't returned to the toy shop, and Daisy told me she had a flat in town she shared with a friend.

Although I'd gotten her number and sent pictures of the receipt I found in *Charlotte's Dollhouse*, she hadn't responded yet.

I couldn't blame her. She probably needed a break.

To reach Hazelhurst, we went on the A14 for a few miles and then exited onto country lanes. I had deep connections to this particular village, one of several ringing the city. My mother had grown up in Hazelhurst, and my uncle still lived in their childhood home. In addition, Kieran's family estate, Hazelhurst House, was the local manor, and we often came out to visit his parents there. I'd catalogued Lord and Lady Scott's thousand-volume library as a side job, which had been an incredible experience.

Today we skirted the village proper to reach Mistletoe Tree Farm, a stone farmhouse, outbuildings, and barns set amid fields lined with evergreens. The parking area was already overflowing so it was difficult to find a spot.

"Everyone had the same idea, I guess," Daisy said with a sigh when we finally slid into a space.

"Part of the fun." As we got out, I took in the throngs milling around to the accompaniment of holiday music over loudspeakers. A draft horse pulling a cart jingled by, and staff dressed in elf, Santa, and snowman costumes directed shoppers. A barn with open doors offered wreaths and a small gift shop featured farm-themed gifts. I definitely wanted to stop at the shop before we left.

"Want a hot chocolate or cider?" Daisy asked as we strolled by a hut serving refreshments.

"Cider would be great." The scents of cinnamon and nutmeg were enticing.

Cups in one hand, pumpkin donuts in the other,

we made our way to the rows of cut trees. "'Norway spruce, Fraser fir, Nords, Korean fir, Lodgepole pine,'" I read aloud from a sign. Nords and Korean fir were new to me and I was curious to see how they differed from more familiar trees.

Finding the perfect Christmas tree wasn't easy. I'd discover a great one, then spot another in the next row that looked even better. I liked full trees—but not too full. There had to be room for the ornaments. While we browsed, I told Daisy about the huge Santa I'd found in the bookshop basement. She laughed when I described his box as a coffin.

"You thought it was a vampire?" Her eyes sparkled.

"Or maybe an ancient mummified family member," I joked. "Cardboard was all they could afford." In many English churches and crypts, like the ones at Hazelhurst House, people were interred in stone and marble coffins instead of buried. "Anyway, it was a fun surprise. He looks great."

"I'll come check him out." Daisy put her hand on a Norway spruce. "I want this one. I love the way it smells."

I inhaled. "Me, too." A head of red hair under a fluffy white beret caught my eye in the next row. "I think that might be Charlotte."

The woman turned and I saw that yes, it was her. "Hey," I called waving. "You made it."

She slipped through the row of trees to join us. "Just got here. I've been at the hospital all morning."

"How is he?" Daisy asked.

"Getting better." Charlotte's brow furrowed. "Not that they let me anywhere near his room." Her gloved fists clenched. "They were acting like I poisoned him."

"By 'they,' you mean the family?" I asked.

She nodded. "Typical behavior on their part. I'm the outsider when actually the exact opposite is true."

"They're trying to bully you," I said. "Try not to let them see it bothers you." Easier said than done, I knew.

Charlotte blinked back tears. "It makes me so angry. They kept me and my grandfather apart on purpose. I wish I could make them *pay*."

This last phrase was delivered with some heat and I noticed people glancing at us. "I totally get it." With a meaningful look around, I said, "We should talk about this somewhere else."

She dabbed at her eyes with a tissue. "Yeah, we should. I'm sorry, it's still so raw. And now Barnaby . . . that whole thing is so bizarre."

She'd heard nothing yet. Wait until I laid my theory on her.

"Why don't we pick out our trees and then we'll go to lunch." Daisy touched a branch on her choice. "What do you think?"

Charlotte readily changed direction. "It's gorgeous. I have my eye on a Fraser fir in the next row. Want to see?"

We went to admire her tree, after which I finally chose a fragrant Korean fir, said to have good needle retention. A helper we flagged carted the trees to a netting machine that prepared them for transport. We bungeed all three to the Mini Cooper roof because Charlotte was driving a small Nissan without a rack.

Once that was done, I said, "I'd like to go into the gift shop before we leave. Do you mind?"

Daisy shrugged. "Fine with me." Charlotte seemed to hesitate, then nodded.

The gift shop held a variety of botanical-themed

gifts, from dried flower wreaths to herbal sachets and tinctures to mugs and pot holders depicting plants.

"Christmas trees are only part of their business," Charlotte said. "They also raise herbs and flowers."

That made sense, since evergreens were so seasonal. We poked around the shelves and racks, making our way slowly to the counter, where a burly, bearded, good-looking man stood. When he spoke, his voice had a faint lilt of the Caribbean.

I picked up a balsam soy candle and inhaled. The scent was so evocative of Christmas—and Vermont. "I really want this scent," I said. "But open flames aren't a good idea in the bookshop."

Daisy shuddered. "I'll say. How about a wax warmer?" She showed me a pretty one decorated with evergreen cutouts. "You could use balsam scent in this." She showed me the wax melts.

I gathered the warmer and melts. "A perfect solution." We'd have our evergreen aroma without endangering the building or the inventory.

As we approached the counter, the man came around to the floor. "Charlotte. How are you?" He took her hand in both his. "I was so sorry to hear about Arthur."

"Thank you." Charlotte gently withdrew her hand. "Andre Lewis, I'd like you to meet my friends, Molly Kimball and Daisy Watson. Andre is a friend of the family."

His laugh was robust. "More than a friend. My late dad was married to Althea and I've always stayed in touch." He nodded at us. "Nice to meet you."

"Andre is also part of the madrigal choir," Charlotte said. "Are you doing that again this year?"

"I am." Andre scooted back around behind the

counter and I set my purchases down. "Wouldn't miss it." A concerned expression creased his brow. "What's this I hear about Barnaby? He's in the hospital?" When Charlotte didn't respond immediately, he added, "I got a text from Althea to the cast, informing us he was ill and to send good thoughts."

Charlotte finally responded. "Last I heard, he was on the mend. He should be out soon."

"Phew." Andre let out a breath. "I'm glad to hear it." He began to ring me up.

"Me, too." Charlotte's smile was tight. Andre didn't seem to know the whole story, and I imagined she was glad. Talk about awkward.

"This place is great." I pulled out a bank card, waiting for the command to insert.

"I'm glad you think so," Andre said. "I've worked hard to diversify what we grow. To add products and events."

"Sounds like what we're doing at the bookshop," I replied.

His brows lifted. "Bookshop?"

"Thomas Marlowe, in Cambridge." I still felt a thrill whenever I said the name of the family business. Was this really my life?

Andre nodded. "I know it, of course. Wonderful store." His grin was wide as he pushed a brown paper bag with handles toward me. "Enjoy."

We called goodbye and left the shop, wandering back toward the cars.

"That was fun," Charlotte said glumly. "I should have known he'd have heard about Barnaby. I'll have to hide my face forever from everyone I know."

"Only until we figure out what happened," Daisy said briskly. "Meanwhile, hold your chin up."

Charlotte raised her chin with a laugh. "Thanks for the reminder. I was starting to feel sorry for myself."

"That's understandable," I said, "You're in a tough spot right now." Changing the subject, I suggested, "How about Bella Mia for lunch?"

"Sounds good." Charlotte glanced behind me with a frown. "Seriously?" She frantically pressed her key fob, making the lights flash and horn blow.

I turned to see a tall woman with a blond bob, dressed country casual in a tweed overcoat, jeans, and boots, striding toward us. The glare on her pretty features could have stripped paint.

"Charlotte," she barked. "Charlotte."

My new friend rolled her eyes, sighed, and turned. "Hey, Dorcas."

I braced myself. Dorcas was Barnaby's mother. My eyes met Daisy's and she made a *yikes* face.

Dorcas halted, gloved hands on her hips. "You're not in jail yet?"

"What?" Charlotte gave a whoop of laughter. "You're kidding, right? I didn't do anything."

One hand came up and Dorcas wagged a finger. "You tried to poison my son."

Tossing her head, Charlotte gave Dorcas a haughty smirk. "Hell no. I *saved* your son. He was trespassing, let's not forget. Next time I'll have him arrested." Her eyes narrowed. "And I know what he was after. Shame on you for sending him to do your dirty work."

Dorcas backed away, hands up, her mouth opening and closing as she struggled to respond. Apparently not able to come up with anything, she turned and fled.

Charlotte watched Dorcas until she entered the gift shop. "Ready for lunch, ladies?" A smile slid across her face as she hit the fob to unlock the door, successfully this time. "You'd think they'd know better by now."

Daisy whistled in admiration. "Remind me not to get on your bad side." She patted Charlotte's arm. "Want to follow us? Honk if the trees start to slide off, okay?"

Daisy found a parking place in front of the restaurant, which meant we could keep an eye on our trees. Charlotte parked in a lot a block down and walked back to meet us.

The mouthwatering aromas of fresh ground coffee, savory soups, and melting cheese greeted us when we walked in. A table near the window was empty so we grabbed it before getting in line to order.

Everything on the chalkboard list looked tempting. I finally decided on tortellini soup and a tuna, tomato, and Swiss panini.

"Get whatever you want," Charlotte said, waving her wallet. "It's on me. And no arguments."

"Thanks," Daisy said. "I'll get you next time."

"Definitely." I liked the idea that Charlotte would be part of our girl gang on Magpie Lane.

Café grandes in hand, we went to our table to wait for the food. "I brought the piece of paper I found in your book," I told Charlotte. "If you'd like to see it." I had tucked the paper into a zipped section of my handbag.

She gave a little squeal. "Yes. I can't believe I didn't notice it before."

"You've had a few things on your mind." I slid the slip across the table.

"That was it for a clue, huh?" Daisy asked, looking on as Charlotte examined the slip of paper.

"So far. There's nothing written in the book that I can see."

Charlotte tapped the paper with her finger. "I think

Grandad set up a scavenger hunt for me. This gives me a place to start at the toy shop."

"A drummer boy toy?" I guessed.

"Something like that." Her gaze was distant. "We have a lot of toy soldiers."

This was exciting. I wanted to jump right up and go look. "Can we help?" I asked.

"I'd love that." Charlotte tucked the paper into her wallet. "It's not much fun doing things by yourself." After a pause, she added, "Sorry. I'm really not on a pity trip."

"We get it," Daisy said. "Everything is more fun with friends."

On impulse, I lifted my coffee. "To friends." We touched paper cups and then, with a laugh, drank.

"Charlotte," a server intoned. "Order is up."

We retrieved our trays and dug into the delicious lunch. "I was wondering," Charlotte said after a few minutes. "What you think about Barnaby getting sick? Any idea where the cakes came from?" She glanced at Daisy. "I know they weren't from your shop."

"I wish the police shared your opinion," Daisy said. "They searched my kitchen and made a big mess." She frowned, a rare expression on her usually cheerful face.

Charlotte gave a gasp. "I didn't know they searched the tearoom. Was it after I went to the hospital?"

"Uh-huh." Daisy's smile was grim yet satisfied. "They didn't find any blue food coloring, that's for sure."

"Do you think the poison was in the frosting? What did the warrant say? Aconite?"

"It could have been in the frosting," Daisy mused. "That would make sense. The sugar would help disguise the taste."

"Aconite has been used in a lot of murders," I said, having researched the poison. "In 1882, Dr. George Henry Lamson was convicted of poisoning a relative with a cake. The motive: inheritance."

Charlotte and Daisy stared at me, wide-eyed. "That sounds a bit too familiar," Charlotte muttered.

I glanced around, making sure no one was listening. The guy on one side was facing away, headphones on, and a noisy group was seated on the other. Still, I leaned across the table and spoke in a low voice. "I'm positive the cakes were meant for you, Charlotte."

Her lips set in a line. "Me, too. The police—and the others—insinuated that I'd left a trap for Barnaby. I told them, I had no idea he was going to break in. I mean, he's a pig when it comes to sweets, but seriously? What if someone else had eaten them by accident? If I'd wanted to target Barnaby, I would have sent the cakes to his lodgings at college."

After letting her words settle, I asked, "Tell me, what did you mean about Dorcas sending Barnaby to do her dirty work?"

"To find the doll. Dorcas needs the money. I know that because she borrowed a huge amount from my grandfather." She paused for effect. "Fifty thousand pounds. Which she never repaid. I have a copy of the promissory note."

"Which means what, she owes the estate now?" I asked.

Charlotte nodded. "I think she thought it would go away when he died. If it had been less . . . much less . . . and she'd been a nicer person, I might have forgiven it." She set her jaw. "The whole family sucked my grandfather dry like ticks on a dog."

An unpleasant but apt analogy. Maybe the cakes had

been left for Charlotte as revenge for not forgiving the debt. In my view, Dorcas was now a strong suspect. She might also be a burglar.

"Get this," I said, excited. "Aunt Violet saw two people near the toy shop the same night Barnaby broke in. Maybe it *was* him—and Dorcas." His sister, Tori, was also a possibility. Was she also dispatched to do Mummy's dirty work?

Charlotte sat up straight. "Did she get a good look at them?"

"Unfortunately, no," I said. "She was too far away, plus the lane isn't that well lit."

"It's something to check out, though," Charlotte said. "Is she going to tell the police?"

"I'll ask her to." It would be simpler if Barnaby told them he'd had a companion. Since they'd entered the toy shop illicitly, key or not, he might be reluctant to get someone else in trouble.

"Thanks. I'd grill Barnaby myself but I can't get near him." She made a humorous growling face, extending her fingers like claws. "Not with his watchdogs keeping me at bay. As you saw earlier."

Charlotte's phone dinged and she looked at the screen. "Oh, good. The locksmith will be there later this afternoon, around five." Her expression became pleading. "Will you come with me to Grandad's house this afternoon? After what happened to Barnaby—and almost to me—I'm starting to wonder. Was Grandad poisoned, too?"

◄●►

After lunch, we drove back to Cambridge, stopping first at Arthur Pemberly's home. Arthur had lived in a three-bedroom, semidetached home in Cherry Hinton, a nice neighborhood several miles from the city center.

I parked in front and Charlotte pulled into the short side drive. Carrying the keys, she waited on the front steps for us to join her. "It's going to be dusty," she warned. "I haven't had much chance to clean lately." She turned the key with a click. "I can't face packing up Grandad's things yet, though my plan is to get this place on the market."

Cherry Hinton was a desirable location and the house, although modest, was sure to be snapped up quickly.

We stepped into a dim, chilly foyer scented with orange and clove. Charlotte picked up loose pieces of mail and set them on a small table next to the pot-pourri bowl. "Yep. Haven't been here for a while." She snapped on an overhead light before leading us through a doorway to the left. "This is the living room," she said. A mix of overstuffed furniture and antiques created a homey ambiance.

Next was the dining room, notable for an elegant ma-hogany table, chairs, and sideboard, and then a fairly modern kitchen. A set of French doors led to a charm-ing, junglelike garden, dormant in this season.

"That was my playground," Charlotte said wistfully, staring out the glass door. "So many memories."

"Are you sure you want to sell?" Daisy asked softly.

Charlotte didn't answer for a moment. "No. But—actually, yes. This place is perfect for a family. It will be much easier to run the shop if I live upstairs. The flat is really nice and quite big. Plus I'll be right in the heart of Cambridge."

"That's why I love Magpie Lane," I put in. "Every-thing is walking distance." One of the reasons, anyway.

Living in a quaint, Tudor-style building from the 1600s thrilled me.

Someone rapped on the front door and Charlotte froze. Guessing she was worried about her estranged family members showing up, I said, "Want me to see who it is?"

She considered that for a moment before squaring her shoulders. "No, I'll go. I have to face them sometime."

"We'll be your backup," Daisy said. We tagged along behind her, ready to do battle if necessary.

Nudging the curtain aside, Charlotte peered out through the front window. "Phew. It's the next-door neighbor. I'll see what she wants."

Daisy and I lingered in the living room while she went to the front door, standing where nosy us could keep watch.

Charlotte unlocked the door and opened it to reveal a short, curvy woman with curly brown hair. "Phronsie. How are you?"

A gust of cold wind blew through the open door, and with a shiver, Phronsie pulled her cardigan closer. "Can I come in for a moment? I won't keep you." Judging by the fuzzy slippers on her feet, she must have run over here on impulse.

"Please do." Charlotte held the door open.

Since it would be ridiculous for us to keep hiding, Daisy and I crowded into the foyer. "Hi," I said. "I'm Molly and this is Daisy. We're Charlotte's friends."

"Nice to meet you," Phronsie said. "I'm next door." She pointed to the abutting wall of the duplex. She appeared to be in her fifties, a kind, comfortable sort of person.

"Want tea?" Charlotte offered. "I can put the kettle

on." She made a face. "There probably isn't milk, though."

Perhaps Phronsie sensed that Charlotte's offer was obligatory because she said, "Thank you, but no. I'm sure you're busy." She took a deep breath. "I know it's none of my business but I thought I'd ask. Have you moved back in?"

"No, I'm still staying in Cambridge, at my rented flat. Why?" Charlotte's eyes narrowed, as if she knew a disturbing reveal was coming.

"Thursday night, the lights were on. All over the house." Phronsie waved a phone. "I have a video of someone at the front door."

CHAPTER 7

"Thursday night?" Charlotte stuttered. "Are you sure?"

That was the same night Barnaby had broken into the toy shop.

Phronsie nodded. She waved the phone again. "Want to see?"

Charlotte shut the door against the wind as we gathered around. Fingers deftly working the screen, Phronsie said, "The camera is for our front door, so I can see who it is from anywhere in the house. Sometimes it will pick up action at your front door, too, if someone comes into our area." A pause. "Honestly, we're not spying on you."

"I wasn't thinking that," Charlotte said. "I'm glad you have it. With the house being empty, I should have put in a camera."

Phronsie gave a grunt of satisfaction. "Here we go." She held up the phone so we could see the video.

A young man walked along the sidewalk toward the camera, smoking a cigarette. Then he pivoted and went back the other way, throwing the butt into the bushes. The last view was of him standing on Charlotte's steps.

"That's Reece," Charlotte said. "Barnaby's roommate at school. Can you send me that video?"

"Of course. I have your mobile number, I think." Phronsie scrolled through her contacts, then sent the video.

Had Reece been with Barnaby in the toy shop instead of Dorcas or Tori? It certainly seemed like a strong possibility.

"Did you see him go inside?" I asked.

Phronsie shook her head. "Later, when I took my boy out for a wee, I noticed the lights in the house were on. Wiggles is my Yorkie," she added.

Thanks for clarifying, I thought but did not say.

Charlotte stared at her neighbor as if trying to process the implications of this information. "Thanks for letting me know. Reece must have been with my cousin, Barnaby. He wouldn't come here alone."

"Oh, yes, I remember Barnaby." The neighbor's expression became sympathetic. "Arthur was a lovely man. He even dog-sat Wiggles for me sometimes. Did you know that? And Wiggles is very, very fussy about who he'll allow to care for him."

"I didn't know, and thank you." Charlotte sounded numb. "I miss him a great deal. He was everything to me."

Phronsie enveloped her in a huge hug. "I'm so sorry, dear." After a squeeze, she pulled back, hands on Charlotte's arms. "Don't be a stranger, all right? If you need something, anything, let me know."

Charlotte gnawed at her bottom lip. "There is one thing . . ." Phronsie's expression was eager, as if she'd been waiting for an opportunity to help. "If you see anyone lurking around outside or inside the house again, will you text me immediately? I'm not sure if you know, but this house belongs to me now. No one should be inside without my knowledge or permission."

Distress crossed Phronsie's features. "Should I have called the police? I'm so sorry—"

"Not a problem," Charlotte said firmly. "Everything looks fine in here. I'm glad you came over and told me about it."

"Phew." Phronsie patted her chest. "I'm so glad. If there is anything else, please don't hesitate to call." She touched Charlotte's arm. "I'll let you get back to . . . whatever."

After the door shut behind Phronsie, Charlotte crossed her arms with a scowl. "I have half a mind to go over to St. Aelred and tell Reece where to get off."

"I don't blame you," I said, thinking how angry and violated I'd feel if someone poked around the bookshop at night without permission. "I think you should talk to Reece and see if he'll tell you what he was doing here. Maybe in a kinder, gentler way, though?" If Charlotte showed up with accusations blazing, Reece would probably recoil and refuse to tell her anything.

Judging by the expressions flowing over her face, Charlotte was waging an internal war. Finally, she said, "You're right. If I antagonize him, he'll clam up. We'll head over after we're done here." A pause. "If you want to go with me, that is."

I wouldn't miss it for anything. "I'm game if you are, Daisy."

She shrugged. "Sure. He might know something about the cakes. Maybe I can get the police off my back."

"Good point," Charlotte said. She ran her hands over her face and shuddered. "I can't believe it. I never thought they would sink so low."

Greed does strange things to people, even seemingly upright and contributing members of society. Entering without permission was the least of it. Things had already escalated to attempted murder.

"Your neighbor seems nice," I commented, changing the subject. "It's good to have another set of eyes and ears on this place."

"It is. Until I put in a camera, at least." Charlotte shook herself, seeming to rally. "We'd better get a move on."

Our first stop was Arthur's study, where Charlotte showed us a copy of the promissory note. As she'd said, it indicated that Dorcas had borrowed fifty thousand pounds, with a promise to make monthly payments.

"Did she make any payments?" I asked.

Charlotte shook her head. "See the date? This is right before he got so sick. She took full advantage, knowing he wouldn't come after her."

"How awful," Daisy murmured. "Despicable, in fact."

Charlotte flipped the folder closed. Then she pulled a few more files from the drawer. "These are going with me. Yes, the attorney has copies, but I don't want anyone pawing through. Or stealing the files." She patted the pile. "Don't let me forget to grab these."

We continued on through the downstairs rooms, making sure the intruders hadn't taken or damaged anything. Then we followed Charlotte up the stairs, to take a look at Arthur's room.

Her steps slowed as she went, revealing a reluctance that I also felt. This was where her beloved grandfather had spent his final days. Walking up these stairs must be a terrible reminder of grief and pain.

I'd experienced something similar after my dad died. He's been at home, in hospice, which had been a blessing for all of us. Still, a heaviness had lain over the house after he was gone, not helped by the fact we were basically trapped inside during a typical Vermont winter. Trapped with our sadness, missing him every day.

The opportunity to move to Cambridge had blown into our lives like a gust of fresh air.

Charlotte paused on the top landing. "I don't know if I can do this."

"You don't have to," I said, taking her arm and steering her to an armchair. The open landing had been set up as a small sitting room. "We can look around, if that's okay with you." I shivered. It felt so intrusive to poke around a dead man's room. Yet how were we going to figure out anything if we didn't?

Daisy hunkered down, taking Charlotte's hand. "With Barnaby being poisoned, we need to see if there is any connection to your grandfather's death."

"What was the cause of death?" I asked, thinking that might offer a clue.

"Heart failure." Charlotte's gaze was fixed on the fingers she'd laced together. "His heart finally . . . gave out."

A chill of realization iced my core. Aconite poisoning could cause heart failure. If Arthur had already been ill, it probably hadn't taken much to kill him.

How perfectly wicked. And they weren't going to get away with it.

With new resolve, I set my jaw. "Which room is his?"

Charlotte remained in the armchair while Daisy and I walked down to the end of the hall. The door was partway open, so I used the back of my hand to widen the gap.

Arthur's bedroom and en suite bathroom overlooked the back garden, tall windows allowing in a flood of sunlight. The bedroom was pleasant, furnished with gleaming dark wood furniture, thick carpet, and two armchairs near a fireplace that appeared to work, going by the ashes in the grate.

A tall glass case on one wall held dolls, stuffed animals, and other antique toys, the doors open and the contents in disarray. One doll lay on the carpet, where she'd fallen. Or had been tossed.

"Three guesses who rummaged through that," I said. "Barnaby must have been searching for the Madame Alexander doll."

"I think so, too." Daisy put on her thin woolen gloves. "We'd better wear these."

"You're right." I fished in my pocket for my pair. We certainly didn't want our fingerprints all over everything, especially any evidence we uncovered.

"His medication is still here," Daisy pointed to the bedside table, where a number of plastic bottles sat.

"We'll start with those," I said.

Working together, we opened each bottle, examining the contents. "This one has capsules," I said, showing Daisy. "The poison could have been added."

"Good point." She opened another bottle. "These are capsules, too."

I pulled out my phone. "I'm going to take pictures. Then we can look them up later." We might discover that the contents didn't match the label. That would be a sneaky way to poison someone.

The hard part was going to be convincing the police to reopen the case. Why would they spend resources on sending these to the lab?

While I snapped shots of the bottle labels and

contents, Daisy went into the bathroom. "Molly," she called. "You need to see this."

"Be right there." I checked my photos to make sure they were clear, then went to join her.

She was standing in front of the medicine cabinet. "Look at that tube."

A white tube was labeled HERBAL EASE-JOINT RELIEF. It had a logo I recognized. "Mistletoe Farm." Where we'd bought the Christmas trees earlier.

"Yep." Daisy pointed. "Read the fine print."

Several herbs were listed as ingredients, including *Aconitum napellus*. Aconite, the same substance that had poisoned Barnaby. In the minute doses used in homeopathic formulas, it was harmless, I'd read. However, aconite didn't have to be ingested. It could be deadly absorbed through the skin, if the dose was large enough.

"I think we might have found our poison delivery system," I said.

Arthur must have applied it himself, obviously not realizing the cream was poisoned. How horribly careless of the poisoner. What if someone else had used it? Or helped him apply the cream? They would have gotten sick or even died as well.

Maybe that had been the plan. Another trap waiting for Charlotte.

Daisy turned away from the cabinet, leaving the door open. "We'd better go tell Charlotte what we found. I'm not looking forward to it."

I wasn't either. This news would blow her world apart even more. Her grandfather might still be alive if someone hadn't tried to escalate the progress of his illness.

Charlotte jumped up from her chair when she saw us come out of the bedroom. "You found something."

Our expressions must have given it away. "We did. Can you come look?"

She gnawed at her bottom lip, clearly reluctant. I got it. A revelation of murder was like a bell you couldn't unring. Not only would it reframe the past, it would release a cascade of consequences in the present. She finally spoke. "Show me what you found."

The bathroom cabinet door was still open. "See that cream?" I asked. "One of the ingredients is Aconitum. The same substance that made Barnaby sick."

Charlotte reared back. "You think something is wrong with the cream? Surely Andre wouldn't sell anything poisonous. It would destroy his business."

"I think someone upped the dosage," I explained. "The homeopathic formula isn't strong enough to make someone sick."

"Did you ever apply it to your grandfather's skin?" Daisy asked.

Charlotte shook her head. "He used it on his hands now and then, for his arthritis." She pointed at the tube with a shaking hand. "You think that it killed him? That little tube of herbal cream?"

"It's a strong possibility," I said. "You said he died of heart failure. That's a symptom of aconite poisoning. If he had preexisting conditions, this could have put him over the edge." Anger clenched in my chest. How devious and horrible. If we were right, we needed to find the killer.

Charlotte put both hands over her face. "What should we do now?"

"I think we should call the police. They might not

believe us, but we need to do something. In case we're right."

After a moment, she nodded. "I'm not eager to talk to them again but I suppose we should." Her tone turned bitter. "Someone might try to pin Grandad's death on me as well."

I hadn't thought of that and it was a real possibility. I also shuddered to think of the results if someone else had used the cream.

Like Charlotte, for instance. That might explain why the killer hadn't removed it from the bathroom after Arthur's death.

Charlotte pulled her phone out of her pocket. "I'm calling now. Do you two mind sticking around? I'd rather not face them alone."

I caught Daisy's eye. "I'll stay. How about you?"

Daisy nodded. "Be glad to. Molly and I are the ones who found the cream, so I think we'd better."

Maybe our presence would convince the police that Charlotte wasn't being hysterical or overwrought. Or trying to point suspicion away from herself regarding Barnaby.

I'd always been inclined to investigate every avenue while doing research as a librarian. Now that tendency was in overdrive after being involved in several murder mysteries. It was exhausting. However, unlike when tracking down arcane knowledge, lazy thinking could get you killed when a murderer was on the loose.

"Sergeant Adhikari, please." Holding the phone to her ear, Charlotte paced around the bedroom.

"Why don't we go put the kettle on?" Daisy suggested, miming the actions in Charlotte's view. She nodded understanding.

"Long as there's a fresh box of tea," I whispered as we left the bedroom.

"Molly." Daisy's elbow nudged my side. "Don't. I'm going to be paranoid now."

"As we should be," I retorted as we tramped down the stairs. "First frosting and then skin cream. Well, vice versa. Who knows what's next?"

CHAPTER 8

Gita Adhikari seemed less than happy about being called out on a Sunday afternoon. The fact they'd sent her indicated to me that the police were taking our concern seriously. That was a very good sign.

"Good afternoon." Gita didn't smile as she stepped inside, accompanied again by Constable Derby. "I understand you have something to show us?"

Although she'd kept her cool while waiting, Charlotte dissolved into tears now that the officers were actually here. "Molly and Daisy found evidence that someone murdered my grandfather, Arthur Pemberly."

Concern creased Derby's brow. "Take a moment, lass," he said, holding out a tissue box that had been sitting on a table.

As Charlotte snuffled and sobbed, dabbing at her eyes, Gita turned her cold gaze on us. As with her superior, DI Sean Ryan, I'd seen two personas: the human and the police officer at work. The latter could be very intimidating.

"Why don't we have a cup of tea while we tell you about it?" Daisy said. "There's a little context here we need to explain."

Gita and Derby exchanged glances. "I could use a

cup," Derby said, rubbing his hands together. "It's a cold one."

"All right." Gita checked her watch. "Long as we're quick about it."

In the kitchen, Daisy had already set the table with colorful pottery mugs and a teapot brewed under a knitted hen cozy. She checked the pot, then began to fill the cups.

"Canned milk," she told Charlotte, indicating a small pitcher. "None in the fridge."

"I already cleaned it out," Charlotte said, sniffing. Her nose was pink. "That and taking out the trash were as far as I got." She accepted a mug of tea with a nod. "Molly, why don't you take the lead?"

Okay. Hopefully my input would lend credibility. Both Charlotte and Daisy were under suspicion for the Barnaby incident.

"Arthur Pemberly died of heart failure," I said. "That's Charlotte's understanding and I'm sure you can check his death certificate." I paused to allow them to absorb this information. "A symptom of aconite poisoning happens to be heart failure. From the search warrant provided to Daisy, we assumed that Barnaby was poisoned by this substance. Am I right so far?"

"So far, so good," Derby said.

"After what happened to Barnaby—and we're so relieved that he's going to be okay—Charlotte started to wonder about her grandfather's death. That maybe something . . . untimely . . . had happened. So we took a look."

Daisy now chimed in. "In the upstairs medicine cabinet, I found a tube of skin cream that contains Aconitum, a homeopathic formula. We are now wondering if the dosage was doctored, resulting in Arthur's death."

"We didn't touch it," I hastened to say. "None of us touched it." In case they thought Charlotte had planted it there.

Gita and Derby stared at each other for a long moment. Then the sergeant said, "I'm not sure . . . We can't order lab work on a whim. There's no budget for that."

Determination flashed in Charlotte's eyes. "Then I'll get it privately tested and send you the report, if they do find something."

An uncomfortable silence fell over the kitchen.

"Don't you have probable cause?" I took up the argument. "One death, one attempted murder, the same substance involved?"

Charlotte leaned forward, her tone urgent. "During the last few months of my grandfather's life, I was barely allowed to see him. He and Althea had gotten divorced, but when he got sick, she moved back in and blocked my access. Why, you might ask? For the inheritance. She didn't know he'd changed his will and written her out."

"That's why I think the cupcakes were meant for Charlotte." Might as well go for it, I figured. "Not to get the inheritance, I don't think that's possible. Revenge, maybe? Dorcas Winters owed Arthur a large amount of money and the estate is collecting. I'm sure Charlotte will show you the promissory note. Plus, if she was out of the way, they'd have more chance to find that doll we told you about."

"That's why Barnaby was in the shop the other night," Charlotte said.

"And, we think," I added, "he wasn't alone. The neighbor here saw Barnaby's roommate hanging around in front the same night. She also said all the lights were on."

Charlotte jumped back in. "Neither of them is supposed to be in this house. I certainly didn't give them permission." She opened the forwarded video on her phone and handed it to Gita. "That's Reece Harrison, Barnaby's roommate at St. Aelred."

The officer studied the video, then handed the phone to the constable.

"If Reece was with Barnaby at the toy shop, then he might know something about the cakes."

Exhausted by my efforts to convince the officers that we were actually offering important information, I slumped back in my seat. We'd given them all we had. What they did with it was up to them.

They were both silent for a moment. "I do hope you're going to change the locks," Gita finally said. "That will help prevent unwanted visitors." This was probably as close as we were going to get to an admission that they were listening.

"I have an appointment with the locksmith this afternoon," Charlotte said. "I'm also looking into getting cameras and alarms. You have to understand that, until recently, my grandfather was in charge of these properties. He apparently didn't see any reason for security measures beyond good locks." She paused. "And considering that my family members are the ones causing problems, I venture to say he was right."

Gita pushed back in her chair. "Shall we take a look upstairs, Derby? Can you fetch an evidence bag?"

The constable swilled down his tea and stood. "Right away, Sergeant."

"I'll go up with you," Charlotte said. "Thank you for your help."

Once they left the kitchen, Daisy refilled her mug and then mine. "I'm glad they're taking us seriously.

Hopefully they'll question Reece and he'll know more about the cakes."

"Yeah, such as if they were left inside or on the steps." I couldn't imagine anyone leaving them outside in case a stray dog ate them. Or a hungry late-night pub patron. I shuddered at the thought. Surely even a killer wouldn't have taken that risk.

Daisy echoed my thoughts. "They must have been inside. So someone else has a key. I certainly don't."

We sipped tea, waiting for Charlotte to finish with the police. Finally we heard voices and the front door closing for the last time.

"You're still here," Charlotte said when she came into the kitchen. "Good." She took a sip of tea and grimaced. "Ice cold."

"Want me to make a fresh pot?" Daisy asked.

Charlotte gathered the used mugs from the table and carried them to the sink. "Not right now, thanks. I want to go over to St. Aelred and talk to Reece." She glanced at us over her shoulder. "Coming?"

We caravanned back to Magpie Lane to drop off the trees and leave the cars. Like much of inner-city Cambridge, the streets around St. Aelred were restricted regarding vehicle traffic. Living in an area like this could be inconvenient at times. It mostly meant that I was staying in good shape by walking or riding my bicycle almost everywhere.

"I'll be back in an hour or so," I told Mum and Aunt Violet. They were in the warm and cozy kitchen with the cats, Mum reading and Aunt Violet knitting.

"We're going over to St. Aelred to talk to Barnaby's roommate."

Aunt Violet's lips pursed in interest. "Are you hot on the trail?"

"We are. We think Reece was with Barnaby at the toy shop. Remember you saw two people that night?" I wound a scarf around my neck. The walk was going to be cold. "I'll tell you all about it when I get back."

"Sir Jon and George are coming over for dinner," Aunt Violet said. Sir Jon was Aunt Violet's longtime friend from college. The Lord of Misrule in that long-ago performance of *Madrigals and Mayhem*. George Flowers, who was in his sixties, was another close family friend. He owned a block of flats on the next street over, and helped us out with repairs and maintenance.

"Awesome. That will be fun." I pulled on mittens. "See you soon."

The three of us set off, Charlotte's brisk pace fueled by her anger. "I can't believe it," she said more than once, clenched fists pumping. "What a nerve."

At least the decorated storefronts, trees strung with lights, and garland draped around lampposts provided cheer. Other pedestrians smiled as they trudged past, arms filled with bags and packages.

I hadn't even started Christmas shopping, which reminded me: "Charlotte, do you have any Sasha dolls with brown hair? I want to get one for my mother."

"I'll check later. If not, I can reach out to my dealer network."

"Thanks." We did something similar at the bookshop when people wanted books we didn't have in stock.

Daisy smiled. "You're buying your mother a doll?"

"I know, that does sound a little strange," I admitted. "Hers went missing so I want to replace it." I rolled my eyes. "It disappeared under Janice's watch."

"What a surprise." Daisy knew all about my difficult aunt.

"You'd be amazed how many adults buy toys for themselves," Charlotte said. "That's why we stock such a big vintage selection. Plus, people like classic toys for their children and grandchildren. Gets them away from screens."

Oh, the simple days before gaming devices, phones, and tablets. I'd heard about them many times from my parents, who had valued books and hands-on activities both indoors and out for fun and education. My screen time had been severely limited and monitored as a kid.

Charlotte stopped on the sidewalk in front of a florist's shop. "Hold on. I want to get something here." A couple of moments later, she emerged from the shop holding a huge poinsettia plant. "For Barnaby."

A few minutes later, we arrived at St. Aelred, one of Cambridge's oldest and smallest colleges. Enclosed by stone walls, the buildings were ancient, with columned porticos and a stand-alone bell tower. The campus was even rumored to be haunted by the ghost of a headless monk.

All visitors were required to enter through the main gate, and as we walked into the porter's lodge, I wondered if we'd be able to get inside. These old colleges had quite a high level of security, instituted to preserve the sanctity of studying scholars—or to protect them from impromptu attacks by barbarians. Or, in this case, the anger of a wronged relative.

"Charlotte Pemberly," she said in an airy voice,

peeking around the plant. "Here for Barnaby Winters. I should be on the list."

The elderly porter checked his computer screen. "Mr. Winters is in the hospital at the moment, miss."

"I know. Isn't it awful?" Charlotte set the plant on the counter. "I'm here to get his rooms ready for his return."

"Ah," he said. "Here you are." He nudged the visitor log. "Sign in, please. Your friends as well." His eyes widened in recognition when he took a good look at Daisy and me. We'd seen him several times during our case involving a St. Aelred student. For a moment, I thought he might say something, but discretion won and he settled for a nod.

We all signed the book and Charlotte picked up the plant again.

The inner court was fairly deserted, only a couple of students making their way from one part of the campus to the other. St. Aelred was set up like many of the older colleges, long blocks surrounding an inner green space. An archway provided access to the next quadrangle and Charlotte headed in that direction.

As always, despite our clothing and the occasional modern touch such as a flag or poster in a window, we might have stepped back in time. Way back. The first colleges founded in the United States were glaringly new upstarts compared to a seven-hundred-year-old institution.

We approached the student lodgings about halfway down one block, a setup called a "stair." Students had individual rooms on several stories with shared kitchens and lounges. In addition to porters, cleaners were provided, something I certainly could have used when

I was at college. Or, to be more exact, my slovenly dorm mates would definitely have benefited from the service.

From our previous visits, I knew that the student doors were locked, a key code required to get in. "Do you have the code?" I asked Charlotte.

She set the plant on the outside steps and took out her phone. "I'm going to text Reece."

Before she could do that, another student arrived. Charlotte gave him a charming smile. "Thank you. Just in time." She picked up the plant, waiting for him to punch in the code. "I'm Barnaby's cousin."

He glanced at her as he worked the keypad. When his gaze lingered, she smiled even wider. "How's he doing?"

"On the mend." Charlotte lifted the plant. "This is for him."

"Nice." The door lock clunked open and he grabbed the handle, standing back to let us in.

We hurried up the stairs before he could change his mind. Once we heard a downstairs door shut, we all started to laugh. "You have a new fan," Daisy said.

"Go on," Charlotte scoffed. "It's the plant. Works every time."

"I'll make note of that," I said dryly.

On the second-floor landing, Charlotte handed me the poinsettia and knocked on a door. Inside, I could hear music playing. She knocked again and this time someone came to answer.

It was Tori Winters, who scowled. "What are you doing here?"

"What a *lovely* greeting." Charlotte's laugh was a silvery little trill that made me admire her even more. If she was upset or worried or angry, that laugh sure didn't reveal any of that. Taking the plant back from me, she said, "I brought this for Barnaby. I thought I could leave it here, with Reece." She elbowed past Tori, using the pot to push her out of the way.

We followed hastily, before Tori could close the door in our faces. "Hi again," I said, as if this was all normal.

Inside the room, four students were seated at tables, tapping away on laptops. One of them, a blond young man resembling an Abercrombie model, rose to his feet, a frown creasing his noble brow. "Charlotte? What are—"

She didn't even let him finish. Dropping the plant onto a table with a thud, she bellowed, "How dare you!" She wagged a finger in his face. "You broke into my shop and my house. Not cool, Reece."

The other students had stopped typing and were watching, mouths hanging open. Reece pivoted toward them. "I guess we're done for now. Come back after dinner, if you want."

They packed up their laptops, pulled on hats and coats, and filed out, casting curious glances back at us. Once they were gone, Reece sighed heavily and folded his arms. "What's this about, Charlotte?" Tori had moved to stand beside him, using identical body language.

The delay and his denial threw Charlotte off course and she sputtered a moment before rallying. "We have video evidence. You were at my house Thursday night. And someone saw you at the toy shop, too." This last was a bluff, since Aunt Violet hadn't identified Reece, or even Barnaby.

Now Reece was off-balance. "So? I was there, yeah. I didn't go inside either time. That was all Barnaby."

Charlotte roared back into fine form. "Phew." She

dramatically wiped a hand across her brow. "I'm so relieved. You didn't sneak off and leave your friend to die."

Tori gasped. "What a horrible thing to say." Her scowl deepened. "Besides, it's all your fault. You left those cakes for Barnaby to eat."

"Right," Charlotte said with an eye roll. "As if I had any idea he'd break in. Now I know, so I'm changing the locks today. And you can tell him—and the rest of the fam—that."

With a grunt of disgust, Reece sat down at his computer. He picked up a bowl and began to shovel noodles into his mouth. "I think it's time for you to leave." He sounded almost bored. "I'm about thirty seconds away from calling security."

"Fine," Charlotte said. "I'm done here anyway." With a flounce, she turned and headed for the door. "Coming, ladies?"

Tori's heels tapped as she ran after us. Leaning out the door, she called, "Isn't it enough that you got everything you wanted?" Her tone was bitter. "You'd better stay away from us from now on. We will be filing a restraining order."

CHAPTER 9

Charlotte held it together until we got outside. "I can't believe this!" she cried, startling several crows perched on the roof. They flew off on heavy, flapping wings, cawing.

"It's not surprising that Reece denied everything," I said. "His best defense was to stonewall you. Plus invoke security, as if you were in the wrong." Personally, I thought he was arrogant and probably lying. I didn't want to fan the flames, however.

Charlotte started stomping along the walk. "I suppose. Hopefully it gave him a heads-up not to try that again." Another few stomps. "I can't believe *they're* going to get a restraining order against *me*."

"They're just trying to intimidate you," Daisy said. "Still mad about the inheritance, obvs."

"That's right," I chimed in. "Don't forget, you won. They can't stand that."

Charlotte's chin came up. "I did, didn't I? Not that they deserved anything from Grandad's estate. If I thought they did, I'd share."

We strode briskly across the court, all of us eager to get out of there. I was looking forward to setting up and decorating the tree when I got back to the shop. First, though, we had something else to do. "Don't forget we have a clue to look for. The little drummer boy."

Charlotte, who was in the lead, threw me a look. "That's right. I definitely need to find that doll first. Before someone breaks in again and steals it."

"You think they'd dare?" Daisy sounded surprised.

"When half a million pounds are at stake, people will do just about anything," Charlotte said grimly. "They already tried to *kill* me, remember?"

The truth of her statement silenced us the rest of the way back to the street. Once we were outside the college walls, Charlotte shrugged her shoulders with a sigh, as if casting off a weight. "Who wants a coffee?"

Peppermint lattes to-go restored our moods as we headed back to Magpie Lane. By unspoken consent, we chatted about this and that, anything except murder and mayhem. Daisy was giving us sugar cookie baking tips when we arrived back at Pemberly's Emporium. "Make sure you chill the dough long enough," she advised. "Otherwise they'll stick to the board."

"I have an idea," I said. "I'll buy them from you."

"Me, too. Problem solved." Charlotte unlocked the front door. "After you."

All looked in order, I was glad to see. Charlotte switched on lights while we set our cups down and took off our coats. "The soldiers are back here," she said, gesturing.

The shop had quite a selection of toy soldiers, ranging from antique tin to modern olive drab plastic. Daisy picked up a tin drummer windup toy and looked it over. "I don't see anything."

Charlotte took the toy and looked at the bottom, then at the drumhead itself. It appeared to be tightly attached. She put it back on the shelf. "I don't want to wreck it."

"Are there any drums?" I asked. Maybe the clue hadn't been literal regarding the "drummer boy."

"Back here." Charlotte now led us to the musical instrument area.

"All right." I picked up a pair of colorful maracas and shook them. "These are fun." There were wood blocks, castanets, eggs to shake, tambourines, and more.

"Focus, Molly," Daisy teased.

I shook them again. "If I worked here, I'd be playing all day."

"Hazard of the job, for sure." Charlotte pulled several drums off the shelf, including a conga, and gave us each one.

"Nothing," I said a few minutes later. Where could Arthur have hidden the next clue? He had really been taking a chance by setting up the scavenger hunt, I realized. What if Charlotte sold an item that held a clue?

We gave up on the drums and returned to the counter to finish our lattes. I glanced around the shop, my gaze falling on the dollhouse. "Can I show you something, Charlotte?" I began walking toward the window. "Was the cake on the table before?"

Charlotte and Daisy peered into the house, at the dining room table set for tea. "I don't remember it being there," Charlotte said.

"What are you thinking?" Daisy asked me.

"Not sure." Actually, I wondered if someone had put the item on the table as a "gotcha." No doubt I was overthinking it.

A windup plush bunny with a drum sat on the window ledge. He wore a blue neckerchief and vest.

Drummer boy. "Um, Charlotte?" I picked up the toy and handed it to her. "Maybe this is it."

Charlotte studied the toy, turning it around in her hand. Then she grasped the top of the drum with her fingers and pulled. It came right off, revealing the hollow interior of the instrument. Daisy and I crowded close. A slip of paper was curled up inside.

After handing us the top of the drum and the toy, Charlotte unfurled the paper. "'We Three Kings.' Okay. Talk about cryptic."

"Do you have any Nativity sets?" I asked. That was the obvious place to look for the three kings referenced in the Christmas carol.

Charlotte shook her head. "They're not toys, so no. Let me think on it." She glanced at the wall clock, which read four forty-five. "It's that late? The locksmith will be here any minute."

I sighed in disappointment. "I suppose I should get back to the bookshop anyway. We're having people over for dinner."

"I have to scoot, too," Daisy said. "Tim is coming over."

"That's fine," Charlotte said. "I have to give this clue some thought anyway. If you have any brainstorms, send me a text." She gave us each a hug. "Thank you so much for today."

⋅•⋅

"You set up the tree." I stopped short inside the bookshop entrance, pleased to see that this task was already done.

"We had time," Mum said. She gestured to several

plastic tubs. "The lights and decorations are in there. Want to help?"

"Sure thing." I hung my coat in the kitchen, grabbed a beer, and returned to the front room. We were closed, so drinking alcohol out here was okay. Mum had a glass of wine. Aunt Violet was making dinner—we took turns—and the cats were supervising us.

Soft strains of classic holiday songs filled the air as we opened the tubs and found coils of lights, the bulbs large and old-fashioned. "I'll get a stool," I said, retrieving one that we used for tall shelves.

When I returned, Mum was opening a smaller box. "Look what I have."

"Mum," I said, breathless. It was the angel we'd used in Vermont and, in that moment, I was transported back to a bittersweet past. Putting her atop the tree had been my favorite ritual, first in my father's arms and later on a stool or stepladder.

"I couldn't leave her," she said, examining her from every angle. "I also packed a few of the ornaments you made."

"Really?" I groaned as I set the stool in place. "Those old things?" She handed me the angel and I hung her on the top upright branch. Mum held up the end of the first light string and I plugged them into the angel's cord.

"How could I get rid of them?" Mum said. "Too many memories."

"That's sweet, Mum."

The things we ended up cherishing the most were not always the most valuable. In fact, to the world they might even seem useless or unimportant. That's why I wanted to buy my mother a duplicate of her favorite doll. So she could relive a happy part of her child-hood.

I handed her the coil and she wound it around the tree and gave it back to me. Working our way down, we got the lights attached. When we plugged them in, most of them worked, a sudden burst of color that made the cats blink. We had some spare bulbs and worked on replacing the dead ones.

Lights done, we paused for a break, drinking our adult beverages. "I had quite the day," I said, going on to relay our visit to St. Aelred and the discovery of the second clue. Aunt Violet slipped in partway through this discussion and sat in the red velvet chair to listen. Both cats immediately crawled into her lap, purring.

"You're trapped," I said with a laugh.

"That's fine." Aunt Violet sipped wine. "The chicken and veggies are in the oven so I don't have to do any-thing for a while."

"I was thinking of taking a trip to Hazelhurst this week sometime," Mum said. "Will you go with me, Molly?"

"Sure." I chose a glass ball and attached a hanger. "What do you want to do there?"

"Visit the graveyard."

"What?" Her answer startled me and I almost dropped the ornament. After a comical fumble, I placed it safely on the tree.

Mum's face set in determination. "I want to visit my parents' graves. It's time."

"Sounds like a plan." Although I tried to sound light, my heart was pounding, the way it always did when Mum talked about her family. I knew hardly anything about them and had learned young not to bring up what was obviously a painful topic. Even now, I was afraid to say the wrong thing although I was bursting with curiosity. What had these people been like? Did they have any redeeming qualities I could be proud of inheriting?

I ventured a comment. "I've never even seen the house where you grew up." All I knew is that Uncle Chris lived there.

"Maybe we can go by," Mum said. "I'd like to see the old place myself."

Aunt Violet lifted her wineglass in a toast that only I saw. She was glad Mum was taking these steps, I gathered. Not so much as to change her mind about the estrangement she'd needed for her own mental health, but to maybe lay that past to rest.

"All right, boys, I have to get up." Aunt Violet nudged the cats aside and stood. "Need to check dinner and I'm out of wine."

I picked up my empty beer bottle. "I'll set the table." And grab another beer.

"I'll keep plugging away here," Mum said.

As for the cats, they followed us to the kitchen, probably hoping it was dinnertime for them as well.

CHAPTER 10

Sir Jon and George blew in through the kitchen French door on a wave of good cheer and cold winter air. "It's a bit nippy out there," Sir Jon said, stamping his feet on the doormat as he handed Aunt Violet a brown-bagged bottle of wine.

George set a bakery box on the counter and unbuttoned his coat. "Victoria sponge."

"Yum." I opened the box for a peek at the two-layer vanilla cake with raspberry jam and whipped cream in the middle.

"Have a seat," Aunt Violet said, ushering them to the table. "I'll bring you a glass of wine."

The men, both around Aunt Violet's age, were a study in contrasts. Shortish and slim with thick gray hair and dapper, Sir Jon was a former MI6 agent-turned-bookseller who owned a shop specializing in spy and adventure books. He still dabbled in cases now and then and was a very good man to know "in a pinch," as Aunt Violet often said.

As for George, he was burly in build, with blunt, pleasant features and a bald head that he covered with a flat cap. Usually dressed in tweed, he looked the quintessential English country gentleman. He was direct, dependable, and kind—and a Brontë aficionado.

"What's new?" George asked, taking off his cap and hanging it on the chairback.

I glanced at Mum and Aunt Violet. "The question is, where to begin?"

He nodded sagely. "Oh, it's like that, is it? Soon as I heard about the poisoning at the toy shop, I said to myself, I bet our Molly is neck-deep in solving that one."

Rather than comment on what he'd said about my propensity for trouble, I asked, "Is that the word on the street, that he was poisoned?" I'd wondered how far word had spread that Barnaby's illness had a criminal cause.

"'Twas the police searching the tearoom that gave it away," George said. He nodded thanks when Aunt Violet set a wineglass in front of him. "Any leads yet?"

"Not leads," I said. "Suspects. Charlotte Pemberly and Daisy."

George sucked in a breath. "Not our Daisy."

"I don't think she's in real danger of being arrested," I said. "Even though the poisoner put one of her cards inside the box of cakes."

"That's bloody rotten." George's face reddened and he snorted like a bull getting ready to charge.

"The police are only doing their due diligence," I hastened to assure him. "I'm keeping an eye on everything, trust me."

"You tell Daisy we have her back," George said. "Actually, I will, next time I go in." He took a sip of wine, glowering.

"She'll appreciate it, I'm sure," I said.

"Any idea about motive?" Sir Jon asked. "I heard

there was controversy around Arthur Pemberly's will. Is that the problem?" His knowledge of the situation didn't surprise me, due to his deep-rooted connections.

"I think so, yes," I said. "Charlotte told me the will was contested and there's still a lot of bad blood between her and Althea's family. Besides the property and business, she also inherited a very valuable doll. She believes Barnaby broke in to look for it."

"Did he steal it?" George asked. "The cheek of the man."

"No, because he couldn't find it," I explained. "And sadly, Charlotte can't, either. Daisy and I were helping her look this afternoon. No luck yet."

"How valuable is this doll?" George filled the wineglasses.

I made a scoffing sound. "You won't believe it. Half a million pounds." I brought up a similar one on my phone and handed it to George. "Charlotte's is not only valuable, it's rare."

"It's beautiful." Mum was looking over George's shoulder. "Ridiculous amount of money, though." She passed the phone to Sir Jon.

"A black-market item, then," Sir Jon said. "Far too distinctive for a thief to sell it openly." Due to his government work, Sir Jon knew all about the black market for books, antiquities, and art. Collectibles as well, it appeared.

"Give me a hand, Molly?" Aunt Violet got up to serve dinner.

I joined her at the stove, to help ferry serving dishes to the table. Thinking we should shelve the discussion of attempted murder, I said, "So, what else is going on?"

Sir Jon sat up straight, clearing his throat. "We have big news." Once we were suitably attentive, he went on.

"I've been asked to reprise my role as court jester for Althea's madrigal dinner. You remember, don't you, Violet? I'm looking forward to my return to the stage."

Aunt Violet exclaimed in surprise, "That's lovely! We'll have to come see you. If we can get tickets," she added.

He waved that off. "I'll get you in."

I was stuck on something Sir Jon had said. "What did you mean by *we*?"

George patted his chest. "I've joined the cast as well. Not sure of my role but I will be singing."

The two men looked at each other and burst into, "God Rest Ye Merry, Gentlemen." Their voices rose and fell in a perfect blend, Sir Jon a tenor and George, bass. On impulse, I added my own alto to the mix, as a counterpoint to the lower notes.

We ended the song in a burst of sound and then started laughing. "I'm impressed," George said. "I had no idea that you had such a nice voice."

My cheeks warmed with pleasure. "I'm better in a group." Solos scared me, quite frankly, ever since music camp, when the teacher said I sounded like a frog in a boot. I'd had hay fever, which explained my croaking, but in my childish mind, audience attention equaled humiliation.

"You should try out," Sir Jon said. "I understand they still need people. We're going to be on telly, I heard, which will be a lot of fun."

Even more reason for me not to join the group. What if I messed up on television? The tabloids would have a field day. I could see it now: *Vermont Beauty Bombs on the Beeb*. Dating Kieran meant I was no longer anonymous or unknown. I was still wrapping my head around being in the public eye.

"Kieran already asked me," I admitted. "He's in the cast, too."

"Even more reason to join then, love," George said. "You'll have a wonderful time together."

"Like Violet and I did in the original show. Hmm, Violet?" Sir Jon's warm gaze rested on my great-aunt, who blushed furiously. "Do you want a part, Vi?"

She shook her head. "Not this year. We're far too busy here."

There was an excuse. "Yeah, I should probably give it a pass," I said. "We're way too busy."

The next few minutes were occupied by getting dinner on the table. Sir Jon carved the roast chicken and we passed around bowls of mashed potatoes, peas, buttered carrots, and gravy.

As we dug in, the warm, savory meal hitting the spot on this cold evening, I mulled over the idea of joining the madrigals cast. On one hand, I'd be singing on stage in a televised performance, a situation that was the stuff of bad dreams. A million ways to make a fool of myself and even embarrass my boyfriend and family.

On the other, joining the cast would give me an opportunity to get closer to the Winters family. Maybe I would be able to figure out what was going on. Who had brought poisoned cakes to the toy shop. If they were still going to search for the doll.

Who had killed Arthur Pemberly.

I hadn't had a chance to tell Mum and Aunt Violet about the cream we'd found earlier this afternoon. To tell Aunt Violet that her old friend had been murdered. Maybe. The police still had to test the cream, I reminded myself. Still, the thought made my midsection tighten and I had to put my fork down.

Mum sent me a concerned look. "Are you okay, Molly?"

"Yeah," I said with a sigh. "Just thinking. Wondering if I should join the madrigals." A real downer of a thought struck me. "What if it's not safe?" Everyone stared at me in confusion and surprise and I scrambled to explain. "I mean, because of Barnaby's poisoning." My voice trailed off. This really was a stretch. Why would anyone at the madrigal dinner be in danger? The poisoning was a family affair, far as I knew.

Sir Jon's smile was teasing. "The only danger I see is our George falling into Althea's clutches. She's quite the man-eater." He hummed a few bars of the Hall & Oates song.

"Three husbands and counting," I noted. "What about you, Sir Jon? You're a catch as well."

"She already tried. I was immune then, even more so now." His gaze slid to Aunt Violet, who flushed again and pretended to chase peas around her plate.

"Well, *there's* a reason for me to join," I said, relief easing my tension. Or was it the heady recklessness of stepping off a cliff? "I need to protect George."

⚬❧⚬

After our guests went home, I headed upstairs to bed, *Charlotte's Dollhouse* in hand, Puck right behind me. He always slept with me, while Aunt Violet was Clarence's person. One of my absolute favorite things was curling up in bed under a down duvet with a purring cat and a book. Before I started reading, though, I found the madrigals announcement looking for singers. I sent a message, mentioning that Kieran, Sir Jon, and George had suggested I try out. Hopefully their names would push me higher up the list.

Charlotte's Dollhouse, cont.

The sun was peeking over London's chimney pots when Charlotte threw back the covers and sat on the edge of the bed. Yawning and blinking, she looked around the room. Then her gaze focused on the dollhouse.

The first thing she noticed was the soldier standing guard on the roof garden. She gasped. How did he get there?

Vague memories of a red rage and hot tears made Charlotte squirm. Had she really thrown the dolls around in a temper? What was Aunt Margaret going to think? She had told Charlotte to be careful with the dollhouse, that it was handmade and quite valuable.

She slid one bare foot down to the carpet. Maybe she hadn't thrown the dolls around. Maybe it had been a dream. A bad dream. She had too many of those lately.

Waking up wasn't much better.

The second foot landed on the carpet and Charlotte padded over to the dollhouse. She plopped onto the floor, her flannel nightgown pooling around her legs, keeping her feet warm.

She bent forward, staring into the dollhouse.

The other dolls were inside.

Mrs. Morton stood by the kitchen table, a chicken in a roasting pan waiting to be put in the oven. Polly was upstairs, standing in front of a mirror.

Charlotte picked Polly up. She really was beautiful with her long, curly blond hair, porcelain face, and blue silk dress. She even wore petticoats and pantaloons underneath.

No one wore those now. Polly was definitely old-fashioned. But pretty. She put Polly back, noticing a blue parasol next to the mirror. How adorable.

In the drawing room, Mr. Bear was seated at a table set for tea. Jingles was across from him, his wooden-bead arms and legs hanging loose.

Charlotte picked up Jingles and shook him, making the bells on his cap ring. She spun him in cartwheels across the rug, his red and green body flashing, and then held him close to her face, examining his painted features and perpetual grin.

The bedroom door opened. "Charlotte?"

Startled, Charlotte dropped the jester and turned toward her aunt. Until she'd moved to London, she hadn't spent much time with Aunt Margaret and Uncle Howard. She barely knew them, in fact. One thing that she was sure of: they were old. Much older than her mother and father.

Smoothing her dressing gown, Aunt Margaret sat on the edge of Charlotte's bed. "I see you're playing with the dollhouse. It was my favorite toy when I was your age."

"When was that?" Charlotte asked, unable to imagine her aunt as a young girl.

Aunt Margaret laughed. "Oh, many moons ago. It's been in the attic for decades and when you came to us, I thought, I'll bring it out for Charlotte."

Although Charlotte knew a polite response was expected, she stubbornly remained silent. The jester stared at her from the rug and she snatched him up and hid his accusing gaze. "Thank you," she mumbled.

"You're quite welcome." Aunt Margaret sounded pleased. "After breakfast, I thought we'd go ice skating and out to lunch. Would you like that?"

"Yes, I would." Charlotte loved ice skating.

Aunt Margaret stood, tightening the sash of her robe. "Wash up and get dressed, then. Wear your wool stockings. I'll see you downstairs."

Jingles had never left the house. Not since the day he had been brought home and propped up under the Christmas tree for Margaret to find.

Now he was riding in Charlotte's coat pocket, taking everything in as she strode along the sidewalk beside Margaret. And there was so much to see. Pedestrians—nannies with prams, schoolgirls arm in arm, serious gentlemen swinging brollies—were an endless river. In the street, delivery vans, omnibuses, and automobiles chugged along, the occasional brash horn making Jingles want to jump. This being daytime, he couldn't move on his own. But still, this was all so exciting. He could hardly wait to tell the others about his adventure.

They entered the park and made their way along the path to the frozen lake. Many skaters were already on the ice and others were getting ready to join the fun. Margaret rented skates and helped Charlotte put hers on.

Holding hands, they gingerly made their way out onto the ice. "You can let go," *Charlotte said.* "I can skate. Really."

"If you're sure." *Margaret looked worried but she dropped Charlotte's hand.*

After a deep inhale, the girl pushed off, one foot in front of the other. It was a sensation like swooping though the air, and Jingles wished desperately he could hold on. Everything blurred as the cold air rushed past.

"Whee!" *Charlotte cried.* "I'm doing it."

"Hurray!" *Margaret called. She soon caught up and the pair whipped around the lake, making a wide circle. When they stopped to catch their breath, Margaret noticed him.* "Is that Jingles?"

Charlotte pulled him out of her pocket. "Yes. I hope you don't mind that I brought him." *She held him to her chest, his nose buried against her wool coat.* "He's adorable."

Margaret didn't say anything for a long moment. "Don't lose him, all right? My son—" *She cleared her throat.* "I've had Jingles forever."

"I won't." *Sounding relieved, Charlotte stuffed him back into her pocket. As they set off again, Jingles thought about the boy. He hadn't seen him for a long, long time.*

CHAPTER 11

"Packages for you, Molly," Mum called after the courier left. She stood behind the desk, sorting through the pile of boxes brought in on a handcart.

"Be there in a minute." I turned back to my customer, a young man buying picture books for his infant daughter. "In this section, we have an array of classics old and new. If you don't see a title you want, we can order it."

"Good to know." He smiled ruefully. "Is there still time to get special orders in before Christmas? I should have started shopping sooner."

"We can do overnight delivery, if need be," I assured him. "The days just fly by this time of year, don't they?"

"They sure do." He started browsing the shelf, so I left him in peace and hurried over to the desk.

"That was fast," I said, reading the labels. I picked up a box cutter. "These are the dollhouse books for my display."

"Fun." Mum was unpacking a box of holiday-themed paperback mystery novels. "Look at these." She held up a couple.

"They are going to fly off the shelves," I commented.

"Maybe put them in the window?" We could stack them under the small, white-frosted artificial tree. The colorful covers would provide an eye-catching contrast.

"Good idea. If we dare to displace Clarence."

"I'll leave him room." If I didn't, he would simply take it. He was lying on the snowman again, the thing almost permanently squashed out of shape.

We worked in silence for a few minutes, ripping open boxes, checking packing slips, stacking books for display. My customer was still happily browsing.

"What do you think about going to Hazelhurst with me this afternoon?" Mum asked. "Aunt Violet said she doesn't mind. Mondays are usually slow anyway."

My heart gave a leap. "Sure. After lunch?" I had a long list of tasks this morning.

"That's what I was thinking." Mum broke down the last box and placed it with the others destined for recycling.

My phone bleeped with a text from Charlotte. *Good news. Barnaby was released from the hospital. I'm at Grandad's getting cameras and new locks put in.*

Glad to hear it. On both counts. Hopefully touch base later?

I wondered how long it would take the police lab to analyze the ointment we'd found. Meanwhile, I had an idea what we could do to keep investigating.

"Mum, do you like the wax melts?" I nodded toward the holder I'd bought at Mistletoe Farm. We had it going today and the aroma of evergreens was heavenly.

"Yes," she said, puzzled. "Why?"

"Well, I was thinking . . . if we have time this afternoon, we could go by Mistletoe Farm. They have a great gift shop."

I'd told Mum and Aunt Violet about the cream this

morning at breakfast, so naturally she put two and two together. Her smile was crooked. "I suppose we can do a little investigating. After we rip the bandage off the wound."

I felt a jolt of compunction. "Are you really sure you want to do this? If you're not ready . . ."

She made a face. "If not now, when? I've already been here six months. Time to stop putting it off."

My customer came up to the desk, holding several picture books. "I found some great ones." He set them on the counter shelf.

"Awesome." Looking at each one, I entered the price into the point-of-sale. *Goodnight Moon. The Very Hungry Caterpillar. Baby Animals*, a touch-and-feel board book. "She'll love these."

"I know," he said with enthusiasm as he pulled out his wallet. "My wife and I had these same books as kids. We're really looking forward to reading to her."

"How old is she?" Mum asked. "And what's her name?"

"Matilda Mary." His face was suffused with pride. "She's a month old tomorrow."

"Getting her off to a great start with books." I gave him the total and he put his card in the reader.

As he walked out, whistling, I thought, *This is why we do this.*

I added the new dollhouse books to the display, then, having a moment to drink a cup of tea, I sat down with a history. Dollhouses, I soon learned, were originally called "baby houses," replicas of actual houses with the goal of showing off household miniatures. Several of the oldest known baby houses were now in German museums, incredibly detailed replicas of early seventeenth-century homes. Included was one purposely built to teach children about household tasks. What a fun way to learn.

Along the same lines was the so-called Queen Mary's Dolls' House at Windsor Castle. Built in the early 1920s for the queen as a gift, this treasure featured working electricity, water, and elevators. Hundreds of craftspeople, artists, and writers (miniatures of their best books) contributed to this masterwork. There were even tiny bottles of champagne in the wine cellar.

In the late nineteenth century, mass production of dollhouses and furnishings helped create a shift from valuable display item to a toy for children. That is where we were today for the most part, although designers still liked to outdo each other with elaborate creations. On a more personal level, there were still beautiful handmade examples like the dollhouse at Pemberly's. Made with love for a special child.

Several customers came in so I shut the history and set it aside. Dollhouses had long captured the imagination of adults and children alike. Who didn't wish they could create a perfect, miniature world and live it in, too? The popularity of dollhouse books, with their living dolls, certainly spoke to a universal fascination with the idea.

We ate a quick lunch of roast beef with horseradish on marbled rye and then got ready to leave for Hazelhurst.

"Are you sure you'll be all right alone?" Mum asked Aunt Violet for about the tenth time.

Aunt Violet cocked a brow. "Did you forget, my

dear," she said in a dry tone, "that I ran this shop by myself for years?"

"No, of course not . . ." Mum exhaled with a huff.

My aunt patted her arm. "You'll feel much better once you get it over with. Trust me."

"I hope you're right." Mum hugged Aunt Violet, who endured the embrace about as well as Clarence did when we held him. Meaning, barely tolerated it. There was no doubt that Aunt Violet loved us, but she had that famous British reticence in spades. Taken to extremes, it made me wonder how conception ever occurred.

After releasing Aunt Violet, Mum dug around in her handbag. "The keys. Molly, do you know where they are?"

I held them up. "Want me to drive?" I was finally comfortable with driving on the left after a few harrowing ordeals behind the wheel, although I still flinched sometimes when entering a roundabout.

Mum gnawed at her lip before grabbing the keys. "Let me. I know the village like the back of my hand."

Maybe driving would give her something else to think about. Aunt Violet's vintage gold Cortina was parked in a garage at the end of the lane and we were soon on our way. As we drove past the tearoom, I saw it was still closed. I should check in with Daisy later and see if she needed help getting ready to open again. The toy shop was also closed up tight, so Charlotte must still be at her grandfather's house.

"Where is the farm?" Mum asked once we were free of the city's gridlock. I gave her directions. "Oh. The Lewis farm."

"Do you know Andre?" He was around the same age as Mum, I thought.

Mum nodded. "He was a couple years behind me in school. Cute kid. Lost his mother young, which was awful. I still remember that day at school. We all heard the ambulance."

"That is awful." After a moment, I said, "His father was Althea's second husband. He's gone now as well."

"She does make a habit of discarding husbands, doesn't she?" Mum's crisp remark startled a laugh out of me and soon she was joining in. "Sorry," she gasped. "It's really not funny."

"No, but it's a pattern." Sometimes it was easier to see them from the outside. Her friends probably thought she had a life marked by tragedy. Guilt at rushing to judgment made me add, "I know I'm jumping to conclusions about Althea. After the way she treated Charlotte, I can't help but think the worst. She barely let her see her grandfather while he was dying."

Mum made a shocked sound. "That's shameful. You told me that he raised Charlotte?"

"For the most part, yes. After she lost her parents."

I cringed. We were back on the subject of loss. So much loss, including in our own small family. Which made me determined to express my feelings while I could. "Love you, Mum," I said fiercely.

She threw me a surprised look. "What did I do to deserve that?"

"Nothing. And that's the point. You're just you, that's all."

"I love you, too." The tightness in her brow and around her eyes eased, which I was glad to see. Despite the pain of her past, we had each other—and my wonderful dad until his death. Nothing could change that.

Despite it being Monday morning, the farm was busy. As on our last visit, music played over loudspeakers and costumed helpers roamed. This time I headed directly for the gift shop. Mum walked more slowly, taking everything in.

"This place is amazing," she said, following me into the shop. "I want to get a wreath."

"We can grab one after," I said, wiping my feet on the doormat. The herbal products were in the back corner so I went in that direction.

"Welcome back!" Andre boomed from behind the counter. Then his mouth dropped open. "Nina? Nina Marlowe, is that you?"

"It is." Mum went to talk to Andre and I kept going. "The farm looks fabulous."

He laughed. "A far cry from when I took it over, for sure. Trying to make it pay for itself."

"I hear you."

They started chatting away, trading memories and updates, while I scanned the shelves for the arthritis cream. There it was, the tubes sold in boxes. *Aconitum Napellus 30C* was an ingredient. Monkshood. The box said the cream was "formulated by hand at Mistletoe Farm." Going by the other inventory, the farm produced a range of herbal products: tinctures, teas, soaps, and salves.

Footsteps approached as Andre and Mum joined me. I waved the box. "You make this here?"

"We do." Andre motioned toward the shelves. "Anything labeled Mistletoe Farm is manufactured here, with many of the plant ingredients grown on site."

Including Aconitum? "What does this mean?" I showed him the ingredient.

"C and X are dilution scales in homeopathy," he explained. "The original ingredient is diluted thousands of times yet retains its essential healing essence."

How could a cream with diluted monkshood kill? It must have been doctored.

"Do you make the homeopathic formulas here?" Mum asked.

"No, we buy those ingredients," Andre said. "Although I've thought of studying homeopathy, I haven't had the time as of yet. The other products are made here, under strictly sanitary conditions."

The door opened and Dorcas Winters stepped in, her glossy bob swinging along the shoulders of a red wool coat. I cringed back, hoping she hadn't seen me. She'd been so aggressive with Charlotte.

"Please excuse me for a minute," Andre said.

After he walked away, Mum and I hunkered behind the display, talking in quiet tones. I ran my finger along the homeopathic ingredient. "They must have added more of this. Undiluted."

"Makes sense," Mum said. "That flower is grown all over the place. It's not rare or anything."

The sound of sobbing caught my ear. Mum and I stared at each other in surprise before peeking out around a display of botanical-themed cards.

"I almost lost him." Dorcas's shoulders were shaking.

Andre gathered her into his arms, patting her back as he tried to reassure her. "There, there. Let it all out. You'll feel better."

Of course they knew each other. Andre's father had been married to Althea, who was Dorcas's mother-in-law. I took a closer look and noticed where his other hand was resting. Or from, er, more intimate encounters.

I could tell by Mum's raised brows that she was thinking the same thing.

She dabbed at her face with a tissue, sniffing, "Everything is going wrong lately. I don't know how much more I can take. It's all because of Charlotte." Her voice was full of venom. "She's the cause of all this."

Mum and I exchanged wide-eyed looks. Charlotte definitely had an enemy in Dorcas.

Andre glanced toward us as he patted her shoulder. "Listen, why don't you go to the house?" he suggested. "Make a cup of tea and put your feet up. I'll be over, after I get someone to watch the store."

"All right. I'll do that." She straightened her coat and gathered her handbag, then left the store, not seeming to have noticed us.

Andre looked over at us as the door shut behind her. "Any luck?"

I tugged on Mum's sleeve. "Wax melts. I'd like to get more." They were on the other side of the store. Hopefully Andre wouldn't think too much about us checking out the herbal ointment. He might put two and two together after the news broke, assuming that the lab did find poison. I preferred to stay on people's good side while investigating.

Mum lifted the packages to her nose. "I like this one." She handed it to me.

Clove, cinnamon, and orange. "Perfect. Let's pay for it and go find a wreath."

◆◆

"What are you doing?" I asked Mum when she opened the Cortina trunk. We were parked in the middle of Hazlehurst, near the church.

"Getting this." She pulled the wreath out, looping it over one arm while closing the trunk with the other.

It took me a minute. *Oh.* She was going to put the wreath on the graves. Even as I thought that, I noticed the decorations in the churchyard, the vases full of holly, other wreaths, and even garlands draped across the stones.

Setting her shoulders, Mum trudged through the arch set between stone walls. I followed with both interest and reluctance. In general, I liked visiting old grave-yards, their leaning stones or elaborate monuments a marker of former lives. I liked reading the inscriptions and thinking about those who had passed this way before, often with twinges of sadness about those who had died too soon. With their recorded dates, art, and often poetic, even humorous, inscriptions, gravestones were valuable historical records.

The one belonging to my grandparents offered nothing along those lines. It was polished and rect-angular, neither large nor small, with only names and dates. Names I only vaguely remembered.

Lilian Evelyn Yates Marlowe. Ralph Thomas Marlowe. Grandparents who I had never met and would never get to know. My eyes watered and I wasn't sure if it was the cold wind or a sudden surge of emotion. I did know that this was sad, a loss, even though it's said, how can you miss what you'd never had? Believe me, you could.

Mum placed the wreath resting up against the stone they shared and stood there, hands folded. Moving around back, I noticed that another name was carved there. My uncle's, with his birth date. No Nina Ellen Marlowe, born in 1970.

Although they'd probably figured that my mother

would join my father in Vermont, the exclusion still hurt. They'd cut my mother out of their lives as cleanly as she had on her end.

My mother was still standing there, staring down at the plot. Rather than ask what she was thinking, I left her alone, wandering off to study some nearby headstones. When I circled back around, she shook herself, as if coming out of a trance, and said, "It wasn't what I wanted but it's what I got." Her eyes were watering too, I noticed. "I tried my best, Molly. I hope you believe me." With a sigh, she looked down at the stone. "No matter what I did, it was never enough. It was only later, after I met your father, that I figured it out. There was nothing I could do to earn my mother's approval. Nothing."

"But why?" Despite the ruminating I'd done on the situation, I still couldn't wrap my head around it. "Why wouldn't she love you? You were adorable and smart and talented."

With a wry smile, Mum shrugged. "I know. Now. As my therapist—"

"Therapist?" This was news to me.

Mum patiently went on without explaining. "As my therapist helped me see, my mother was mentally ill. So was her mother, before her. She had a personality disorder where she always needed an enemy to fight— an in-group and an out-group. I was the target. Chris, she adored. Dad tried to placate her, to keep her from going too far, I realize now."

A wave of indignant anger gusted over me. If only my grandparents were still alive. I would tell them where to get off, respect my elders or not. "That's not fair."

Mum's smile widened. "I always used to say that.

And she'd respond that life wasn't fair. So one day, I said, when I was oh, about four, that it was up to us to make it fair, then."

My mouth dropped open in admiration. "Awesome. What did she say?"

Now Mum laughed. "She just stared at me. She had no idea what to do with me. That was probably when she started telling me I was too smart for my own good."

"Too smart to control, you mean."

"That, too." Mum sighed. "Anyway, I didn't come here to rehash past grievances. I'm trying to let it all go, once and for all. My life has been wonderful. I really have nothing to complain about."

Maybe so, but I could see what a loss it was, that she'd never had a close relationship with her parents. This realization made me appreciate my own sweet mother and father even more.

"Want to go by the house?" Mum asked.

"Your childhood home?" My pulse leaped. Another piece of the puzzle to be filled in. "Sure." Then I added, worried, "Do you really want to?" Was she ready, I meant.

Mum shrugged. "In for a penny, in for a pound, right? Might as well finish the memory tour."

As I followed her out of the cemetery, I glanced back at the stone. "Your loss," I mouthed. Maybe it was strange to say that to two people who were already dead, but it was true. Lilian and Ralph had lost their daughter and had never even met their granddaughter—me. Life was hard enough. Why did some people make it more difficult by mistreating those they supposedly loved?

I couldn't help but think of Charlotte and her horrible

relatives by marriage. In her case, hatred had escalated to attempted murder. I shivered at the certainty that there would be another attempt. Where and when was the question. Could Daisy and I keep her safe?

CHAPTER 12

The Marlowe house was on the outskirts of the village, a charming thatched cottage with a peaked roof and diamond-pane windows. The thatched roof featured fancy ornamentation along the ridgeline, the signature of a master at work.

"Wow!" I exclaimed as Mum pulled up in front. "It's gorgeous."

"Dad designed the roof." Mum shut off the engine. "He regarded our house as an advertisement for his work."

"So Chris took over the family business?" Until I'd moved to England, I hadn't even considered that thatching was a profession, an ancient and skilled one, too.

"He did." Mum opened her car door. "Why don't we take a walk around the garden? Chris won't mind. He's been asking me to come over for ages."

He has? I didn't say that out loud, though. Mum had her reasons for not wanting to visit and I respected that. I was dying to go inside, though, to be honest. Not only was it a family home, it was enchanting.

Growing up there must have been like living in a fairy tale. One with an evil witch. "Mum, were you Snow White?" Oops. Had I really asked that?

She paused, her hand on the picket-fence gate. "Pretty much." She laughed. "Your dad kissed me awake."

I rolled my eyes. "Please, Mum. Too much information."

We slowly walked up the path toward the front door taking everything in. Even in this dormant season, it was apparent that the grounds were well cared for. Rosebushes were neatly trimmed, the flower beds tidy for the winter, the grass like shorn green velvet.

"Mum loved her garden," my mother said, stopping beside an extensive border. "She was out here almost every day puttering around. She really had a talent."

How generous of Mum to praise Lilian. As I was about to say so, the front door of the house flew open.

Aunt Janice came out onto the step, arms hugging her midsection against the chilly air. Startled and taken aback, we stared at her in surprise. My aunt and uncle had separated last summer, after which my aunt had taken up with another man. That had ended badly due to the other man's death. Hearing that they might reconcile had not exactly been welcome news.

A therapist might say that my uncle was seeking the familiar because my aunt was as difficult as his mother. She was a snob and a social climber with a spiteful tongue and an air of superiority.

"Nina," she said with a sniff of disdain. "What are *you* doing here?"

Mum is one of the most even-tempered people I know. However, even a low kettle boils at some point. Her fists clenched and an expression of sheer rage flashed over her features.

"A better question is, why are *you* here? Did my brother actually take you back?" Mum's voice was laced with doubt and scorn.

Aunt Janice shifted her feet, a tell if I'd ever seen one. "Um . . . not exactly. Not yet."

Mum grunted as she ascended the steps and pushed past Janice. We were going inside, I guessed. I scooted along behind her before she could change her mind. I had to see the house.

"Hello, Molly," Aunt Janice said, a sheepish look on her face.

"Hey." I didn't linger to chat.

The cottage was everything the exterior promised. Low, beamed ceilings, stone fireplaces, and plaster walls over wide-board wainscoting gave a cozy feel. The front rooms had been knocked into one at some point, extending across the front to encompass a living room and dining room. A winding staircase was revealed behind a half-open door.

Mum made a beeline for the stairs, with me on her heels. Aunt Janice ran after us, calling, "Where are you going? Hold on, Nina. We need to talk."

Ignoring her, Mum continued upstairs. We arrived in a square hall with several doors off it. A couple of armchairs and a bookcase made this landing into a cozy nook.

Mum went directly to a certain door. Her old bedroom, I guessed. Loud panting noises behind us notified me that Aunt Janice had followed us upstairs.

"Nina," she said again.

The door squeaked as Mum pushed it open. I crowded behind her, peering over her shoulder. "It looks the same," she said. "Most of my things are gone, of course."

I saw a charming room with white-and-gold French provincial furniture, a faded yet plush floral carpet, and white curtains with bobbles.

"We use it as a guest room," Janice said. She barged by Mum into the room and started to straighten the already smooth quilted spread.

I thought Mum might take offense at the *we,* but she didn't even look at Janice when she entered the room. A little wooden jewelry box sat on the long bureau and she opened the lid. Music tinkled as a little ballerina spun around. She closed the lid and ran a finger along the top. "A Christmas gift when I was ten."

"Do you want to take it?" Janice sounded eager, as if she wanted to make amends.

Mum shrugged, her gaze skittering around the room. Then she methodically began to open and close the bureau drawers. "Have you seen my Sasha doll?"

"Sasha doll? No." Janice's cheeks reddened. "It wasn't in the trunk?" The shrillness of her tone was a dead giveaway that she was lying.

"No, it was not." Mum leveled a look at my aunt. "Can you give us a moment, please?" When Janice balked, Mum pulled out her phone. "I'll give Chris a ring, see what he says."

"All right. All right. I'm going." Janice bustled with great umbrage toward the door. "Why you're here now after thirty years, that's what I want to know. I've been taking care of this house for most of it. Your ailing parents as well."

Mum rolled her eyes. Janice thumped down the stairs, sighing and muttering. Once she was really gone, Mum went over to the bed and crouched down. She flipped the covers up and half-crawled underneath, sprawling on her stomach. Did she think her doll was under there?

A few minutes later she crawled back out, dust bunnies clinging to her coat. She picked one off and dropped it on the floor. "I guess Janice isn't the best housekeeper, huh?"

She was holding a stack of notebooks. Before I could ask, she said, "These are my journals. I kept them under a loose floorboard." She hugged them to her chest. "My first poems. I was positive someone would have thrown them out by now."

"Janice would have, I bet. If she knew where they were." My gaze fell on the wooden jewelry box. "Can I take that?" Because it was Mum's, not because I owned much jewelry.

"Help yourself." Mum started toward the door. "I've seen enough for one day. Let's get out of here."

Janice popped out of the kitchen when we reached the bottom of the stairs. "Cup of tea?"

"No, thanks," Mum said, clutching the notebooks to her chest. "We need to get back."

Janice arched a brow. "Oh. To the bookshop?" Her dismissive tone made me bristle and I bit back a sharp retort. Just another of her games, I reminded myself.

As I followed Mum toward the door, Janice pounced on me. "Are you still seeing Kieran Scott, Molly? How's it going?"

"Fine," I gritted out between clenched teeth.

"His mother, Lady Asha, is so lovely." As if I didn't know her name. "We're on so many committees together." Right on my heels now, she picked up a bundle of tickets from a table beside the front door. "We're selling *Madrigals and Mayhem* raffle tickets to benefit local children's programs. The main prize is two seats in the front row. It's almost impossible to get tickets to the dinner, you know. After word got out that the BBC would be filming this year."

"I don't need tickets to attend," I said. "I've been

asked to perform." Not that I'd auditioned yet or even heard back. It was worth the stretch to see her eyes bug out in disbelief.

"Oh, that's amazing. I didn't know you could *sing*." There it was again, the dismissive and demeaning tone. Rudeness was her default setting and it was infuriating.

Mum turned. "You remind me so much of my mother, Janice." In contrast, her voice was perfectly neutral, which only increased the impact of her words. "Believe me when I say that's not a good thing." She opened the door. "Coming, Molly?"

∘◦∘

"That woman." Mum was gripping the steering wheel like a newbie driver, she was so tense. "I can't believe Chris is even thinking about reconciling. She hasn't changed a bit."

"Yeah, she's a royal *B*, not to mention that she cheated on him." I still held the jewelry box, and I opened the lid to listen to the music. "Name that tune," I said, closing the lid again. Something classical was all I knew.

"Swan Lake." Mum's tight jaw eased. "I loved that jewelry box. My favorite gift that year. Well, besides the books from Uncle Tom."

"That's right. You got to meet him." I was sad that I'd never known Uncle Tom, who had been a children's book expert and, by all accounts, a wonderful person.

Mum shared some of the favorites gifted by my great-uncle and that occupied the rest of the ride back to Cambridge. As we bumped down Magpie Lane's cobblestones, I noticed the lights were on in the toy shop. Charlotte was back. Even better, the open flag was out at the tearoom and I saw people inside. Great news for Daisy.

Carrying our finds from the Marlowe house, we entered the bookshop a few minutes later, calling out in unison, "Aunt Violet. We're home."

My phone bleeped with a notification and I stopped to read the message. *Hello, Molly.* Madrigals and Mayhem *tryouts are tonight. See you then.* An address and time followed.

Nerves knotted in my belly. The moment of truth—or my complete humiliation—would soon be at hand.

An early December dusk was falling by the time I stopped to take a break. While waiting for additional dollhouse-themed books to arrive, I'd decided to include books about dolls on my stepladder display.

On our shelves, I'd found two Raggedy Ann titles, *Raggedy Ann in Cookie Land* and *Raggedy Ann in the Deep Deep Woods.* Johnny Gruelle's magical illustrations were among my favorites. *The Story of Holly and Ivy,* a Christmas-themed story by Rumer Godden, was also perfect, and so was *Miss Hickory,* a Newbury Award–winning winter tale by Carolyn Sherwin Bailey.

Fresh cup of tea in hand, I curled up in the red chair with *Charlotte's Dollhouse.* The shop was cozy and bright, redolent of the cinnamon wax melts. Lights on the Christmas tree reflected in the window glass and Santa stood vigilant, a beacon of cheer. Samuel Barber's *Die Natali* provided seasonal background music.

Charlotte's Dollhouse, cont.

Jingles found himself the center of attention with the other dolls that evening, a very gratifying experience. "You got to go outside," Mr. Bear said, envy in his voice. "I haven't been outside for ever so long."

"And even then we only made it to the garden," Mrs. Morton put in. "What was it like? Tell us every detail."

Jingles did his best. "The motorcars race along the streets," he said. "And there are so many of them now. A few times I thought we might be struck down."

"Motorcars?" Polly lifted her nose. "I want to hear about the ladies' fashions. Were they wearing fur muffs?"

"Of course," Jingles said slowly. What was a fur muff? He didn't want to ask and spark the bisque doll's disdain.

"I want a muff for Christmas." Polly clasped her hands. "To go with my coat. And a new hat."

"I like motorcars," the Lieutenant mused softly. "Wish I could go for a ride."

"Please, both of you," Mrs. Morton said. "Do go on, Jingles. Where did you go? What did you do?"

Jingles told them about skating and then the visit to the restaurant, how Charlotte had ordered hot cocoa with whipped cream. "She sat me on the table and I fell face first into the whipped cream," he said. "It was delicious." The other dolls laughed.

"Good job, mate," the Lieutenant said.

Mrs. Morton peered closely at his face. "I still see some." She lifted her apron and scrubbed at his cheek.

"I heard something important," Jingles said. "In the restaurant." He stopped talking, a serious—for a jester—expression on his face.

"Do go on," Mr. Bear said after a moment.

Jingles leaned forward and whispered. "Charlotte is an orphan."

Mrs. Morton's hands flew up. "What? Oh, that poor thing."

"No wonder she's bad tempered," the Lieutenant said.

"Two ladies at the table mentioned it while Charlotte was off washing her hands," Jingles said. "Her father was lost in the War." The Lieutenant saluted his memory. "And her mother died from the influenza."

The dolls fell silent, contemplating this sad story.

"That's why she's here, then," Polly said. "She has no one else. Only Margaret and Harold."

"And us," Mr. Bear said stoutly.

"I wonder how we can help," Mrs. Morton said. Mrs. Morton loved nothing more than an opportunity to do someone good.

"She seemed to enjoy my company," Jingles said modestly. "Maybe we should take turns spending time with her? Let her know that she's among friends."

"I like it," the bisque doll said. "Maybe I'll have an opportunity to view the latest fashions."

"It's not about you, Polly," Mrs. Morton said.
"This is what I think we should do."
They all leaned close and listened.

The shop door opened with a jingle and I looked up
to see Charlotte, bundled up in a white down coat with
a fur-trimmed hood, matching Uggs on her feet.

"Hey." I closed the book and stood. "How are you?"
I crossed my fingers that there wasn't more bad news.
How much could one person take?

Charlotte shrugged. "Okay, I guess." She picked up
a book from the display, *The Magic Nesting Doll* by
Jacqueline K. Ogburn. "Nesting dolls are so cool."

Joining her at the display, I said, "They really are."

She began to leaf through the pages. "We have some
at the store. They come in all kinds of themes now—
animals, dinosaurs, even Egyptian pharaohs. The smallest one is a mummy, like in a sarcophagus. It's a hoot."

"Pharaohs?" *Kings.* "We three kings."

Charlotte gasped. "The clue." She snapped the book
closed and placed it on the shelf. "Let's go." She opened
the shop door and ran out.

"Mum," I called, racing for my coat, which was
behind the counter. "I need to go over to the toy shop
for a few, if that's okay."

She looked up from the computer, where she was entering daily sales. "Fine with me."

By the time I caught up with Charlotte, she was
standing in front of the toy shop, keys in hand. "Grandad knew I loved those dolls," she said, inserting the
key. Above the door, a camera mounted stared down at
us. "It makes sense that he included them in the scavenger hunt."

Inside, we didn't bother to take off our coats.

Charlotte went directly to a section featuring colorful wooden toys and plucked the Pharaoh nesting doll off the shelf. She opened the dolls, one, two, three, revealing the last one, a mummy as promised, and another slip of paper.

I couldn't hold back a shout of triumph. "We found it."

Charlotte unfolded the paper and read, "'We travel afar.'"

"I guess we should have seen that one coming. 'We three kings of Orient are, bearing gifts we travel afar.'" I looked around the shop. There were toys from all over the world. Geography games, globes, and planes, trains, and automobiles, too. "Where to begin?"

"Exactly." Keeping the clue out, Charlotte put the dolls together. "At least we're further along than we were five minutes ago." She set the pharaohs on the shelf. "By the way, I'm moving into the flat tonight. Want to see it?"

"Sure. I can only stay a few minutes, though." I touched her arm. "I'm going to try out for the madrigals tonight."

"Althea's madrigals?" Charlotte threw me a look of surprise. "I didn't know you liked to sing."

"I do, but that's not the reason," I explained. "It's a way for me to get closer to the family. Without them guessing what I'm doing."

"Oh. To investigate, you mean. Hmm." She tilted her head. "You'd really do that for me?"

Um, yeah, because someone tried to kill you and if I can prevent another attempt— I didn't say that, though. "It will be fun. Kieran is in the cast, as well as a couple of other friends."

A wry smile curved Charlotte's lips. "I hope so, for

your sake. When I was in the madrigals last year, she was a nightmare."

"What a surprise." I sighed. "Forewarned is forearmed, right?"

"Hopefully." Charlotte placed the paper clue on the front counter. "Let's go up."

I followed her into the break room, where she opened a door to reveal a staircase.

"The only exits are through the store," she said as we began climbing. "That's why the flat was never rented. I'd have to reconfigure the back area and I'd rather not right now."

"It's really convenient living above the bookshop," I said. "Plus it saves money." Cambridge rents were prohibitive, even if we wanted to move.

"Hopefully I can keep a good work-life balance." Charlotte flicked on a light switch, revealing a large room set up as a studio apartment. "I have trouble with that sometimes."

"So did I, until Aunt Violet barred me from the shop after hours."

"I need an Aunt Violet. So, what do you think?"

"It's fantastic." Along one wall, a galley kitchen was charmingly old-fashioned with a small AGA and deep porcelain sink. One corner held a wide daybed piled with cushions, and a seating area featured a comfortable-looking sectional. Dormer windows overlooked Magpie Lane and the small back garden.

"Just right for one," Charlotte said.

I went to one of the front windows. "That's my bedroom," I said, pointing. "We can signal each other."

She pretended to point a flashlight out the window. "SOS means bring wine."

"Or we can use BYOB," I joked. Having Charlotte living on the lane was going to be fun. I envisioned us getting together at the tea shop, for meals at home, or at the pub. "You should come to our next darts night at the Magpie." My friends were flexible when it came to enlarging the group on our outings.

"I'd love to. Let me know when."

"Will do." I remembered what I wanted to tell her. "Mum and I went out to Mistletoe Farm today. We checked out the skin cream like the one your grandfather had. Not that we figured anything new out, exactly. Andre told us that he buys the homeopathic remedies already formulated and blends them into his creams. I bet someone added undiluted aconite."

Charlotte winced. "Poor Grandad. Who would have ever dreamed that someone would do such a thing?" She put a hand to her mouth.

"I know. It's awful." I would be glad when the case was over and our most vital decision was which wine to drink. "Another thing: I saw Barnaby's mother at the farm. She seemed to be a very good friend of Andre's, if you know what I mean."

Her head lifted sharply. "Dorcas? Hmm. Interesting. I had no idea they were more than acquaintances." She grimaced. "Althea monitors Dorcas's every move. Every time she starts dating someone, Althea does her best to trash the guy and break them up."

"Seriously? That's awful." Dorcas was a middle-aged mother and still being bullied.

"That's Althea for you. She likes to control every detail of everyone else's lives." Charlotte turned away from the window. "I'll walk you down."

I was halfway across the lane when I saw Uncle

Chris's van in the alley. Uh-oh. I had a feeling about why he was here. *Aunt Janice.* She must have complained about us.

As I drew close to the front door, he emerged from the alley, hands tucked in his jacket pockets. Despite my wave and smile, his expression remained stoic.

"Is your mother around?" he asked. "We need to talk."

CHAPTER 13

I opened the shop door, allowing him to go first. "She's probably in the kitchen. Go on back."

He stomped through the shop and, after locking the door, I followed.

When I entered the kitchen, Mum and Uncle Chris were facing each other in a standoff. "Molly, please," Mum said.

I folded my arms. "I'm not going anywhere. I was there today, remember?"

She turned back to Chris. "What exactly did she tell you?"

He had taken off his tweed cap and was now rotating it in his hands. The poor thing was going to be mangled by the time he was done with it. "She said you came to the house and insulted her. That you were rude." A pause. "What were you doing there?"

Fire sparked in Mum's eyes. "It was my home, too, Chris. I could have fought for half, remember? I have every right to visit and collect my things."

"We brought Mum's jewelry box home," I put in. "She's allowed to have it, right?"

"Molly," Mum said tersely, motioning as if to brush me aside. "It's not *her* house," she told Chris. "Why should she have any say about my presence there? Besides, she stole my Sasha doll."

Uncle Chris grabbed this diversion like a lifeline. "Come on, Nina. Why would my wife want your doll? You're really reaching."

"Who knows?" Mum's tone was dismissive. "She's always been jealous of me."

Uncle Chris scoffed. "Jealous of you? Why? I'm your brother. It's not like you were competing for me."

Actually, in Janice's eyes, they might have been. Mum was blood, Janice a newcomer. My guess was that she was horribly insecure.

My mother had another theory. "Because I'm a poet. Because I've been published. She's always wanted to write, remember? I told her to sit down and do it, then." She laughed. "She didn't like that. Seriously, Chris, there's room in the world for more than one poet."

He waved a hand. "That aside, what about what you said to her?"

Mum blinked. "Said to her? Oh. You mean that she reminded me of our mother?" Her grin was wicked. "Surely you think that's a good thing. You were Mum's favorite."

His mouth open and shut as he tried to formulate a response. Don't even try, buddy, I wanted to tell him. She's smarter than you.

Uncle Chris slapped the rumpled cap on his head. "I need to get going. See you later."

Mum's smile was sweet. "Will we still see you at Christmas?"

No, please, no. It wasn't him or my cousin, it was Janice I hoped to avoid.

He didn't say one way or another, though. Merely mumbled something inaudible like, "We'll see."

"I'll let you out," I offered.

He was silent as we retraced our steps through the shop. I unlocked the door and opened it for him. "Have a good night," I said cheerfully.

"You too, Molly," he grumbled. Then, halfway through the door, he stopped and turned. "You know, Janice isn't such a bad sort. She feels really bad about all this."

That was a start. "I'm pretty sure that if she apologizes, Mum will accept. I mean, I'm new here, but it's obvious that she's hostile toward Mum." When he started to protest, I shook my head. "Don't. Family shouldn't be about competing or jealousy. Life's too short."

As I shut the door behind him, I thought, case in point, Charlotte's step-relatives. They'd rather kill than get along.

∙●∙

"Thanks for coming with me," I told Kieran as we bicycled along the path. The tryouts for *Madrigals and Mayhem* were being held at Lilly Maxwell Hall at St. Hildegard's, too far to walk but less than ten minutes by bicycle.

In Vermont, bicycling at night in the winter would seem ludicrous, not to mention dangerous. In contrast, Cambridge had plenty of bike lanes and decent lighting. Living here was great for my thighs.

"No problem," he said, edging over as a group of bicyclists headed our way, lights and reflective clothing flashing. "Happy to provide moral support."

"Or immoral support," I quipped.

He grinned. "That, too."

My heart began to thump when the towers and

halls of St. Hildegard's came into view. "I'm nervous," I admitted. "I haven't been on stage since college." I winced. "I could use some of that immoral support right now."

"Okay." He halted his bicycle and I stopped beside him.

A few wonderful kisses later, despite the hinderance of our helmets, and I felt much better. "I have an idea," I said with a giggle. "We'll have to take kiss breaks backstage between acts."

"Lord Nightingale at your service," he said, sketching a bow. "Ready?"

I inhaled a shaky breath. "As I'll ever be."

We parked our bicycles in a rack outside the hall and made our way to the theatre. Double doors stood open and a peek inside revealed a spacious room, a stage at the far end, polished wood floors, and finely carved plaster cornices. Long red velvet curtains adorned tall windows and the stage. A few short rows of chairs had been set out; the rest, along with tables, were stacked against the wall.

"Name, please?" Tori Winters sat on a stool inside the door, attention on the clipboard she held. Then she looked up and recognized me. "What are *you* doing here?"

"I'm trying out for the madrigals." Was she going to turn me away because of my friendship with Charlotte? I hadn't thought about that possibility. I felt terribly exposed, as if she could sense my motivation, namely, a desire to investigate her and the rest of her family.

"She's with me," Kieran said, putting an arm around me. "I suggested she try out."

"Huh." Tori's gaze flicked between him and her list. The hand holding the pen didn't move.

"Sir Jon and George Flowers also recommended I try out." I tried to dial back the pleading in my voice. "I mentioned that when I signed up."

Other people wanting to audition were lined up behind us now, probably wondering what the holdup was. I could hear muttering and feet shifting.

An older woman crossed the wide room, her heels tapping. Trim and petite, a sheaf of bobbed gray-blond hair sliding over one eye, she wore a designer wool suit and an air of authority. This must be the famous Althea Winters.

"Tori." Her tone was clipped. "Let's move it along." She moved to stand behind her granddaughter. "What's the problem?"

"Nothing," Tori mumbled, reluctantly making a check mark with the pen.

In an attempt to wrest control of the situation, I said brightly, holding out my hand, "You must be Mrs. Winters. Violet Marlowe says hello. I'm Molly Kimball, her great-niece."

Althea's eyes flicked over me, up and down, her face softening, showing dimples and a warmth in her gaze. "How is Violet?" Her handshake was firm for someone with such small hands and tiny fingers.

"She's wonderful, thanks. I'm helping her run the bookshop now."

"Oh, yes." Althea released my hand and gestured, indicating that I should move along. "Go wait with the others." She nodded toward a cluster of people near the stage.

As Kieran and I edged by, hands linked, Althea cried, "Kieran! What brings you here tonight? You silly boy, you're already in the cast."

"I'm here to support Molly," he said, smiling politely.

Althea looked down at our connected hands, a sour-lemon expression pursing her lips. "How nice. Say hello to your mother for me."

Feeling somewhat buffeted already, I went to get in line. Kieran found a chair, giving me a thumbs-up before taking out his phone. He really was going above and beyond, sitting through auditions.

Then Althea approached him, clipboard in hand. They chatted for a moment and then he reluctantly accepted the clipboard. He put away his phone and sat with an ankle crossed over the opposite leg, knee bouncing and pen tapping.

She'd roped him into scoring the singers, I guessed. Our eyes met and I shook my head. He rolled his eyes and shrugged. I flashed both hands at him, hinting that he should give me a ten. He nodded.

Other people joined the line. I glanced at the clock, wondering when we would start. I couldn't wait to get it over with.

And naturally, I had to visit the restroom. I tapped the shoulder of the young man ahead of me. "Can you hold my place? I need the loo."

"I'll try," he said.

"Do you know where they are?" I asked.

"Out in the hallway." He turned back around.

I hesitated, thinking I should wait. Then I checked out the line again. Why be uncomfortable? Worst case, I'd end up last.

Kieran looked over as I walked across the long expanse to the door. He probably wondered if I was making a run for it. "Be right back," I mouthed.

The main door was shut now, Tori having left her station, and I slipped out into the hall. There was the sign. I hurried down the corridor, shoes squeaking on the polished tiles.

After emerging from the restroom a few minutes later, I saw Reece Harrison talking to Dorcas Winters near the entrance doors. They didn't seem to notice me, thankfully, so I put my head down and motored along.

"Can I have a little longer?" Dorcas said, speaking in a low yet carrying voice.

Reece crossed his arms. "A better question is, will you deliver?"

Interesting. Did Dorcas owe Reece money, too? Pretending I hadn't heard a thing, I picked up my pace and swept past the pair, hoping neither would recognize me. I felt their gaze on me as I opened the door, but didn't turn around.

Inside the room, the first singer was on stage, warbling about chestnuts roasting on an open fire. I dashed across the floor and cut into line, to the glares of those behind me. The guy actually indicated I should go ahead of him, signaling that my move was cool.

A glance over my shoulder to check on Kieran informed me that Tori was now sitting next to him. Reece and Dorcas also came in, Reece sitting on Tori's other side and Dorcas sitting in the front row.

On it went, singer after singer performing their choice of holiday song. Meanwhile I reviewed my choice, panicked when suddenly I couldn't remember the first line.

Breathe. You know it by heart. I should, because it was one of my father's favorites. He had loved music from the 1940s.

"Molly Kimball," Althea said. "You're up."

I charged up the stairs to the stage and then crossed

the seemingly vast acreage to the middle. Me, standing alone. A few rows of chairs out front, curious eyes watching. A huge room beyond, the ceiling lost in shadows.

"Any time, Molly," Althea said dryly.

Kieran flashed me a thumbs-up, which made me smile. Buoyed by the affection we shared, I opened my mouth and began to sing "I'll Be Home for Christmas." Images of Dad and Vermont flashed through my mind, and a poignant sense of love and loss and longing infused my voice. No performance had ever been more heartfelt.

After I stopped, the room was silent. Kieran was staring at me with amazement. Tori's mouth was gaping. She clamped it shut and made a note.

"Thank you, Molly," Althea said. "Next?"

I gladly exited the stage. There were still more people to go, so I found a chair and sat, to wait until Kieran was finished. My phone vibrated. A text from Kieran.

Awesome job. You're a shoo-in.

You're biased.

True, but you blew everyone away.

I sent him back a string of emojis 'cause I couldn't write what I wanted: *Love you.* We weren't there yet.

After the final singer, the judges conferred, which meant more time hanging around. A text came from Daisy.

We still on for the Magpie?

Absolutely. Be there soon.

As I typed that, the group broke up. As I made my way toward Kieran, Althea intercepted me. "Very nice, Molly."

My heart leaped. "Did I—"

Her smile was close-lipped. "We'll let everyone know once we make the final determination."

"Okay. Thanks for including me." So why had she come over?

"I understand you've been hanging around with my granddaughter."

My eyes went to Tori, who was laughing as she chatted with Reece and Kieran.

"Charlotte," she clarified. "Charlotte Pemberly."

"Oh. Yes. Charlotte. I met her the other day. Nice to have another shop owner on Magpie Lane." I was treading carefully, pretty sure that she wouldn't like me raving about how wonderful Charlotte was. I wouldn't care, except I wanted to get into the madrigals.

She leaned closer. "Please don't take this the wrong way, but Charlotte is a bit of a fantasist. A very imaginative young woman." She shook her head sadly. "Her poor grandfather had his hands full."

CHAPTER 14

Daisy and Tim were waiting at the pub, seated near the roaring fireplace. "Sorry we're late," Kieran said, taking off his coat and hanging it on the back of a chair.

"They roped Kieran into judging," I explained as I hung mine on an adjacent seat. "Everyone else left right after their audition."

"So how was it?" Tim asked. "Did you get in?"

"Tell them, Molly," Kieran said. He checked the contents of their glasses. "I'll go get a round."

"Half-pint of bitter for me," I said, sitting. "Thank you."

The other two told him their drinks and Kieran went up to the bar.

"The audition went well," I said. "They haven't decided yet, though."

Daisy groaned. "Aw? Seriously. Way to torture a person."

"I agree." I fiddled with a coaster. "You won't believe what Althea Winters said to me." I gave them the gist of her ludicrous and slanderous comments and also mentioned Tori's attitude toward me.

"Sounds like going into the lion's den," Tim said, picking up his glass. "Sure you want to do this?"

Kieran returned with a tray and I glanced up at him. "Long as I have Kieran to protect me."

"I'll be armed and ready, with my fake sword." Kieran passed the drinks around. "Anyone want food? I'm starving."

"So am I." All I'd been able to eat before the audition was a bowl of soup and toast.

The outside door opened, momentarily distracting us, and Tori and Reece came in. They settled at a nearby table, Tori seeming to pointedly ignore me. That was fine with me.

My question was: why were they in Magpie Lane? There were dozens of pubs closer to St. Hildegard's or St. Aelred's. Maybe I should warn Charlotte, my *fantasist* friend. She hadn't imagined the poisoned cakes, that was for sure. Grabbing my phone, I sent a quick text: *Reece and Tori are at the Magpie. Might be heading your way.*

We studied the menu cards and ordered fish and chips all around.

"My favorite meal," Daisy claimed. "I might even have it at my wedding."

Kieran and I exchanged glances. "What'd we miss?" I asked.

In answer, Daisy let go of Tim's hand raised hers above the table. A modest yet lovely diamond ring graced her third finger.

We hooted in excitement. "Hurray! You did it!" I cried.

When people looked over, Kieran lifted his glass. "Daisy and Tim are engaged!" he bellowed out.

Congratulations, cheers, and shouts filled the room. All the locals knew Daisy and Tim.

Once the hubbub died down, I asked, "So when did this happen?"

"Earlier this evening," Daisy said. "We were wrapping presents in his flat when he got down on one knee." Her joyful laugh pealed out. "I thought he was after the tape, which had fallen onto the carpet."

Tim took up the tale. "She handed me the tape and then noticed I had a ring box in my hand."

"That tape went flying. Again." Daisy put a hand to her mouth. "I couldn't utter a word, I was so gob-smacked. I finally said, yes, of course."

Her fiancé kissed the side of her head. "I know some people like to make a big production of it, but to me, the moment was perfect. Daisy and I at home, happy and relaxed, talking about our families and Christmas."

My eyes met Daisy's and she winked. She'd thought he would ask during a night out, while dining in a fine restaurant. Instead he'd chosen a simpler yet more meaningful moment.

A server brought our food, accompanied by four shots of whiskey.

"What's this? Tim asked, pointing at the shot.

"I want to do another toast," Kieran said. We picked up our glasses. "To my best friend and his future lovely wife," he said. "May you be blessed with happiness, long life, and many bairns." Kieran was reverting to his Scottish roots with that last.

Still holding her shot aloft, Daisy burst out laughing. "What?"

"Did I forget to mention it?" Tim joked. "I want at least twelve."

We all laughed. "Well, two or three might be all right." Daisy smirked. "Long as you help change their nappies."

"I'm an old hand at nappy changing," Tim said seriously. "Ask my mum."

"Ooh. Secret talents," Daisy cooed.

"You have no idea." Tim's smile was roguish.

"Okay, you two," Kieran said. "Bottoms up."

We drank and then dug into heaps of piping-hot chips and lightly breaded slabs of haddock. I'd gotten accustomed to using vinegar instead of ketchup and I sprinkled plenty on.

Between bites, I checked in on Tori and Reece, sitting nearby, chatting quietly. His phone buzzed and she pulled back with a frown. "Got to get this," he said, getting to his feet. He slid around the table and walked toward the restroom hallway, talking. She slumped back in her chair, lips pouting, staring angrily at the fire.

After about five minutes, she lurched out of her seat and stormed off in his direction.

"What's going on?" Daisy whispered to me. "Lovers' quarrel?"

Maybe. There was more than love between that pair, what with break-ins and Barnaby's poisoning. Not to mention Reece's cryptic conversation with Dorcas.

I put my napkin down. "I feel a strong need to use the loo." Kieran and Tim gave me puzzled looks. "Joking. Be right back."

Tori and Reece were standing at the end of the hall, near the exit door. I interpreted their body language easily—the hunched shoulders, clenched hands, and deep frowns of an argument.

"Tell me what's going on." Tori tugged at his sleeve. "I know you're hiding something."

He pulled his arm away. "It's better you don't know, trust me."

Tori barked a laugh. "If only I could."

Reece grumbled an inaudible reply, then started stalking down the hall toward me.

"Wait, Reece. I didn't mean—" Tori saw me and stopped, frowning.

Busted. I ducked into the ladies' room and then into a stall. I'd wait here for a couple of minutes and hopefully they'd be gone when I emerged.

The restroom door creaked open, followed by footsteps. I cringed. Was that Tori? Hopefully I could out wait her.

I heard a sob, followed by sniffing. When it continued, I pushed out. "Hey. Are you okay?"

Tori wiped away smudged mascara. "Not that great, to be honest." She blinked rapidly, tears flooding. "I think I just broke up with my boyfriend."

"That sucks. Or does it?"

My blunt remark startled a laugh. "Yeah, it sucks. He's my brother's best friend, which means he's always around." She grabbed another paper towel out of the dispenser. "Plus I love him." Her voice broke on the word, *love*.

Considering her attitude at the madrigals tryout, her willingness to confide in me was surprising. Although, willing ears work when your heart is crushed, right?

"I'm sorry," I said awkwardly. "If you want to talk . . ." I felt I should offer although inside I was screaming, *Please, no. Not right now. I'm trying to have a night out.* Unless she knew who had poisoned Barnaby and possibly Arthur Pemberly. That I would listen to any time.

She crumpled the towel and tossed it in the can. "Thanks. I appreciate that." With a sigh, she shuffled for the door. "But I'm going to go home and try to get some sleep."

"Sounds like a plan," I called after her. "Take care."

When I arrived back at our table, Kieran said, "Guess what? I'm going to be best man."

"Awesome." I pulled my chair up to the table. "Talking about wedding plans?"

Daisy smiled at Tim. "We're thinking June. Which isn't much time, when you think about it."

Tim pretended to wince. "Don't get too fancy on me, woman."

"Even the simplest wedding takes a lot of planning," Daisy said with mock umbrage. "Doesn't it, Molly?"

"I wouldn't know, but I'm guessing yes." I picked up my beer. "Here's to the wedding. May the sun shine on your day and your love."

They all toasted with me. "I want you to be my maid of honor," Daisy said.

I was touched that she'd choose me from among her other friends and relatives. "Really? I'd be, well, honored." I gave her a hug.

"What happened in there?" Daisy tilted her head toward the restrooms. "Reece came storming out and then Tori, a few minutes later."

"She and Reece just broke up. I saw them arguing and after he left, she told me about it in the bathroom." I shrugged. "And that is totally lame. No big revelations about Barnaby or Arthur, unfortunately."

Kieran put an arm around my shoulders. "You'll get there, Molly. I have faith in you."

I snuggled against the warmth of his body. "I hope so."

CHAPTER 15

Early the next morning, I tiptoed out of Kieran's bedroom, intent on my errand. My plan was to nip over to Tea & Crumpets to buy coffee and treats. Smiling as I crammed my feet into boots, I pictured Kieran's surprise when I served him breakfast in bed. Neither of us was due at work until ten, which gave us plenty of time for a lazy morning.

Like me, Kieran lived above his business. His flat, while not huge, was charming with its thick ceiling beams, wide-board floors, and exposed brick. He favored squashy leather furniture, and a bicycle carcass hung from the ceiling, a project in process. It was a gravel bike, he told me, as opposed to road, mountain, fat tire, or the cruisers so common to Cambridge streets.

I buttoned my coat and slipped out, leaving the flat door unlocked. I'd only be gone ten minutes. As I hurried down the stairs and out into the frosty morning, my thoughts turned to the previous night. Daisy and Tim were engaged. How wonderful. We'd had such a good time discussing the wedding, with Kieran throwing in ridiculous and hilarious suggestions. He'd also offered he use of Hazelhurst House, his family manor, and that had not been a joke. The evening had ended up being the perfect distraction from thoughts of murder and mayhem.

I'd even forgotten to incessantly check my phone for news about the madrigals tryout.

I was almost at the tearoom when a sharp banging noise caught my ear. I stopped and glanced around, unable to tell where it was coming from.

Rap, rap, rap. There it was again. This time I looked up and over.

Charlotte was at the second-floor window of the toy shop, face practically pressed to the glass. Thinking she was only trying to get my attention, I waved and kept going.

Rap, rap, rap. This time she shook her head and pointed. Then, frustrated, she heaved at the window and finally got it open a crack. "I'm locked in the flat. Can you help me?"

I glanced at the front door. Surely the shop was locked. I dithered, not sure what to do. Break in? Call the locksmith? Find a ladder? She'd never fit through that crack, however.

"Check the doors," Charlotte said. "I didn't lock the flat door. I think someone broke in again."

"What does the camera show?" I asked.

She shook her head. "Nothing. They either damaged them or covered the lens somehow."

"Okay." I took reluctant steps toward the front entrance, still occupied by this new dilemma. How were we going to get to Charlotte?

Reece and Tori. Had they done something? They'd been at the pub, only a few doors away. When I reached

the front door, I looked up. There was a piece of cloth
draped over the camera. I stood on tip-toe and tried to
pull it down but only snagged it worse.

Thinking of fingerprints, although they were un-
likely due to gloves or mittens, I carefully turned the
knob by using the stem.

The door swung open. It was unlocked. So someone
had been inside.

I retreated back to the lane. "Charlotte, the door's unlocked. I'll be right there."

She gave me a thumbs-up. "I'm calling the police."

Once inside the store, I had another shock. The
place was ransacked. Toys and boxes were scattered all
over the floor, requiring me to pick my way through.

What a mess. I hoped nothing was broken.

"Meow." I turned to see Puck trotting through the
store toward me.

"What are you doing here, buddy?" He must have
slipped out of the bookshop and then followed me. He
was sneaky that way. He rubbed against my ankles
and I bent to pat him. "Listen, we have an emergency.
Mom's busy."

First I shut the front door, which I'd left ajar in my
haste, and then rushed to the rear of the store, Puck
right behind me.

All was well in the break room—except for the cabinet blocking the upstairs door, which opened outward.

What if a fire had broken out? She might have been
trapped.

"Molly." Charlotte pushed the upstairs door open as
far as it could go. "What's blocking the door?"

"A cabinet." I put my shoulder to the tall, heavy case.
"Hold on. I'll give it a try." The cabinet moved exactly
one inch, then a couple more. After leaning my full

weight on it, it finally moved enough that she could slip through the crack in the door.

Charlotte, dressed in a long T-shirt and plaid flannel pants, ran a hand over her tangled hair, staring at the cabinet. "Who did that? It's scary to think they were inside the shop while I was sleeping." She noticed Puck and snapped her fingers. "Hey, cutie."

"He followed me in." Had Reece and Tori been the intruders? Even though they'd broken up—according to Tori—they might have teamed up to search for the doll. Or it might have been Barnaby, even Dorcas.

"There's more," I said, dreading the next reveal.

Her hand paused while patting Puck, her eyes flaring wide. "What do you mean?"

My answer was to gesture for her to follow me into the shop.

"What the—who did this?" Charlotte gave a shriek of sheer rage. Her eyes were wild as she glanced around at the disarray. She began to run around in a panic, giving little grunts of dismay as she picked things up.

"Charlotte. Hey, Charlotte." Finally I whistled, two fingers in my mouth. "Hold on. Wait for the police. Don't touch anything." I had another thought. "Oh, and if there's video from last night, save the files for them. Someone draped cloth over your outside camera."

The mention of the camera successfully diverted her attention and she ran over to the inside one to check it. "They did that here, too." She pointed at a camera mounted high on the wall in the corner of the room.

"You really need that alarm system." Cameras and new locks hadn't prevented someone from getting in and causing havoc. How *had* they gotten in? "Hold on. I'm going to check something." I went to the rear of the store, to a storage room.

"Puck, stay back." A pane of glass had been broker allowing the intruder to unlock the window and clim' inside. Charlotte came up behind me. "So that's hov they got in."

"The front door was unlocked, so I think they wen out that way." I started toward the window, stopping when my feet crunched broken glass. "Don't come an closer." Charlotte was barefoot.

She retreated. "I'm going to go up and get my phone Police should be here soon."

"I'll wait out front." I paced around the shop floo waiting for her to come back down. Puck jumped u onto the counter, as if surveying his new domain.

Kieran. He was going to wonder what had happened to me.

I'd left a note saying, *Stay put. Be right back*, in cas he woke up.

"Molly." He sounded groggy. "Where did you go?"

"Well, I was on my way to the tea shop to get u breakfast when I ran into a situation at the toy shop." gave him the details. "I should probably wait here fo the police. I'm a witness."

"Think Reece and Tori had anything to do with it?"

Trust Kieran to put two and two together. "I thin! it's a strong possibility, despite their argument. The were probably looking for the missing Madame Alex ander doll. It's worth a lot of money." My heart sank What if they had found the doll? It would disappea again, this time for good.

"I'm gonna get dressed and come over," Kieran said "Wait there and I'll get your coffee and something tc eat."

"Aw. Thanks." His thoughtfulness touched me.

A few minutes later I spotted him loping down the

lane toward the tea shop. He saw me in the window and waved. What a great guy.

The dollhouse was beside me so I decided to check it out. Puck, naturally, joined me. There was such detail in the furnishings, as in *Charlotte's Dollhouse*. The time and care that went into it. This house, modeled after mansions of the day, had two staircases, a smaller one off the kitchen for the staff.

Hold on. This was too creepy. A model dresser that held miniature plates was now in front of the staircase. Had someone moved it on purpose? Well, of course they had. I was thinking in relation to what had just happened to Charlotte.

Someone was definitely messing with her. Beyond the crimes they were committing, of course. First a tiny cake on the dining room table and now this. I took photographs, as proof, Puck managing to insert himself into the shots.

Lights flashed as a panda car eased down the lane. The police had arrived.

I was about to call Charlotte when she strode into the room, now fully dressed. "That was quick," she said, peering outside.

We both groaned softly when Sergeant Gita Adhikari got out of the car. The upside was that she was familiar with every twist of this case. Her expression was grim as she started toward the door, Constable Derby at her heels. He moved ahead to open the door for her.

"Good morning." The sergeant's keen gaze swept the shop. "What happened here?"

Derby pulled out his device, ready to take notes.

Kieran chose that moment to show up, bag in one hand, tray with cups in the other. He shifted the bag and knocked.

"Get rid of him, okay?" Gita ordered.

"Of course." I scurried toward the door. "They want to talk to us alone," I half-whispered. Behind us, Charlotte was showing the officers around the shop as they gradually made their way to the back.

"No problem." Kieran handed me the tray and then removed a cup for himself before passing over the bag. "Catch up later?"

"You don't want something to eat?" I held the bag out. By the aroma, I could tell he'd bought egg and bacon sandwiches. My mouth was watering.

"All right, I'll take one. There are two more in there, for you and Charlotte." He took a foil-wrapped package, then kissed me. "Keep me posted."

I unwrapped my sandwich and took a big bite, chewing hastily, and swallowed a slug of coffee. Puck was eyeing me piteously so I broke off a piece of egg and gave it to him. Then I wrapped my sandwich again and tucked it back into the bag. Still carrying my coffee, I hurried after the others, who were standing in the break room, looking at the cabinet.

"Molly discovered the situation while I was still trapped upstairs." Charlotte pointed at the cabinet. "That was blocking the door."

The officers turned to me. "Tell us how you happened to come along," Gita said.

Even though she wasn't accusing me outright, it felt that way. I supposed it was their method, to get under people's skin and make them get defensive or blow up. I wasn't going to let her do either.

"I'd just left Kieran Scott's flat and was on my way to the tea shop," I said. "Charlotte rapped on the upstairs window to attract my attention." Between sips of coffee—I really needed my java right now—I took them through my every move.

"I think they went out the front," I said. "And came in this way." I led them to the stockroom, where cold air was blowing through the broken window.

"Looks like it," Derby said. "I'll dust for prints. Though they probably wore gloves." He slipped out of the room and a moment later we heard the front door shut.

"Thanks." Gita turned to us. "Any idea who could have done this, Ms. Pemberly?"

Charlotte set her jaw. "The same people who broke in last time. Barnaby Winters and, we think, Reece Harrison, his roommate, who was at my grandfather's house that night."

"Or it might have been Tori Winters, Barnaby's sister," I added. "She was with Reece at the Magpie last night."

"Still looking for the doll?" Gita asked. "The one you think is here somewhere?"

"Uh-huh." Charlotte pulled her sleeves down over her hands. "And harassing me, too."

Her remark reminded me. "They moved something in the dollhouse again." As we walked out front, passing Constable Derby on his way to the broken window, case in hand, I told them about the cake. "Today I found a cabinet in a very interesting position."

Puck was sprawled in front of the dollhouse, one paw resting on a doll. I hoped he hadn't been batting it around. Gita smiled at the sight, which helped lighten the atmosphere. "He belongs at the bookshop, doesn't he?"

"He does." I gently moved him aside. "He followed me here."

"I wish cats could talk," Charlotte mused. "He could probably tell us a lot."

"Me, too." I showed them the cabinet in front of the back stairs.

Charlotte huffed. "That wasn't there yesterday."

Gita's brows rose. "Are you sure?"

She huffed again. "No, I don't memorize the position of every piece of furniture." She reached for the cabinet, stopped only by my hand on her arm. "I'd never leave that blocking the stairs like that."

"In case the dolls needed to go upstairs?" Gita's tone was arch.

"Someone put a cake here, too." I directed them to the dining room table. "I noticed it after we found the poisoned tea cakes. At the time, it was a stretch but now . . . I know someone is messing with Charlotte. Beyond breaking in and trying to steal, I mean."

"Head games," Charlotte muttered. "They're not going to get me." She spotted the to-go order on the counter. "Is that for me?"

"Yes. I think it's coffee." Still drinking mine, I wandered back over. "Egg and bacon sandwich in the bag." I found mine and took another bite. "Hope you don't mind," I said to Gita. "Haven't had breakfast yet."

"You go ahead." The officer still stood near the dollhouse, arms folded, appearing to be lost in thought.

Officer Derby bustled out from the back room. "I got nothing. Which is to be expected. I'll do the front door as well."

"And the cabinet." I pointed to the dollhouse. "Pretty hard to use gloves while moving dollhouse furniture around."

He halted, confused. Gita gestured. "Over here.

Ms. Pemberly thinks someone was playing around inside."

"Okay. Can't hurt." He put his case down on the front window ledge and extracted fingerprinting supplies. "That cat should probably move."

I snapped my fingers. "Puck. Come." He threw me his famous look of disdain. "I have egg." That got his attention. He ran over to me, mewing.

Gita's phone rang, and she walked toward the back to talk, where she had more privacy. Constable Derby carefully fingerprinted the cabinet. Judging by the muttering under his breath, he found a clear print.

Charlotte stopped eating to smile. "Hurray," she said under her breath. "Maybe we finally got a break."

"I hope so." I remembered the security cameras. "Was there anything on video?"

"No." She sighed. "Whoever covered the cameras was careful to hide their face. Look." She brought up the video. Someone approached and then, after a rustling noise, the screen went black. "I already forwarded these to the officers."

"Maybe the time stamp will help, if nothing else." The person had come by at 2:00 A.M., I noticed. If it had been Reece and Tori, where had they been between nine, when we saw them, and two? It was too cold to hang around outside for hours, that was for sure.

Brisk footfalls announced Gita's return. "Ms. Pemberly," she said. "I have news."

Charlotte threw me a scared look as she set down her sandwich. "What is it?"

Gita inhaled. "They found aconite in your grandfather's tube of cream. Enough to kill an adult."

CHAPTER 16

Charlotte made a choked sound, her shoulders hunching as if in pain. "Grandad . . . Someone poisoned him?"

"It's a possibility," Gita said. "Unfortunately, it may be hard to prove without further physical evidence."

I knew what she meant. Charlotte's grandfather had been buried months ago. They'd have to exhume. If that would even work. Some poisons didn't leave enough traces to be detected later.

"I will be talking to the family again," Gita said. "We'll try to trace the purchase of the cream."

"They still make it at Mistletoe Farm," I said. "I saw some in the gift shop." Gita eyed me with suspicion, probably wondering how much snooping I'd done. "They have great Christmas scented wax melts." The explanation fell flat, even in my own ears.

Gita sucked in air. "First, I'd like to get statements about today's events. Then I'll be following up with you both about finding the cream. Molly, take me through today. Quickly, if you please."

While Constable Derby took notes, I retraced my movements from when Charlotte called to me out the window. Meanwhile Charlotte sat behind the counter, a huddled ball of misery. Discovering that we'd been right about her grandfather's death was a serious blow.

This news confirmed that Charlotte was in the killer's crosshairs, at least to me.

"Did you see anyone in the lane last night?" Gita asked. "Or hear anything unusual?"

"Not a thing. Except for seeing Reece and Tori at the pub. This isn't their neighborhood."

"All right, Miss Kimball," Gita said. "You may go. We'll circle back to you concerning the cream you found at the Pemberly home. Will you be around?"

"At the bookshop all day," I promised.

Before leaving, I went over to Charlotte. Puck was now in her arms, purring. He always seemed to know when someone was hurting. "I've been dismissed. Touch base later?"

She looked up at me, her face miserable, and nodded. "Do you want Puck?" Despite the question, her arms tightened and he rubbed his head against her chin.

"He can stay here for a while. Give me a buzz when the police leave and I'll come get him." Although Puck was capable of crossing the lane by himself, I still worried about him.

Taking the remains of my breakfast with me, I left the toy store. Outside, I was hit with sudden exhaustion. If only I could crawl back into bed and sleep. Instead I had to saddle up and face a busy shopping day.

◆◆◆

"Molly!" Aunt Violet cried when I walked through the shop's front door. "Have you seen Puck?" She was practically wringing her hands. "He slipped outside earlier and I haven't seen him since. Please forgive me."

"No worries," I hastened to assure her. "He followed me across the street. I was on my way to the tea shop but Charlotte waylaid me." While taking off my coat and switching my boots for loafers, I explained the situation. The shop wasn't open yet so we went back to the kitchen, where Aunt Violet turned on the kettle. "He's staying with her right now," I concluded. "I'll go over and get him later."

"Phew." Aunt Violet put a hand to her chest. "I'm so glad. Not about the break-in or the cream being poisoned. Oh my. That poor thing. It's coming at her from every direction."

"Yes, it is." I sipped coffee, thinking. "We need to catch whoever is behind the poisonings. Otherwise, I'm worried there will be another attempt on Charlotte."

"I don't like saying it, but you're right," Mum said. "I don't get it, though. The estate is settled, isn't it? Why go after her now?"

I mulled her question over. "No idea, except for the missing doll. I think the killer is trying to find it before Charlotte does. Otherwise, you're right. I doubt she left anything to Althea or her family in her will." If she had one.

Aunt Violet brought a teapot to the table and sat. "I can think of another possibility. Maybe Charlotte knows something about the murder of her grandfather." She put up a hand when I started to protest. "She might not *know* that she knows. The killer is worried about getting caught."

Her theory had merit, and with the discovery of the

poisoned cream, even more worrying. "I'm sure of one thing," I said. "They all resent Charlotte, especially Althea. She wouldn't let Charlotte visit very often when Arthur was sick."

My great-aunt swore under her breath, something that we didn't hear very often. "What a terrible woman."

"Selfish, for sure." I checked my phone again. "Speaking of which, still no answer about the madrigals tryout."

"How did it go?" Mum asked.

"Great. I think. I sang 'I'll Be Home for Christmas.'" We shared a sad smile. "That song was one of Dad's favorites," I explained to Aunt Violet.

Someone rapped at the front shop door. "I'll go," I said, jumping up. Maybe Charlotte had brought Puck back despite my offer to retrieve him later. "You two sit."

Charlotte wasn't at the door. Instead it was Detective Inspector Sean Ryan, Gita's superior. I guessed that with the proof of murder, the case had been bumped up to him.

"Hello, Sean," I said when I opened the door. "I see they brought out the big guns." I called him Sean because of the somewhat awkward fact that he'd dated my mother several times. Not to mention that we'd worked together on three cases so far. Not by his request. I'd somehow ended up in the middle of murder, as I had again. Quite by accident.

"Miss Kimball," he said crisply, as he stepped in, removing his hat. So we were on professional footing today, not in friend-of-the-family territory. "I'm here to ask you a few questions."

Mom popped out of the back, her face suffusing with

a glow when she saw him. "Sean." Then she took in his demeanor and formal dress. "Oh." She pivoted on her heel and marched off, leaving him staring after her in dismay.

"Come on in," I said, already weary from the day's twists and turns. Still looking in Mum's direction, he'd almost bumped right into old Saint Nick. "Watch out for Santa."

"Is there somewhere private we can chat?" he asked. "The shop is opening soon, right?"

"It is. I guess we'd better go into the kitchen."

He followed me through the store. "Sorry," I told Mum and Aunt Violet when we reached the kitchen. "The DI and I need to talk privately."

"Not a problem." Aunt Violet got right up, tea mug in hand. "We'll move out to the shop."

She and Mum edged past, Mum doing her best to pretend Sean wasn't standing right there. Though I liked Sean, when he wasn't interrogating me, I could sympathize with my mother. Christmas was bringing up lots of bittersweet memories of my father. I didn't blame her for feeling conflicted or confused. Especially with Sean's flip-flopping between friend and foe. Well, friend and officer of the law.

I motioned toward the table. "Have a seat. Would you like a cup of tea?" I felt the teapot. It was still warm.

"If it's no trouble." Sean took out a tablet and placed it on the table, along with his phone.

"Not at all." I retrieved a mug and filled it, letting him add his own milk. Then I sat opposite and tried to collect my thoughts.

"I'm going to record this," he told me. "Any objection?"

"No, of course not. Please do."

After a few preliminaries—names, date, time—we began. I had expected him to ask about today but instead he focused on Barnaby. I guessed the discovery of the tainted cream had led them to try to connect that to the cakes.

"Take me through the morning you found Barnaby Winters at the shop."

I explained the sequence of events culminating in our discovery of the stricken young man.

"Did you see the card with the cakes?"

"I did. It was from Tea and Crumpets." My heart rate jumped. "Daisy didn't make those cakes."

"You sound pretty certain. How do you know she didn't?"

"Well, she said so. It was the frosting. She never uses that color blue. Plus, why would she? She had no motive to poison Barnaby or Charlotte."

He didn't respond, only made a note.

"I thought the police didn't find anything at the tearoom." Maybe they had but Daisy didn't know it. Had the killer planted poison somewhere?

"Miss Kimball. Please. Now that this is my case, I'm going over everything again."

I tried to swallow the arguments crowding to my lips. The last thing I wanted to do was make things worse for Daisy or Charlotte.

"The skin cream you found at Arthur Pemberly's dwelling. Can you explain how that came about?"

"Sure. It all started when we found out Barnaby was poisoned with aconite. Charlotte started to wonder if her grandfather was also a victim." I outlined my train of thought and the events that led to the discovery of the tainted arthritis skin cream.

He let me speak, interrupting now and then with a clarifying question to separate the factual from the speculative. As we went along, understanding dawned and I could clearly see the direction he was headed in.

Sean Ryan believed Charlotte was the killer.

CHAPTER 17

The worst part was, I could see his logic. He believed that Charlotte had left a trap for intruders, knowing that sooner or later someone would try to find the doll. She'd also set Daisy and me up to make the discovery of the cream. The fact was, she benefited most from her grandfather's death. Even if she hadn't visited much, it only took once for her to give Arthur the cream.

Every fiber of my being screamed *no* in response. I'd been there, I'd witnessed Charlotte's reactions, the pain she felt over her grandfather's untimely death.

Arguing with a detective inspector wasn't the best course of action, I reminded myself. As in past cases, I needed to do some digging and present what I'd learned. Sean Ryan might be maddening at times but he was fair. I had to give him that much.

"That's it for today," Sean said, closing the tablet case. "Thanks for your time."

I hopped up from my chair. "She didn't do it." So much for keeping my mouth shut. "I know how bad it looks for Charlotte. I get it. Other people have motives, too. Strong ones."

He regarded me steadily, his expression inscrutable.

"We follow the evidence, Molly." Then he threw me a bone. "The investigation is far from over."

"Good to hear." Maybe I could find more of the evidence he needed, proof that Charlotte was innocent. As soon as he left, I was going to do a deep dive on the Winters family and anyone close to them. Andre and Reece, for example.

"Be in touch if you come across anything of interest," Sean said. "And be careful."

"Oh, I will." As he exited the kitchen, I picked up his mug and carried it to the sink. Another cup of coffee and I would get to work.

When I returned out front, mug in hand, the shop was open but empty. Even more so without Puck, who was still at the toy shop. Even Clarence seemed to miss him, nosing around the corners and checking the window and the red chair for his presence. "He'll be back soon," I told him. "Pleased that you missed him." Clarence lifted his face as if sniffing and stalked away, tail swinging.

A text arrived with a ping. Daisy. *I've been summoned for an interview at the station.*

Anger and dismay made my stomach clench. Sean Ryan really was going over old ground with a fine-tooth comb. *DI Ryan was just here. He's in charge now. Keep me posted, 'k?* She sent back a thumbs-up.

Putting my phone aside, I opened a browser on my laptop and entered "Althea Winters" into the bar. Why not start at the top? As the saying went, a fish rots from the head down.

My phone pinged again. Finally. The results of the tryouts.

Molly, we are pleased to let you know that you have been selected . . .

"Yahoo!" I bellowed. "I made it into the madrigals."

Mum and Aunt Violet poked their heads out from the shelving. "Congratulations," Aunt Violet said. "Well done."

"Good job, Molly," Mum said. "We'll definitely come see you perform."

"I'm counting on it." Turning back to the laptop, I scrolled through the search results. Ah. Here was a bio.

I skimmed over the description of her upbringing near Cambridge, attendance at St. Hildegard's, and appointment as professor. The many credits for plays produced and music consulting gigs on films and television shows.

I wanted the good stuff—details about her personal life. Althea's first marriage was to a man named Harvey Winters, who died twenty years ago. He was a member of Parliament and owned a family property called The Bells, built on the site of a former abbey. Althea had obtained her university degrees and teaching position under the name of Winters and kept that surname despite two later marriages, I noticed.

Naturally I went down this trail and looked up The Bells. It was now a bed-and-breakfast with six guest rooms. Hmm. I looked up the hosts. Definitely not Althea.

Had she sold it after his death? Maybe so. I returned to the personal history and learned that Althea and Harvey had one son. Looking up his name, I found an obit from five years ago. He'd left a wife, Dorcas, and two children, Barnaby and Victoria. Tori.

Althea then married Andre's father, mere months after Harvey died. That was quick. Finding a pad of paper, I began to jot down dates.

The pattern was repeated again, with Arthur. Althea

was widowed and then she married Charlotte's grand-father.

I wondered what the cause of death was for husbands one and two. Obituary time. Husband one died of a heart attack. Okay, that could definitely be poison. Husband two died of natural causes. Like Arthur. Maybe husband two had health problems nudged along with judicious amounts of something deadly.

Repelled by the idea and needing a break, I pushed back from the desk and picked up my coffee. Cold. I decided to make a fresh cup.

The door opened and I halted, my priority being to wait on whomever. Charlotte walked in, holding Puck in her arms. She let him down with a laugh. "He does not like being carried."

"Tell me about it." I waved my mug. "I was going to get a warm-up. Want something to drink?"

"I'll take a coffee." She waved when we walked past Mum, who was still shelving. "Hello, Nina."

"Nice to see you, Charlotte." Mum looked at me. "Can you please bring me a cup of tea? I'm ready for a break."

"Sure thing, Mum." I knew what she really wanted—to sit in on an update from Charlotte. I couldn't blame her.

Charlotte looked around the kitchen while I brewed the hot drinks. "Love this building." She peered out the French doors at the view of the garden. "I should put in something like this. My back garden is totally neglected. A bunch of weeds and a trash bin or two."

Unlike the elaborate gardens at Arthur's residence. "We sit out there a lot in nice weather. Our little piece of paradise." I filled a mug with a tea bag and a fresh

French press with boiling water. The cats had followed us so I gave treats to Charlotte and let her hand them out, earning purrs of appreciation. Hearing purrs always made me feel better.

"Maybe I should get a cat." Charlotte patted each in turn. "Thanks for letting me borrow Puck today. Thank you for visiting, Puck."

He blinked at her as if to say, *no problem.*

"He was a stray. Clarence has been here since he was a kitten. We'll ask around, find you one. Or two."

"I'll start with one." Charlotte left off patting and came over to the counter. "Can I help?"

"You can carry these." I placed a tin of cookies in her hands, then poured our coffees. Retrieving milk from the fridge, I offered it to Charlotte before adding splashes to Mum's tea and my mug. The mugs went on a tray and Charlotte toted the cookies.

"Thank you, love." Mum accepted her tea. "How are you, Charlotte?" Her bright eyes conveyed that she was eager for details.

Charlotte rolled her eyes. "I scarcely know where to begin. As Molly probably told you, I was trapped in my flat this morning." She quickly covered up to when I'd left, then said, "They really grilled me about the cream. Even though we reported it, Molly, they acted like I poisoned it." Her lips pouted in a frown. "A senior officer came by. DI Ryan."

I took a breath, trying to still my leaping pulse. They *were* leaning toward Charlotte as a suspect.

"He's very good," Mum said, as if trying to convince Charlotte. "Very fair." She seemed to have gotten over being miffed that his visit was official, not personal.

I threw her a smile. "As if you're unbiased." When

she elbowed me in response, I added hastily, "He is. Both good and fair."

Charlotte's gaze flickered between us. "And you know that how?"

"Those cases Daisy told you about . . . he was the lead investigator each time." I grimaced. "He wasn't that thrilled when I put my nose in, to say the least. Our first murder was right here at the bookshop and Aunt Violet was a suspect. How could I sit back and let her be railroaded?"

"I thought he was fair." Her brows drew together in confusion.

"He is. I meant to say, I was worried about that happening. We were new to Cambridge so I didn't know how things worked. Not that I'd dealt with the police in Vermont." Not beyond an incident or two when my friends and I had been partying in the woods as teenagers.

She stared into her cup, seeming to absorb what I'd said. "Anyway, he questioned me thoroughly. Asked if I'd used or applied the cream and if not, why not? I explained that Grandad preferred to do things for himself. One reason why being sick was so irksome for him. When I did see him, he kept fretting about the shop, worried that closing it had been the wrong decision." Her features creased in pain. "I should have moved back sooner. I was so selfish. So worried about my job. I might have saved his life."

Charlotte began to weep. Mum scooted her chair over and put her arm around her, making soothing sounds. She didn't offer platitudes or false reassurances. There was nothing anyone could say to make it better and Mum didn't even try.

I gritted my teeth, feeling both helpless and frustrated. We couldn't change the past, so the only option was to find Arthur's killer—before they succeeded with Charlotte.

Mum and Charlotte were still talking, Charlotte's tears seeming to have eased, and so I went back to my research. This time I tried a different approach. What exactly did we know? The cream had come from Mistletoe Farm, where it was formulated. Had it been doctored with poison there or after purchase?

We'd already learned that Dorcas was close to Andre, the farmer. He was a madrigals performer, so he also knew Althea. That gave him proximity to the case. A motive was still a mystery. Reminding myself to keep an open mind, I focused on Andre and the farm. What facts did the research show us?

On a *Madrigals and Mayhem* social media page, I found pictures of Andre performing last year, including taking a bow with Dorcas and Barnaby. Barnaby had also been in the cast—and so had Reece, who was in another picture. Mustn't overlook Reece. He was Barnaby's partner in crime, maybe literally, and was dating Tori. Definitely close to the family as well.

"Whatcha doing?" Charlotte scooted a rolling chair closer. Her eyes and nose were red but otherwise she looked better. Mum was waiting on someone I hadn't even heard come in.

"Background research." I flipped through the pictures I'd found. "Trying to find connections." I went through my reasoning. "Reece seems to be around a lot."

"He is." Charlotte sipped her coffee. "He and Barnaby

are best friends. And you already know about him and Tori. She's always had a huge crush."

And now she was crushed by the breakup. Sighing, I opened the photo albums on the farm's social media page. Lots of photos. I scrolled down, hoping something relevant would catch my eye.

"Hold on," Charlotte said. "Go back. Is that the production area?"

"It is." Someone had taken photos of the setup where creams and other herbal products were prepared. The workers were garbed in white overalls, plastic caps over their hair.

"That's Reece. The photo with two other workers."

I enlarged the photo to get a better look at the faces. "I'll take your word for it. I've only seen him in person twice." Viewing him on grainy home cameras didn't count.

"Read the caption," Charlotte said.

"'This summer's team at the Mistletoe Farm production area includes Reece Harrison, chemistry student at'—Chemistry student! Ding, ding, ding." Reece might well know how to extract aconite from monkshood flowers or how to obtain the concentrated poison.

Charlotte nodded slowly. "Very interesting, my dear Watson."

"Hey, I'm Sherlock." Thinking of what Sean Ryan had said before he left, I decided to email this photo to him. He needed to see it. "Wish I could talk to Reece. I need an excuse to get into the college, though." There was no way he'd add me to his list of visitors.

"Hmm. I wish you could, too. I'm definitely not welcome. That last visit to Barnaby's building was pushing it."

An idea flashed into my mind. "The bookshop

has library privileges." We enjoyed this courtesy at all the Cambridge colleges. "I could pay a visit to the St. Aelred library and then go by the lodgings after." Getting inside Reece's building might be a challenge. I'd figure that out later.

"Perfect." Charlotte sighed. "I wish I could be there." She checked her mug, then took a sip. "What are you going to ask him?"

I had no idea. "I try not to overthink it," I said. "Kind of go with the flow." This lax—some might say careless—approach had always worked. I talked to people, tried to read their body language and listened to nuances in their tone and wording. "Don't worry. I won't make things worse." *I hope.*

◆◆

Thoughts, worries, and theories chased themselves around my mind as I walked over to St. Aelred College later that afternoon. Would I be able to talk to Reece? He might not be there, for one thing. Another possibility was that I wouldn't be able to get into his building.

Was he guilty of murder? If so, why would he kill Arthur? He didn't have anything to gain that I could see. Had Althea convinced him to make the poison on her behalf?

Or had it been Tori? Somehow I couldn't see her as a manipulative and beguiling seductress in a *The Postman Always Rings Twice* scenario.

Dorcas, maybe? The beautiful older woman, a Mrs. Robinson type, preying on his sympathies? In that case, Althea was a more likely target. Talk about an overbearing mother-in-law.

A simpler answer would be Barnaby, the best friend.

If not for the fact that Barnaby had gobbled down cakes poisoned with the same substance. Reece was lucky he hadn't eaten any.

Handy that, using the same poison. Aconite ran like a deadly thread through the story.

The winter dusk was already falling, streetlamps glowing gold in the blue light. The Blue Hour, it was called. So many connotations there. Here we were in the most festive time of year and I was chasing down a killer.

Buck up, Molly. I tried to push off the mantle of gloom settling around my shoulders. Winter days in Vermont had been short and frigid, the lack of light closing in like a prison. At least England wasn't quite as cold and spring would arrive much, much sooner.

Plus I had so much to be thankful for. A dream business, a wonderful boyfriend, and dear family and friends. Except for Janice. There always had to be one fly in the ointment, right?

A big, noisy one she was, too. I smiled, picturing a fly with Janice's face.

As I entered St. Aelred's Way, a truck with a wood-slatted cargo box bounced along the cobblestones toward me. When it passed by, I noticed it was from Mistletoe Farm, Andre at the wheel. He must have been delivering Christmas trees.

Before going into the lodge, I pulled my identification and Thomas Marlowe business card out of my wallet. To give truth to my ruse, I probably should stop by the library first. That would give me a chance to warm up and gather my thoughts before tackling Reece.

I had barely stepped through the door when blue lights strobed around the room. Instead of flashing past, the vehicle halted at the gate.

"What's going on?" I asked the porter, the same elderly gentleman who had assisted me before.

His face was grim as he put down the phone receiver. "We've had an . . . an accident this afternoon." He clamped his mouth shut, not willing to divulge details to an outsider.

"I'm sorry." I placed my cards on the counter. "I'm here for the library. From Thomas Marlowe, the bookshop."

The porter barely glanced at my identification before pushing the ledger toward me. "Sign in, please. Do you know the way?"

"Sure do." I signed my name and purpose and then tucked away the cards.

"Please excuse me, then. I must attend to a pressing matter." He glanced toward the lane, where another emergency vehicle was pulling up.

"Thank you." Slinging my bag strap over my head, I hurried to the door, not wanting him to change his mind for some reason.

In the main court, I noticed students running along the paths in the direction of the second court where the students lived. Too fast for mere eagerness to get inside someplace warm. "What's going on?" I called to a young man.

He barely broke stride. "Reece Harrison. He . . . he . . ." The student visibly gulped. "He's *dead*." He turned and ran.

CHAPTER 18

Reece is dead. Unlike the student disappearing into the distance, I halted, unable to move. A cascade of emotions washed over me. Shock. Sorrow. Sadness. And the unnerving feeling that a killer had just beaten me to the punch. I was too late.

Whatever Reece knew, it was beyond reach now.

Had the killer been cleaning up loose ends? Or had someone sought revenge after learning that Reece killed Arthur and tried to poison Barnaby?

Or maybe it was an accident and I was jumping to conclusions. Lurching into action, I followed the student through the arch into the next court. Here I saw people clustered near the entrance to Reece's building. The gate to the lane was open and medics were pushing a gurney through, the glow of emergency lights and streetlamps lighting their way. A couple of officers followed, striding with authority.

"Help is on the way," a student said as I joined the group.

"Too little, too late," another remarked. "I heard he . . ."

"No, don't say that." A young woman burst into tears. "It can't be true."

Another student put his arm around her. "I'm afraid it is."

She leaned on him. "I was supposed to meet him, like, right now." She began to wail.

"How did everyone find out so fast?" I asked the first student. "Looks like the police and medics just arrived."

"His roommate found him," he said. "Barnaby Winters? He had barely called nine-nine-nine when Percy Bellows, who is in Reece's study group, walked in. Percy told his roommate, who told . . . well, you get the idea."

"I sure do." Barnaby had discovered the body and Percy had told everyone about it. "What happened?"

The student shook his head. "Don't know exactly. He said there wasn't any blood. He was just sitting at his desk, all slumped over." Horror infused his tone.

Was it something he ate? I wished I could ask someone. Maybe Percy, if I could find him.

The crowd parted, falling silent as the medics and officers made their way to the building entrance. *Sergeant Adhikari.* I ducked behind a taller student, hoping she wouldn't see me. How could I explain this coincidence? To be honest, it wasn't one. I had planned to visit Reece today.

What if I'd been the one to find him? The thought was horrifying.

"Molly. Molly." Still caught up by dreadful imaginings, it took a while for the voice to penetrate. Finally I tuned in when a woman tugged at my sleeve. I turned to see Tori Winters, her eyes huge with shock and fear.

"Come with me," she pleaded, tugging at my arm again.

"What? Where?" I was taken aback that she was

seeking my help. Surely as Charlotte's friend, I was the enemy. Maybe she'd softened toward me after our encounter at the Magpie, when she'd been so upset. Or not. With the Winters family, it was always complicated, I gathered.

Her face screwed up in distress and she began to shiver. "Reece. He . . . I heard . . . please." She turned to look toward his building, where a constable was now standing guard.

"You want to go inside? I don't think they'll let us."

Not bothering to respond, she began walking in that direction. I hurried along behind her out of concern and yes, curiosity as well. Looking straight ahead, Tori plowed through the crowd, heedless of the people she jostled or annoyed. I followed, wincing, shoulders raised in apology.

The constable took a step forward when she saw Tori barreling toward her. "You can't go inside right now," she said, putting up a hand.

Tori stared up at her, blinking. "What if I live here?"

"The answer is still no." Softening slightly, she said, "That may change soon. Hold tight."

With a huff, Tori stalked away. She pulled out her phone. "Barnaby. Pick up." She disconnected and tried again. This time he answered. "Finally. What's going on? You can't talk? I'm outside the building." She listened for a second. "What do you mean they want to talk to me? What did you tell them?"

I stood right beside her, trying to listen. Barnaby was practically shouting when he said, "The noodles. I said you brought them. I'm sorry. Really I am. Got to go." He cut the call off abruptly.

"Noodles?" I asked. Tori was standing stock-still, a vacant expression on her face.

Her mouth dropped open. "No. How could . . . they weren't . . . I didn't . . ."

"Tori. Please. Tell me." I snapped my fingers in front of her face. "I can't help you if I don't know what's going on." And maybe not even then.

She set her jaw. "Reece was eating noodles when he . . . Noodles I happened to buy."

Poison again. Had to be. "Dry noodles?"

"Yes. You boil water—"

"Got it." How could someone poison dry noodles? It had to be in the seasoning.

Tori's phone rang in her hand. She stared at the display before answering. "Barnaby? Who is this?" A pause. "But I don't know anything." Her shoulders slumped. "Be right there. I'm outside, in the court." She thrust her phone into her coat pocket. "I've been summoned." The pleading note returned to her voice. "Will you come with me?"

"To be questioned?" My mind began to race. "They won't want me there."

"I don't care." Tori's mouth set in a line. "I'm not under arrest or anything so they'll just have to deal."

In that case . . . "Okay, I'll go with you."

When we approached the door, the constable said, "Name, please." When Tori told her, she stood aside to let her enter. As I followed, she shifted her stance. "Hold on."

"She's my friend," Tori said. "I'm not under arrest so I'd like her to come with me. For moral support." Her voice rose. "Do you have a problem with that? My boyfriend is dead and I'm very, very upset."

The constable glanced around, no doubt gauging the possibility of an ugly scene. The other students were watching so she relented. "Go ahead. Try to stay out of the way."

"You bet." I sidled past before she could change her mind.

We tromped upstairs to Reece's room, passing a student wearing a leather jacket and jeans sitting on the steps and holding a tablet. "Hey, Percy," Tori said.

He rubbed a hand over his spiky brush cut, eyes behind black-rimmed glasses following us as we went by. Percy was in Reece's study group, the student outside had said, and he had come along right after Barnaby found Reece. The police must have parked him here for further questioning.

Tori knocked on the room door and a few seconds later, it opened slightly, revealing Constable Derby. "Yes?"

"I'm Tori Winters. You summoned me."

He opened the door barely wide enough for her to go in. Rebuffed by his cold stare, I didn't try to follow.

"I'll wait, Tori," I called. Hopefully she wouldn't be held up for long. Since I was already here, I might as well hang out and gather every detail possible.

The door shut firmly and I sat down on the stairs, a few steps up from Percy. He had his head down, reading, so I pulled out my phone. Judging by the gathering in the court, the news was out, which meant I could talk about Reece's death.

Creating a group text, I sent a note to Mum, Aunt Violet, and Kieran, giving them the update. I didn't contact Charlotte yet. This wasn't news I wanted to break to her over a text or even a phone call. Or Daisy. She was with the police right now, being interviewed.

Why Reece? Unless . . . the targeted victim could have been *Tori*. She'd brought the noodles, she said.

That didn't mean they'd come directly from the store to here. She could have been storing them at her place. Wherever that was. I wasn't sure if she lodged at St. Hildegard's or if she lived with her mother.

I must have sighed or grunted or something because Percy glanced up at me. "You all right?" he asked.

"Yeah, I guess so." Now I definitely sighed. "I can't wrap my head around it." Reece's death, Barnaby's poisoning, Arthur, the shenanigans at the toy shop . . .

"Me either," he said. "I'm in total shock." As people do when they've had a traumatic experience, he began to tell me about it, seeming to find relief in verbalizing the event. "It was a normal day, you know? I came over to check in with Reece, to finalize a . . . a couple things. I know the downstairs code, so I was able to come up without calling." Distress darkened his eyes and he swallowed. "Walked in and first thing I saw was Reece at the table with his head down, as if he was sleeping. Thought he was drunk, which wasn't like him, not at all, but I joked, 'Little early, isn't it?' Then I noticed his cousin, Barnaby, standing there. He goes, 'He's not drunk, he's dead, you ass.'"

"Whoa, harsh," I muttered.

Percy waved that off. "I don't blame him, he was in shock. He called nine-nine-nine right away and although he suggested I take off, I hung around. Thought they might want to talk to me." His expression became disgruntled. "They did, for a minute, then told me to wait." He shifted on the step as if uncomfortable. "I'd like to get out of here someday."

"Police stuff can take a long time," I said, hoping this wasn't true in Tori's case. "Did you see a bowl of noodles on the table?"

He drew back. "Noodles? What are you talking about?"

"Nothing. Tori said . . . never mind." If the noodles had been sitting there, Percy hadn't noticed. To change the subject, I said, "So you were in Reece's study group." That's what the student outside had said. "Was that for a certain subject or did you just hang out, like a study hall?"

"Study group?" He gave a dry laugh. "Yeah, sort of. We did, um, special projects." His amused eyes invited me to ask more.

"Like what?"

The downstairs door opened and someone came up the stairs, moving fast with energy and purpose. By unspoken consent, we fell silent, waiting for the person to reach us.

My pulse jolted when Detective Inspector Sean Ryan came into view, his sharp gaze raking over us. "Miss Kimball." He bit out the words. "What are you doing here?"

Feeling soundly scolded, I hurried to explain. "I'm with Tori Winters. Who is in there." I pointed a shaking finger at the closed door. "She asked me to wait." Instead of stopping while ahead, I bumbled on. "I was on campus to go to the library. You can check the book in the lodge." The hesitation in my voice made it sound like a lie. Which it sort of was. "Then I noticed the commotion and came over to check it out. That's when I ran into Tori. And found out about Reece."

Percy sat listening, chin propped in his hand, no doubt wondering how a police officer knew my name.

Ryan lifted one brow, one of his trademark gestures. "I see." He squinted at me. "I think it best that you leave."

"Absolutely." I scanned the step, making sure everything was in my bag, before standing to button my coat. With as much dignity as I could muster, I headed down the steps, edging past Percy and Ryan.

To my dismay, Sean Ryan followed me down the stairs to the vestibule. "Miss Kimball. Hold on a moment."

I slowly turned to face him. "Yes?"

"Tell me again why you're here." His tone was gentle.

Although highly tempted to double down, I wanted him to trust me—and listen when I passed information along. He had the power to actually arrest someone. I didn't. "I wanted to talk to Reece. But I was too late."

His head went back. The fact I'd readily admitted what he suspected startled him. "Okay." Brow furrowed, he gnawed at his bottom lip for a moment. "Seriously, Miss Kimball. Be careful." He put up a hand. "I'm not trying to be patronizing. This . . . situation is a hornet's nest."

"Yeah. It is." I gestured toward the door bar. "Can I go now?"

I was halfway across the court before I stopped to take a breath, my cheeks stinging as if they'd been slapped. DI Sean Ryan had only been doing his job, I reminded myself, both in questioning me and warning me. I shouldn't take it personally. This rationale was somewhat comforting, as was the thought that, if he could intimidate innocent me to this degree, the killer didn't stand a chance.

My phone buzzed. Daisy. Calling, instead of texting. My heart clenched. "Hello?"

"Molly? Hey. Are you okay?" To my relief, she sounded normal.

"Not really. But first, tell me: How did the interview go?" I held my breath.

"Fine." She gave a little laugh. "Actually, it was cut short. One of the officers told me they'd tracked the cakes to another bakery."

My head swam with the release of tension. "Oh, I'm so relieved."

"What's going on?" she asked. "You sound funny."

Glancing around the court to make sure no one was nearby, I started walking slowly toward the lodge. "It's Reece. He's dead." I could barely get the words out.

"No!" she cried. "I don't believe it."

I swallowed hard, trying to moisten my dry throat. "Neither can I." Who would be next?

◆◆◆

When I got back to Magpie Lane, I went directly to the toy shop. I couldn't put off telling Charlotte. Thanks to social media, the news was sure to get out any minute about Reece Harrison.

All the lights were on, including colorful strings around the front window. Charlotte had moved the dollhouse to a more prominent spot and the giant bear usually looming behind the counter was now next to it. That eye-catching display was sure to lure shoppers inside.

I rapped on the glass, then tried the handle. It was locked but I saw Charlotte hurrying to open the door. "Molly. Did you go to St. Aelred?" She sounded slightly breathless.

"I did." How to begin? Stalling, I took off my bag and plucked the hat off my head. "I have news. It's not good."

She'd been fidgeting with stuff on the counter and

now her movements stilled. "What do you mean? What happened?"

"Reece." I stepped across the floor to join her, placing my bag on the floor. "Reece," I said again, the rest of the words refusing to come. Instead they sat like a rock in my chest.

Charlotte's fingers tugged at her sleeves, pulling them down over her hands. "Uh, about that." Her gaze skittered away. "I went over to St. Aelred this afternoon." The story came out in a rush. "I was out doing errands, last-minute things I needed, planning to open tomorrow, you know. I went right by there and I said to myself, 'Why not try to see Reece and Barnaby?'"

There were a lot of reasons why not, including being kicked out the last time. Oh, and the attempted murder here in the shop. Not to mention that talking to Reece had been my mission, as we decided, and she could have blown it for me.

"Why did you do that?" I asked. "The plan was for me to go."

She had the grace to look sheepish. "I know. I'm sorry. It was an impulse."

And a huge mistake. "How did you get in?" I asked. "Last time . . ."

Charlotte tugged at her braid, her smile sly. "I managed to talk my way in. How else? The porter there is the sweetest man. Then, when I got to their building, I hung around until someone else was going in and followed." Dimples flashed. "Easy peasy."

Dread built inside me with every word. Was Sean Ryan right to suspect Charlotte? Was she about to confess to murder?

CHAPTER 19

"Did you see Reece?" Afraid to hear the answer, I barely managed to choke out the question.

"I sure did." Her chin went up. "He denied all knowledge of the cream. Said he'd never even been inside Grandad's bedroom or bathroom." She leaned forward, eyes gleaming. "He knows something, though. I saw the realization on his face. His eyes widened and then he glanced at his phone."

Had Reece contacted the killer? Even if so, they would have had to work awfully fast to bring poisoned noodles over. Unless Charlotte had brought them with her.

"Did you bring Reece a gift?" I asked.

Confusion creased her brow. "A gift? No. A kick in the pants would have been more like it, the way he's been acting."

Or a bowl of poison? I inhaled, wondering if I should continue—or exit and call Sean Ryan. I decided to live dangerously.

"So what did you do?" I asked. "After he denied knowing anything."

Her shoulders lifted. "Nothing. I told him to watch

his back. I mean, if he confronted the killer, he might be next, right?"

A final inquiry. "Was he eating anything?"

"No. Why?" Charlotte frowned. "You've been asking the strangest questions, as if you think *I* did something." Hands on her hips, she said, "'Fess up, Molly. What's going on?"

Tell her or not? Either way she was going to be angry with me. I'd questioned her as if she was a murder suspect. Which was a reasonable concern, I reminded myself. People all around Charlotte were being poisoned. All I had to prove otherwise was our friendship and my sympathy for the loss of her grandfather.

Still, I felt about an inch high, like shrinking Alice in Wonderland.

I took a deep breath, steeling myself to drop a bomb. "I didn't get a chance to see Reece, as we planned, because he's dead."

She recoiled, her eyes flaring, all the color leaching out of her face. "What?" She gripped the counter to hold herself upright. "No. I don't believe it."

"Neither did I." I grunted a dry laugh of disbelief. "I was on my way to the library when I saw a student running across the court. I asked him what was going on and he told me." Maybe I could bury my blunder in this barrage.

She leaned on the counter, transfixed by my story.

"Tori was there, outside, and she called Barnaby. He told her Reece had been eating noodles—"

"Noodles? They were poisoned, too?"

"Apparently. Barnaby . . . found him. The police wanted to question Tori for some reason and they booted me out of there."

The color returned to her cheeks like a flood, and for a moment I thought she was going to tear into me about my insinuations. Instead she put shaking hands to her face. "I can't believe it. Poor Reece. Why would someone kill *him*?"

"I have no idea. It might have been a mistake, except I gather he liked noodles. He was eating them when we took the poinsettia over, remember?"

"Maybe. If you say so." She stared into space, stunned. "That makes three people now. And each time, I was there. Oh, Molly, I really made a mess of things going to see him today."

"You didn't know," I said. "It was a coincidence. Had to be." It couldn't be a frame. Charlotte had visited Reece on the spur of the moment. Plus if he'd made the noodles himself, they had to have been already tainted. Dismay churned in my stomach. What if another student had eaten the noodles first? Or Barnaby or Tori? The killer didn't seem to care about risks to bystanders. Truly malevolent.

An engine grumbled and I turned to see a familiar striped vehicle easing down the lane. "Here come our friends," I said. The police must have gotten wind of Charlotte's visit to Reece. "Brace yourself."

I considered making a run for it, knowing that Sean Ryan's tolerance toward me was wearing thin. Then, thinking better of it, I stood my ground. I hadn't done anything wrong, although if I'd known that Charlotte had gone to see Reece, I might not have come over. Stayed away until the dust settled. She was really in the thick of it now.

This time, Sean and Gita were in the car. The big guns.

"Come clean," I warned Charlotte as the officers

approached the toy shop. "You don't want to get caught in a lie. Not by these guys."

She was literally wringing her hands. "Should I call an attorney? What if they arrest me? I'm innocent, Molly, I am."

I had faith that our local force wouldn't railroad an innocent person, but it wasn't my neck on the line. "Maybe you should. You have a right to representation."

Charlotte picked up her phone. "I'll call the lawyer who helped me with the estate. She might be able to give me a referral." Gita Adhikari rapped on the shop door. "Molly, can you get that?"

Feet dragging, I went to answer. "Hello."

The officers exchanged glances. "Molly, what are you doing here?" Sean gritted out between clenched teeth.

"Visiting Charlotte." I stood back to let them enter. "I take it this is about Reece?"

Not bothering to respond, they brushed past me. Charlotte was still on the phone. "Thank you," she said, writing something on a scrap of paper. "You're a lifesaver. I'll give him a ring right away." After disconnecting, she looked up, a triumphant smile on her face. "I'm not answering any questions without my attorney present."

Sean and Gita stood stunned for a moment, then Sean said, "That's your prerogative, Miss Pemberly. I'll expect you down at the station forthwith. Have your attorney ask for me."

As for me, I crept across the floor toward the door, ready to make my escape.

"Molly—Miss Kimball." Sean's voice stopped me.

I pivoted. "Yes?"

"We'll be over in a minute to talk to you." Sean

folded his arms, giving me a crooked smile. "Unless you're also planning to lawyer up?"

"Not at the moment. No need." Then, because I couldn't resist, "That might change, of course."

Before he could respond, I practically ran out of the building. Charlotte wasn't the only one neck-deep in this mess. Maybe I should hole up in the bookshop until the case was solved.

Thomas Marlowe was closed, so I used my key to get in. Mum was behind the counter at the computer. "Molly. What's the matter?" She knew me too well.

"Everything." I crossed to the counter, shedding my bag and coat as I went. "There's been another murder. And Sean Ryan is coming over any second to question me."

Mum took this extraordinary outburst in stride. Standing, she smoothed her wool skirt. "I'll put the kettle on."

∗∗

After the police finally left, I curled up in the red armchair for a comfort read I desperately needed. I'd been thoroughly grilled about my visit to St. Aelred, and every move I'd made while there. Every word that Tori had said. Her protests of innocence and her plea for me to go inside the building. Then my visit to Charlotte. I didn't relay our conversation, though, or my briefly suspicious thoughts about her impromptu visit to St. Aelred. I had been trying to tread the fine line between being transparent and honest and throwing my friend under the bus and it had been exhausting.

I'd been able to turn the tables a bit, when I changed the subject to Reece's employment at Mistletoe Farm.

I had the impression they hadn't known about it until I sent the photograph of Reece at the production facility to Sean Ryan. Gita's quickly suppressed surprise at my sleuthing skill was gratifying. I'm petty like that.

Most of all, though, I was upset and angry right now. About Reece, a young man lost. Barnaby, who had barely survived. And Arthur, who had been a wonderful man. One only needed to look at the toy shop to know that. Justice needed to be served—and soon.

With a deep sigh, I opened *Charlotte's Dollhouse*, wishing that I could step into the pages of a book for a while. The last time I'd read, the dolls had been plotting.

Charlotte's Dollhouse, cont.

The next morning, Charlotte opened her eyes. And screamed.

The five dolls were sitting on the comforter in a circle, facing her.

Charlotte pushed herself to a seated position. "Who did this? Who put you on my bed? Aunt Margaret!" she cried. "Aunt Margaret!"

When Aunt Margaret came, Charlotte pointed to the line of dolls smiling so innocently. "The dolls. They weren't on my bed last night when I went to sleep. Did you put them there?"

Aunt Margaret's mouth opened and it seemed like she didn't know what to say. Picking up the bisque doll to make room, she perched on the bed. "Let me tell you a secret."

Charlotte leaned forward, eager. "A secret? About the dolls?"

"Yes." Her aunt fiddled with Polly, fluffing

her silk skirt and straightening a ruffle along the bodice. "They're magic." She walked Polly along. "At least I always thought so. When I was your age, I often found them in odd places." She flopped Polly onto her face on the bed. "In positions I hadn't left them in."

Charlotte's eyes were saucers. "You mean they move on their own?"

Aunt Margaret picked Polly up. "I think they might. What other explanation could there be?" She held out the doll. "Polly is what is called a fashion doll. Fashion dolls have been used for hundreds of years to display the latest fashions."

Charlotte eyed Polly's long, full dress dubiously. "I think she needs new clothes, then."

Aunt Margaret burst out laughing. "You're right. Her hemline is far too long." She smiled. "I have an idea. Why don't we bring her with us to the dressmaker's? Polly can get a new Christmas dress, too."

"A new dress?" Charlotte clapped her hands. "When are we going?"

"After breakfast." Aunt Margaret placed Polly on the bed.

Charlotte slid the covers back, careful not to dislodge the dolls. "See you later," she told them. "I'm going to wash up and go down to breakfast." Then she reached for Polly. "You're coming with me today."

Polly had never ridden in a motorcar. The last time she'd been out of the house, she had been a passenger in a carriage drawn by a matched pair of white horses. The carriage had been lovely with its tufted cushions and upholstered walls, the springs rocking gently as they rolled along the London streets. She'd felt like royalty, like a princess from a storybook.

The automobile wasn't bad, though. They sped along the streets so fast Polly felt like they were flying. And the horn was magnificent. The first time it blew, Polly would have jumped if she could move. Charlotte's laugh made her realize there was nothing to be afraid of. The second time was a thrill and she tried to memorize the sound so she could demonstrate it for the other dolls. Jingles would be so envious.

They pulled up in front of a fine establishment offering dressmaking and alterations. Polly thought she might have been here before, although the dresses in the window were awfully short, revealing the mannequin's ankles.

Oh my. Fashions had changed. Polly felt like a frump.

Inside, the shop was as she remembered: bolts of beautiful fabrics—silks and satins, georgette and chiffon—along the walls, a seamstress with a tape around her neck and pins in her apron, and plenty of mirrors in which to admire oneself.

"Christmas dresses for two?" the seamstress asked, her gaze raking over Aunt Margaret and Charlotte as if sizing them up. Which she probably was.

"For three," Charlotte said, holding Polly out. "My doll needs a new dress as well."

The seamstress took Polly in her callused yet gentle hands, turning her over as she examined her. *Waiting for her decision, Polly held her breath. How could she bear to wear these old rags now?*

"She hasn't had a new outfit since 1890," Aunt Margaret said with a laugh. "Well past time, isn't it?"

"She's lovely," the seamstress said. "She'll be the belle of the ball in her new dress."

I closed the book there. Time to get ready for the first rehearsal of *Madrigals and Mayhem*. I was getting a new dress soon as well, I thought with a smile, but I would be going retro, to the Renaissance period.

CHAPTER 20

Once again, Kieran accompanied me by bicycle to Lilly Maxwell Hall for the first rehearsal of *Madrigals and Mayhem*. As we dismounted in front, another cyclist hummed toward us. They drew close and I recognized George by the flat tweed cap he often wore. "Hello there."

George hopped off, agile for a man in his late sixties. "Molly. You decided to join us." He nodded at Kieran.

"Well, it's more like I passed the audition." I clicked the bike lock and tested it.

We waited until he secured his bike, then entered the building together. "What's your role?" I asked. "We're Lord and Lady Nightingale." My assigned role had come through on another message, and I was happy to be paired with Kieran.

"Nice." George knew the way so we followed him through the building. "I don't have my assignment yet. Althea said she was working on a part that would showcase my talents."

Although he seemed pleased, I was alarmed. Considering Althea's track record, she should come with a warning label: Biohazard.

We reached a set of double doors and George pulled one open, gesturing for us to precede him.

The cast and crew were clustered near the stage, and as we approached them, Althea broke away and trotted toward us, an eager expression on her face. She held out a hand. "George. There you are." She put her arm through his, drawing him back toward the others. "I can't wait to show you the script. It's hot off the presses tonight."

Althea had barely spared us a glance. "What are we? Chopped liver?" I muttered. Kieran threw me a confused look. "Old saying."

Dorcas was standing beside a chair, passing out folded, photocopied booklets that I guessed were copies of the script Althea had mentioned.

"Is this different than the last script we had?" a young woman asked. Besides Kieran and me, Sir Jon, Dorcas, Andre from Mistletoe Farm, Barnaby Winters, and George, there was a mix of students and older people.

No Tori. Grieving over Reece? I couldn't blame her.

"We've made a few changes," Althea said. "After everyone has a program, we'll go 'round and introduce ourselves. Then we'll do a read-through and blocking. Crew, get ready to take notes."

After everyone was introduced, Althea gave us an overview of the story. "The scene opens at the court of Queen Elizabeth." She patted her hair. "I am playing the queen. Judi Dench will have nothing on me."

"*What?*" Dorcas's voice was a barely contained shriek. She began to frantically leaf through the booklet. "This isn't my play."

"It mostly is." Althea's teeth were gritted. "I rearranged a couple of roles. You and Andre are now the star-crossed lovers."

Dorcas sent her mother-in-law a troubled look as she flipped through the pages. Andre stood close, murmuring reassurances into her ear.

"Onward." Althea tossed her head. "George is the Stranger from the North, who sets the court on its ear with revelations of long-guarded secrets. You." She pointed at me and Kieran. "Lord and Lady Nightingale. When the play opens, you are estranged. On the way to reconciliation, you suffer misunderstandings."

I'd pictured Kieran and me together throughout, glued at the hip. My own fault for not reviewing the actual script first. No choice but to roll with it now.

"We also have a very special performer this year," Althea said. "Reprising his role from the first madrigals dinner we put on at university. I present to you Sir Jon, our Lord of Misrule and Master of Ceremonies."

Sir Jon, who was wearing a jester cap, bowed as everyone clapped. Our eyes met across the circle and I waved, glad to have him here. Considering recent events related to the Winters family, I wondered if his role here was more than jester. Was he also investigating? It wouldn't be the first time he'd worked for law enforcement agencies since retiring from Her Majesty's service.

"I'd also like to introduce my grandson," Althea said, radiating pride. "Barnaby, please step forward." He did so sheepishly, ducking his head so a sheaf of hair hung over his eyes. "This is Barnaby's second year with the madrigals. Barnaby is playing the role of a handsome rogue."

One who hits on me, I noticed while flipping through the script. *Ugh.* The sacrifices we must make during an investigation.

"The songs will be a mix of madrigals written and

performed for Queen Elizabeth and classic Christmas carols," Althea said. "Although some of our carols aren't period correct, they are beloved and atmospheric. The first song is 'All Creatures Now Are Merry-Minded.'"

With that, she lined us up in two groups and we marched through the room singing, converging at the feast table on the stage. From here, featured actors would get up to recite lines and sing in solos, pairs and groups. In between, there would also be trumpets and a minstrel playing a lute. The musicians weren't at this rehearsal. While the audience would enjoy an Elizabethan feast, we would not, although there would be food props such as a fake boar's head and ale and wine on our table. The last song was "God Rest You Merry, Gentlemen" as we proceeded offstage and out.

After a two-hour rehearsal, I was wiped, dying to get through the last hurdle, a meeting with the costume master, and go home.

"What'd you think, Molly?" Sir Jon asked. "Glad you joined our little band?" He still wore the jester hat, the bells jingling with every move.

"It's fun so far," I said. Which was true, despite my being tired. The songs were lively and there was a great deal of wry humor in the dialogue. Althea and Dorcas were talented writers, even if one or both were killers.

"Talk soon," Sir Jon said with a nod. "I'll bid you good night." He strode away, heading for Althea, who he engaged in conversation. If he was investigating, he was doing it with great charm and panache.

"Molly Kimball?" Toby, the wardrobe master, called my name.

As I made my way backstage, I passed by Dorcas and Andre, sitting together on chairs. A phone rang loudly and Dorcas dug around in her handbag. "Got to take this," she said.

"Hello? This week. Yes." She strode away.

Andre glanced up at me, and seeing that Toby was talking to someone, I perched on the vacated chair. "I'm so sorry about Reece," I said. His brows drew together, as if surprised by my condolences. "Someone told me he worked for you." Of course, I'd actually seen the photos online. I had also seen Andre's truck at the college the day Reece died.

Andre rubbed his beard. "Yeah, yeah. For a while. It's a real loss."

"It is," I murmured. How could I bring up seeing his truck? "We love our tree," I said, a sideways approach. "I noticed that you delivered trees to St. Aelred. While I was on my way to the library. Do all the colleges buy from you?"

His expression was puzzled. "Not all of them. Mostly the smaller ones."

"That's great." Dead end. Except that he was now leaning away from me, as if he wanted to distance himself. He pulled out his phone and began to scroll.

"Molly?" Toby called again, sounding impatient this time.

"That's my cue." I got up and hurried off. He didn't even look up. Dorcas was now hurrying back to her chair, an annoyed expression on her face. She threw me a scowl, probably wondering what I had been saying to Andre.

Toby stepped backstage and I followed. The costume area was a curtained-off section used for fittings. The master checked his clipboard, then showed me a photograph. "This is the concept we're going with. What do you think?"

The colorful brocade dress was full-skirted and Medieval in style, worn with a pointed hat trailing scarves. "It's great. I've always wanted to wear one of those princess hats." That's what we called them as kids.

Toby hummed agreement before starting to measure me. "We'll order the costume for you, and it should be here by the next rehearsal. You can try it on and see if it needs any alterations."

"Wonderful." Toby was obviously good at his job.

Someone called his name from outside the curtain. "Excuse me a minute. I'll be right back."

I stood listening to the life of the theatre outside my enclosure. Footsteps tapped and then a man said, "Yeah, we're almost done. I know. Raw deal." A pause. "Yeah, it isn't fair. Just hang in there, okay? It will blow over. Talk to you later."

Being nosy, I peeked out of the curtain. Barnaby was standing nearby. He startled when he saw me. "Didn't know anyone was there."

I might as well grab the opportunity. "Barnaby. How are you?"

A hand went through his hair, pushing his fringe out of his eyes. "I'm okay." His feet shifted.

"We were pretty worried about you," I said. "Daisy and I. No lingering effects?"

Barnaby shook his head. "Nope. All better." He grimaced. "Not that I like thinking about it. Still can't look at a cake."

"Don't blame you a bit." I lowered my voice. "I was sorry to hear about Reece. What a shock."

He nodded. "It sure was. He was fine when I left. Never expected to find him . . ." The expression in his eyes was haunted and I wished I could read his mind.

Had he put two and two together, namely that both the cakes and soup were poisoned, maybe—probably—by the same hand? Did he have any theories about why Reece had been targeted?

"Tori said it was the noodles."

He reacted as if I'd lobbed a firecracker at his feet. "What? No. When did you talk to her?"

"I saw Tori outside the building that day. She was so upset." I shook my head. "Later, it looked like the police were blaming her. Which is ridiculous." This was a half-truth. While I thought the motive of a breakup was thin, Tori wasn't totally off the list of suspects. She'd been around when Barnaby was poisoned and had probably visited Arthur along with the rest of the family.

His brow furrowed. "I certainly don't *want* to think that she did it. She and Reece were pretty tight."

Except they'd broken up. "Me either."

Barnaby lifted one foot. "Not to be rude, but I really need to get going."

"Of course." I gave him a big smile. "See you at the next rehearsal. This is going to be so much fun." I ducked back inside the dressing room.

Toby burst back through the curtains. "Sorry. I just need one more measurement and you're all set."

While he measured my arm, I pondered my conversations with Andre and Barnaby. Nothing conclusive, unfortunately. Oh, well. I'd have other opportunities.

•◊•

When I got home, I puttered around the bookshop, not ready to go to bed yet. Charlotte called my cell while I was unpacking new stock, so we'd be ahead in the morning.

"How are you?" I asked, almost afraid to hear the answer. I hadn't gotten an update concerning her interview with the police, which hopefully had been conducted with an attorney present.

"Still a free woman," she said breezily. "The reason I called is, she finally came in. I know it's late, but do you want to pop over and see if you like her? Maybe have a drink?"

"Hold on. What are you talking about?" I was totally confused.

"The Sasha doll. The one you wanted for your mum?"

"Oh. I almost forgot about that." I took the last books out of the box. "I'll be right over. So the interview went okay?"

"It was fine. I have the feeling they're looking at someone else. Before you ask, no, I don't know who it is."

I did. Tori Winters.

A couple minutes later, I put my coat on again and said goodbye to two disgruntled cats. "I'll be right back, 'kay? Keep an eye on things." I swear they both curled their lips.

Charlotte hurried to unlock the toy shop door for me. "There you are. Come on in."

Following her, I took a quick detour to the dollhouse. This was the house I pictured when reading *Charlotte's Dollhouse*. My friend also reminded me of the main character or vice versa. Both could be emotional and dramatic. With good reason, I acknowledged. Both had suffered major losses. I was the opposite, tending to shut down and become almost stoic in the face of an emergency or loss. Maybe that was my English side.

To my relief, the dollhouse looked as I remembered it. No new warnings of harm to Charlotte or anyone else.

"Come look," Charlotte called.

I turned to see her placing a doll with dark hair on the counter. About sixteen inches high, she wore a blue gingham dress, white shoes, and a somber expression on her finely carved face.

"She's in perfect condition," Charlotte said, displaying the doll for my inspection. "A real find." She handed Sasha to me.

I smoothed her hair, which was artificial yet silky. "She's beautiful. Mum is going to love her."

"She even came with instructions and the original box." Charlotte showed these to me and I tucked her back into the box.

"This reminds me," I said. "We need to keep going with the clues to find your Madame Alexander doll." The last clue had said, "We travel afar," and there were lots of travel-themed toys in the shop to investigate.

"We definitely should. Later this week?"

"Definitely. The sooner, the better." I was worried that the family was still after the doll. Why would they give up now?

Someone rapped on the door. "Uh-oh," Charlotte said. "I didn't lock it."

Then the new arrival cupped their hands around their face and peered inside.

Tori Winters.

"I wonder what she wants," Charlotte said. "Should I have her come in?"

"Why not? There are two of us," I joked.

"What's up, Tori?" Charlotte asked after opening the

door, cool as can be. You'd never know they were practically sworn enemies.

Tori shivered, wrapping her arms around her torso. Under her furry hat, her dark eyes shone with fear and desperation. "The police think I killed Reece. Someone is trying to frame me."

CHAPTER 21

I was right—Tori was the police's primary suspect. Then the second part of what she'd said penetrated. "What do you mean, they're trying to frame you?"

She threw me an irritated look. "Exactly what I said. I didn't kill Reece. I loved him."

I refrained from pointing out that love didn't mean innocence. As Reece's significant other, she would be high on the list of suspects.

"But you broke up," I blurted. So much for restraint.

Another frown. "You sound like you think I did it."

"Hold on." I put up a hand. "Let me take a step back. What evidence do they have that you killed him?"

"The noodles." Tori shrugged. "I always buy that brand. It was our favorite." Her scowl deepened. "Not anymore, needless to say."

Charlotte had been watching us volley shots back and forth. "Who knew about the noodles? Besides you and Reece, I mean."

Tori gave her question some thought. "A lot of people. I keep some in my room at school and at home. Plus the students in the study group. They've seen us eat them a million times."

"I saw him eating them, too," I remembered. "Remember, Charlotte? When we visited with Daisy."

"Not really," Charlotte said, glaring at Tori. "I was too busy being threatened."

"You deserved it." Tori's stare back was equally ugly.

"Guys. Guys," I said, waving my hand. "Focus."

Tori blinked. "Sorry. Yeah." She swallowed. "So, they think I killed Reece. Yes, we broke up. We would have gotten back together eventually. It was what we did." A sob convulsed her chest. "They don't believe me."

I gestured toward Charlotte, who set a box of tissues on the counter. Grabbing a couple, I handed them to Tori. While she dabbed at her face, I glanced at Charlotte, wishing I could ask her a few questions. Did she think Tori was guilty? If so, did that mean Tori had also poisoned the cakes and the cream? Did Charlotte even want to help her cousin?

Charlotte folded her arms. "Okay. Tell me something. Why are you here?"

"I was hoping you could help me," Tori mumbled.

"How?" Charlotte drilled down.

Tori crumpled the tissues and tossed them toward a wastebasket. They missed, so she scooped them up and dropped them in. "I thought . . ." Tori pivoted on her boot heel and started striding toward the door. "You know what? Forget it. You can cheer when they lock me up and throw away the key."

Charlotte ran after her, touching her arm. "Hey. Wait. I didn't say we wouldn't help you. I wanted to find out what you have in mind."

Tori stopped moving. "Someone tried to pin Barnaby's poisoning on you, right, by leaving the cakes here. It's the same with the noodles. They're associated with me. Maybe it's the same person?"

Although I believed Charlotte had been the intended target when it came to the poisoned cakes, I decided to play along. "Assuming you're innocent, who else has a motive?"

"'Assuming'?" Tori shook her head as if befuddled. "Charlotte, did you know about Barnaby and Reece's side business?"

"No. What are you talking about?" Charlotte returned to the counter, Tori following.

Her cousin glanced back and forth between us. "Don't tell anyone, okay?" When we agreed, she said, "They were paying students to write papers."

The study group. "You mean cheating." As someone who had done all her own work in college, this scenario disgusted me.

Tori's cheeks pinked. "I suppose you could call it that."

"You think one of his . . . um, *team* killed him?" I asked. "Why, though?"

She shrugged. "Reece could be harsh. He fired people if they didn't perform. He'd get mad when he had to edit their work too much."

"And they couldn't do anything about it," I guessed. "They were as guilty as he was."

"Uh-huh. A lot of students are broke, so they depend on the money."

We stood in silence for a long moment. Could Tori be right? Maybe Reece's death had nothing to do with the Winters family. Jury was still out on that one for me. Although if Barnaby had been the intended victim . . . which would mean Charlotte hadn't been . . . This was confusing.

One thing was consistent, though: the poison. If it was a monkshood derivative and if a student had killed

Reece, then the killer had somehow known about the other incidents.

"What do you want us to do?" Charlotte asked. "I'm not allowed anywhere near St. Aelred. You do realize that?"

Tori looked at me. "Molly? Can you help me? Us?"

I bit my lip, thinking. Tori's theory could be totally wrong. It didn't explain Arthur's death, for one thing. However, talking to other students, especially those close to Reece, might uncover additional clues. "Okay. I'll do it. What did you have in mind?"

◆◆◆

By the time I crawled into bed, I was both cranked up and exhausted. Once I'd agreed to help, Tori had lined up a meeting in the morning with Percy Bellows, the student who'd been sitting on the lodging stairs with me after Reece's body was discovered. I'd also hidden Mum's Sasha doll in my room, glad that I'd been able to sneak her into the bookshop.

"I want this to be over," I told Puck, who was curled up beside me on the duvet. He stretched out a paw and tapped me on the arm, then closed his eyes again. "I'll go to sleep in a few minutes. I'm going to read for a while first." That always helped.

Charlotte's Dollhouse, cont.

Instead of being banished upstairs after the dressmaker's, Polly was allowed to accompany Charlotte to dinner. What a banner occasion this was turning out to be! She could hardly wait to tell the other dolls all about it.

"How was your day?" Uncle Howard asked after their plates were filled and grace was said. With his wire-rimmed glasses, stern expression, and formal dress, Uncle Howard was a very dignified gentleman. He reminded Polly of Mr. Bear.

"We had a wonderful time, Uncle," Charlotte said. "I'm going to have a beautiful new dress for Christmas and so is Polly." She held the doll up for her uncle's inspection.

"It was a real treat, going to the dressmaker." Aunt Margaret's cheeks were flushed, her tone almost girlish. "I haven't seen such nice fabrics since before the War." She giggled. "The seamstress actually asked if Charlotte and I were mother and daughter. Can you imagine?"

Charlotte audibly sucked in a breath and the hand holding Polly let go. She fell down, down, down to the floor. Splat. Right on her face.

"You. Are. Not. My. Mother." Charlotte shoved her chair back with enough force to knock it over. "My mother . . . my mother . . . is dead." She burst into noisy tears and ran from the room, leaving Polly behind.

"Oh, dear," Aunt Margaret said. "I didn't mean . . ."

"I know you didn't, my dear," Uncle Howard said.

The dolls had been tidying the dollhouse when the bedroom doorknob rattled. "Positions, troops," the lieutenant called. "On the double." He threw himself flat on the roof, where he'd been polishing his rifle.

"Roger that," Mr. Bear said as he dropped the duster.

Mrs. Morton closed the oven and sat at the table and Jingles dropped the lid onto the rubbish bin. "I can't wait to hear about Polly's adventure," he said.

"Shush," the lieutenant warned.

The door flew open and Charlotte burst in. Without even bothering to take off her shoes, she threw herself across the bed, sobbing so hard her teeth chattered.

"Oh, my," Mrs. Morton whispered. "Things have gone wrong." Her heart clenched. And where was Polly? Was the bisque doll lost or hurt?

Although Polly lay unseen under the table, she could hear everything Aunt Margaret and Uncle Howard said. She listened intently, trying to commit every word to memory. The other dolls would want a full report.

"Everything was going so well," Aunt Margaret said, near tears herself. "Or so I thought. Charlotte was starting to warm up to me. We had such a good time ice-skating and going to the dressmaker."

"It will take time, my dear," Uncle Howard said in a soothing voice. "Losing both parents is a terrible blow. Not to mention that she barely knows us." His voice softened. "Which is one of my regrets. I let business get in the way of seeing the family more often."

Aunt Margaret was silent for a moment. "I feel bad about that, too. I should have gone down to

see them. Or had them here to stay." She gave a
deep sigh. *"I'd better go talk to her. Hopefully
she'll forgive me."*

Someone knocked on the bedroom door. *"Go
away!"* Charlotte shouted. *"Leave me alone!"*

The doorknob twisted and the door opened a
crack. Mrs. Morton gasped in relief when she saw
Polly, apparently unharmed, peeking around the
door. *"It's me. Can I come in?"*

Charlotte turned over on her back and stared
at the doll. Then she sniffed mightily. *"I suppose."* She rolled over again, hiding her head
with her arms.

The door opened wider and Aunt Margaret
came in, holding the doll. She sat on the edge
of the bed, smoothing Polly's skirt. *"I'm sorry,
Charlotte. I know I can never replace your dear
mother. Or your father."*

Charlotte lifted one arm to look at her aunt.
"No one can."

Aunt Margaret sighed. *"Isn't that the truth
of it? Those who are left behind must make the
best of things."* She paused. *"My son fought in the
War, too."*

"You have a son?" Charlotte sounded interested.

"No, he's gone. Killed in battle."

"That's what happened to my father." Charlotte's voice was tiny. *"In France."*

"I know, love. I'm so sorry." Aunt Margaret
put Polly aside and got up. The dolls quivered
when she came over to the dollhouse. Who was
she going to choose?

She picked up the Lieutenant and brought him over to Charlotte. He stood straight as he could, chin up, rifle over his shoulder. "My son, Robert, used to play with this doll. He was his favorite."

"Really?" With a sniff, Charlotte sat up. She picked Polly up. "Do you think Polly had a good time today?" She walked the doll over to the Lieutenant, who hoped Polly would think he looked handsome. Was that a wink? He was almost sure . . .

"I'm sure of it." Aunt Margaret, sensing the storm was over, sounded relieved. "In fact, her outing has given me an idea. Why don't we take the Lieutenant with us tomorrow, to visit the soldier's memorial in Whitehall."

The Lieutenant's chest filled with pride. He was going to have a chance to honor peers lost in battle. And Robert . . . his favorite person.

"Tomorrow is Robert's birthday," Aunt Margaret said. "That's why I want to go."

"Can we bake a cake?" Charlotte asked. "To celebrate?" She glanced over at the other dolls. "Mrs. Morton can help us."

Mrs. Morton had to restrain herself from jumping for joy. When was the last time she had gone down to the kitchen? Being literally woolly-headed, she couldn't recall. A long time ago, anyway.

"I love that idea. Why don't we have his favorite dinner, too? He loved roast beef and Yorkshire pudding."

"So do I," Charlotte said. She looked at the dolls again. "Can Mr. Bear be our butler? I want him to have a chance to help."

Mr. Bear's button eyes gleamed. He'd always longed for an opportunity to use his service skills.

"Why not?" Aunt Margaret laughed. "We'll invite all the dolls to dinner." She bent over and kissed Charlotte's head. "There's rice pudding if you'd like to come down and have some."

"Rice pudding, hurray!" Charlotte scooted to the edge of the bed. "I'm coming." She held up the dolls. "I'm going to put them away first."

After Aunt Margaret left, Charlotte went over to the dollhouse. She sat Polly and the Lieutenant on the floor, then placed the other dolls beside them, similar to the way they'd once sat on her bed.

"You must be wondering why I've called you together tonight." She'd heard grown-ups talk this way.

The dolls were calm on the outside, bursting with excitement on the inside. Jingles itched to dance and tumble. As soon as Charlotte left . . .

"I'm sorry I was mean to you," Charlotte said. "I love the dollhouse and I love you. Thanks for being my friends." She picked each one up in turn and hugged them.

The dolls beamed, happy to have a new person to play with them. Even better, to take them downstairs and out into the world for new adventures.

Jingles was so thrilled, he couldn't suppress a jingle of his bells.

Charlotte, who was on her way to the door, to

go down for pudding, regarded them with wonder. "Maybe you are magic."

Mrs. Morton liked to think so.

THE END

I smiled as I closed the book. After reading this book as a child, the idea of magic dolls had stayed with me. Now that I was older, I saw the poignant message, the theme of loss and new beginnings and new friends. I'd experienced this myself and I hoped that Charlotte would as well. She'd had so many losses.

I prayed there wouldn't be any more.

CHAPTER 22

Tori had arranged for me to meet Percy Bellows at the Cambridge Market. Located in Market Square near the Guildhall, trade had been conducted in this spot since the Middle Ages. This morning, with Christmas music playing, the smell of roasted chestnuts and mulled cider drifting, and stalls heaped with evergreens and colorful wares, it felt like stepping back in time.

At first, I'd thought the location was an odd choice, because it wasn't exactly private. But as I moved around the circuit, stopping to buy two ciders and hot donuts, I realized the hubbub and movement were a perfect cover. Everyone was too busy to pay attention to anyone else.

Percy was sitting on a bench, head bobbing as he listened to earbuds, a tablet open in his lap. I sat beside him.

"Here," I said, holding a cup out to him. Removing the buds, he regarded the cup dubiously. "I bought it right over there. Hot cider."

"'Kay, thanks." He took the cup and, when I displayed the bakery bag, took a donut.

"How are you?" I asked, figuring we should warm up a little before plunging into twenty questions. He mumbled something that sounded like *fine*. "Going home for break?"

He nodded. "Later this week. My folks live in London."

"Nice. We're having a family gathering at the bookshop. Thomas Marlowe," I added.

His wary features broke into a smile. "Love that place." He regarded me with assessing eyes. "That's your shop?"

"It is. Mum and I are partners with my great-aunt." We'd made it official a couple of months ago. "Been in the family for four hundred years."

"Cool." He took a bite of donut. "That's what I love about Cambridge. We're sitting right where people used to dine on pasties and eel pie."

The original street food. "Now we have kabobs and dim sum." And lots of other choices, including a noodle stall. In light of Reece's death, I wasn't going to mention that.

"Eating outdoors never loses its charm." He finished the donut, using a napkin to wipe sugar off his fingers.

"I agree." Diving in, I asked, "You probably wonder why I wanted to meet you."

"Tori told me." Percy shifted, sitting back and stretching his legs. "You're trying to help her out. What are you? A modern-day Nancy Drew?" He raised his brows.

"Sort of, I guess. Not that I try to be. Things just happen." I took a sip of cider. "So. Reece. Tori told me about his, um, enterprise. Was anyone involved angry with him?"

Staring at the ground, he thought for a long moment. "I can't think of anyone in particular. I mean, he could be a bit of an arsehole. Don't blame him, really. He had to make sure people produced a good product." His smile was wry. "No AI or plagiarism. Or sloppy sources."

"It sounds like hard work," I said. "Don't *people* have enough to do already?" Although I was pretty sure Percy was involved, I didn't want to verbalize it.

He shrugged. "The money's good. Better than clearing tables in the dining hall."

"I get that." Not that I agreed with what was essentially cheating. If the paying students couldn't cut it, too bad. Us smart poor people had enough hurdles already. Why help the lazy and entitled? "Who came to the rooms? I mean, going back a day or two." The tainted noodles might have been sitting there for days, even weeks. I doubted it though, not if Reece ate them as frequently as Tori claimed.

Percy listed several names I typed into my notes. I'd ask Tori who they were later. "Is that it? Anyone that seemed out of place?" I was groping here, hoping for a clue.

"Hmm. There was one guy, I don't know his name. Older, with a beard. He came in as I was going out, to class." A pause. "The day Reece . . . It was later, when I came back . . ."

I got the gist. Who was the man? Andre, maybe? I gave him a couple of descriptive details. "Was that him?"

"Probably. Reece wasn't happy to see him, I could tell."

It sounded like Andre had come by Reece's rooms before or after delivering trees. Had he poisoned Reece? How, though? Would Reece have accepted a packet of noodles from him?

"Is there anything else? Anything at all that seemed strange to you?"

"Um, not really." He squirmed a little. "Except . . ."

I remained silent, in what I hoped was an encouraging way.

"Barnaby's mother came by with a box of goodies a few days ago. A care package, she said."

"Dorcas Winters?" I asked to confirm.

"Uh-huh." He rubbed his cheek, the gesture signaling to me that there was more to this seemly innocuous and generous act.

"Was Reece there?" I asked, hoping he would fill in some details.

He shook his head. "At class."

"Did you see what was in the box? Any noodles?"

His head jerked around. "You think—"

"I don't know," I said honestly. "I'm just trying to put the facts together."

He looked up, as if checking his memory. "There were homemade cookies, crisps, chocolate bars, cheese and crackers, and yeah, a couple packets of noodles." He shifted his bum on the bench. "I had a few cookies. Barnaby offered them to me." One knee bounced.

"What is it, Percy?" I said in a soft, coaxing tone. "Is there something else?"

Percy huffed a sigh. The knee stilled. "Yeah. It was weird. Dorcas and Barnaby looked through Reece's desk."

"Right in front of you?"

"Yeah. I was back at my table, working."

"Did they say what they were looking for?"

"Nope." He spread his hands wide. "Sorry."

The knee started again and I decided to put him out of his misery. "Thanks for talking to me. I appreciate it."

His smile was apologetic. "Not sure if it helped."

With that, he got up, tossed away his trash and took off, earbuds in place again.

I sat on the bench for a while after Percy left. In a nearby tree, tiny birds twittered and hopped, and church bells chimed in the distance. At the market, people came and went, vendors and customers calling out cheerfully. The haddock was really good today, apparently.

My meeting with Percy had brought me back to square one: the Winters family.

Reece being poisoned by a student had been a theory, something to check out. With three closely related poisonings, the direction of guilt seemed obvious. The question was, which of the family members had done it? Or had it been Andre? The police thought it was Tori in this latest crime. Far as I knew, they still suspected Charlotte concerning the cakes.

Tori had also been at the shop the morning we found Barnaby. Had she come by to see if her plan had worked? If Charlotte was dead?

Her distress over Reece had seemed genuine, though. Unless she was a great actress. Maybe he hadn't been poisoned because of the breakup. Maybe Reece had known something about Barnaby's poisoning. Or Arthur's death. Perhaps even both.

He knows something . . . I saw the realization on his face. Charlotte had thought the same thing. As a close family friend, Reece had been in a position to observe the killer at work.

I popped my empty cider cup into the bakery bag and stood. Maybe I'd take a circuit of the market before I went back. Buy a pound of that haddock for dinner. Then I needed to get back to the shop before we opened.

~•~

Aunt Violet carried a tray out of the back, signaling it was time for midmorning tea break. Was it that time already? We'd been slammed since opening the doors this morning. Sales were definitely ramping up as the holidays approached.

Mum called a cheery "Thank you, come again," to the customer, who was now exiting. "Perfect timing, Vi. I'm parched."

"Not surprising," Aunt Violet said as she poured. "They're a chatty bunch this morning."

"By the way, the toy shop is open." I added milk to my mug. "I told Charlotte we would spread the word."

"Good for her." Aunt Violet adjusted the cozy on the teapot. "It's wonderful to have another thriving business in the lane. That shop has always been a draw."

Mum gathered the packing slips to update the computer inventory while drinking tea. "How are we doing compared to last year? Any idea?"

Aunt Violet scooted her chair over to a file cabinet and pulled out a ledger. "Before you brought me into the twenty-first century, I logged daily sales in here. They're tallied by the week and month so I could compare from year to year."

Mum took the ledger and began leafing through. Once she found the right page, she checked it against a report on the screen. "We're definitely up compared to this week last year." She tapped on a calculator. "Over twenty percent."

"Fantastic." I'd had the impression that business was

growing. This data proved it. "It must be the Santa," I joked. He stayed lit day and night, a friendly presence at the front of the store.

"Santa and everything else," Aunt Violet said. "I'm so thankful you two decided to join me. I don't know where I'd be if you hadn't." Her voice shook slightly. The bookshop had been in danger of closing, thanks to an unscrupulous relative. We'd soon sent him packing.

"Aww." I went over and gave her a hug. "We love you. We're so glad you invited us to come."

Aunt Violet, a typically reserved and unemotional Brit, merely patted my arm. "I . . . er . . . yes." After I let go, she said, "I do wish your Uncle Tom was here. We had such a good time. We'd wear Santa hats and, with his white beard, little ones thought Tom was the real deal."

Santa hats sounded fun. I thought I'd seen some in the cellar, among the Christmas decorations. "Hold on. I'll be right back."

When I ventured into the basement this time, I was armed with a large, bright flashlight and a mental map of the cobwebs. As a result, I made it over to the shelves unscathed and web free. *Ka-dunk. Ka-dunk. Ka-dunk.* Puck had caught wind of the expedition and followed me.

"Where did I see them?" I muttered, opening several boxes. "Aha." The hats were in a box of costumes and I pulled out three, one for each of us.

Another box caught my eye and, curious, I opened it. Mistletoe. Artificial, naturally, since the real stuff would have dried up and deteriorated.

Mistletoe. This could be interesting.

I tucked the box and the hats under my arm and picked up the flashlight. "Come on, Puck." When he didn't follow, instead choosing to nose around behind a shelf, I threatened to turn the lights off. Finally he padded up the staircase and slipped past me, depositing sticky strands of cobweb on my jeans leg. Cats.

The mistletoe I left in the back hall, to put up somewhere out here. It wasn't for the customers, it was for us. Wherever it ended up, I'd maneuver Kieran under it for a few kisses.

Out in the shop, I gave Mum and Aunt Violet a hat, then pulled one on. "We should wear these every day until Christmas." I studied my reflection in nearby cabinet glass, making an adjustment. "Cute."

"Do I have to?" When we insisted, Mum reluctantly tugged it on.

"You look adorable," I said. "I hope Sean Ryan stops by and sees you in it." If he was going to hang around so much, we might as well try to enjoy his company. I'd get him and Mum together under the mistletoe somehow.

"That's all I need," Mum said. "I'm too old for this foolishness."

Aunt Violet had already donned her hat and was flitting about like an elf. "If I'm not, then you aren't. We must make an effort to get into the spirit." The shop door opened just then and a customer walked in, a good-looking middle-aged man. Aunt Violet hurried over to Santa and draped an arm around his shoulders. "Welcome. I'm Violet, one of the big guy's helpers. What can I do for you?"

The customer laughed as he pulled out his phone. "Well, Violet, I've got quite a list. Think you can help me fill it?"

"Absolutely." Aunt Violet glanced over her shoulder and winked at us as if saying, *This is how it's done.*

Mum fiddled with her hat. "Point made. Bring on the Christmas cheer."

I found the perfect spot for the mistletoe in the kitchen, on the private side of the door. I hopped up a stepladder and suspended the string from a beam.

That task accomplished, I made sandwiches and carried them out to the shop, along with a bag of crisps. "The mistletoe is hanging in the kitchen," I said, pulling a chair up behind the counter. "In case you want to kiss someone." I planned to maneuver Kieran under there the next chance I had.

Both Mum and Aunt Violet pretended not to hear me. "How did your meeting with the student go this morning?" Aunt Violet asked.

"Pretty well." I thought back to what Percy had told me. "I went into it thinking one of the other students might be guilty. Instead, the trail leads back to the Winters family." I told them that Dorcas had brought noodles and then she and Barnaby had searched Reece's desk.

"Reece was also in the middle," Mum pointed out. "He worked at the farm making creams and he helped Barnaby search for the doll."

"Agree." I nibbled on my sandwich half, thinking. "He might have known too much. Maybe he tried to take advantage somehow."

"You said Dorcas is in debt?" Aunt Violet confirmed. "And she brought some noodles to the room?"

"Deeply in debt. And yes, so she makes sense as a suspect for Reece. Sort of." I still didn't have a strong motive for Dorcas to kill Reece. After another bite, I said, "Definitely not for Barnaby's poisoning, though. If Dorcas left poisoned cakes at the toy shop, surely she would have warned him? She probably sent him there to look for the doll, which she needs to get out of debt."

"In my eyes, Althea is the strongest suspect for Arthur's death," Mum said. "Don't forget, she had already buried two husbands." Her mouth twisted in distaste and I guessed what she was thinking. Dad's death had been a tragedy, and as a loving wife, she couldn't imagine wanting him to die.

Mum's comment reminded me of George, who I guessed was Althea's next target. Before I could talk myself out of it, I took out my phone and sent him a text.

Watch out for Althea. She's already lost three husbands, remember?

His answer came right back. *Thanks for the warning but I can handle myself, love.*

No doubt her previous victims had thought the same, until she'd beguiled them into marriage. I'd have to keep a close eye on George, whether he wanted me to or not.

CHAPTER 23

Later that afternoon, business slowed enough that I had time to pop over to the toy shop to help search for the Madame Alexander doll. We needed to find it before someone else did—or made another attempt to harass Charlotte.

"Hey, Molly. Thanks for coming over." Charlotte was standing behind the counter, putting a lid on a board game. She added the game to a stack already sitting there. They all had a travel or geography theme, I noticed. "Did you see Percy?"

"I did. He had some very interesting things to say." I took off my coat and hung it over a tall stool, then pushed up my sleeves. "I'll fill you in while we work. Where should I start?"

The clue in the nesting dolls had been *We travel afar*.

Charlotte picked up the games. "Nothing in these so they're going back on the shelf. How about the train sets?"

I groaned. The shop offered a wide selection of train cars, tracks, and miniature buildings and the like. She'd already pulled the boxes off the shelf.

"I know. It's a lot." Charlotte set her jaw in determination. "You start at one end, I'll work from the other. If customers come in, I'll wait on them, if that's okay."

"Of course. I'll pretend I'm organizing the inventory."

While we opened boxes, carefully looked inside each toy, and reassembled, I shared my conversation with Percy and what I'd learned.

"So Dorcas brought the noodles," Charlotte mused. "She must have poisoned him." She deftly arranged loose pieces of track in their slots.

"Maybe. Someone else might have put the noodles in the box. Or the ones he ate might have already been in the room." I opened the next set. *Great.* Boxcars with doors that opened. I'd have to look inside each one.

"True. Dorcas visiting might be a coincidence." Charlotte placed a lid on a box. "Are you going to tell the police?"

I peeked inside a boxcar, which was empty. "Think I should? Sean Ryan hasn't been very happy with me and how I keep showing up in this case." At this point, he was probably regarding me as a royal pain.

"He might not be aware of her visit," Charlotte said. "Barnaby isn't going to rat out his mother, that's for sure. And Tori might not know about it."

"Good point. Maybe I should call him." I shelved the box of train cars. "What's the story with Tori, anyway? She was adopted by Dorcas and her husband?"

Charlotte also took a break. "She was actually adopted by a Winters cousin. When that couple, who were older, couldn't handle her, Dorcas and Rob, Althea's son, took her in. Rehoming, they call it." Charlotte sounded angry. "As if she were an unruly pet."

I couldn't speak for a moment. "How awful." Tori

must feel like a parcel that'd been passed around, as unwanted as a white elephant gift. "Does Tori know her bio parents?"

"Her mother died of an overdose. Her father has always been out of the picture."

"Oh, Charlotte." My heart twisted with grief and anger. No wonder Tori had been difficult. She'd been grieving. Just because a parent was troubled didn't mean they hadn't bonded with their child. And now she was living in a nest of vipers, if Althea was anything to go by.

"How did rehearsal go?" Charlotte levered herself to her feet. "Want a cup of tea? I'm ready."

"Sure." As I trailed behind her to the back, I told her about the first session, including how Althea had rewritten the play to give herself a starring role. "I think she's after my friend, George Flowers."

Charlotte paused while filling the electric kettle. "Not George."

"You know him?"

She turned off the tap and placed the kettle on the stand and switched it on. "He was the shop handyman. Lovely man."

"He's our handyman, too. And a good friend of the family. Anyway, we have to keep him out of her clutches."

We wandered through the shop while drinking our tea, stopping to put things away. Several toys hung from the ceiling and a jaunty red airplane caught my eye. It was large enough for a toddler to sit in it and push themselves along. A sign reading *Not for Sale* was attached to the nose. *We travel afar.* Except for the rocket ship right beside it, that airplane was the embodiment of that phrase.

I pointed upward. "What's the story with that?"

Charlotte craned her neck, studying the plane. "That was Grandad's, my dad's, and mine. He told me never to sell it."

A thrum of excitement beat in my veins. "It makes sense, then, that the doll would be inside it. He wouldn't put something so valuable in a toy that might be sold."

She was still staring at the airplane. "True. I'll go get the stepladder." She handed me her mug and trotted toward the back room.

I put the mugs on the counter and returned to the spot, waiting for Charlotte to return with the ladder. She set up the folding triangle and clambered up to *not a step*.

"Be careful," I warned.

"I know, I need a taller one. Hold on to it for me, will you?" She reached for the airplane, which was held up by cord looped over two hooks. While I steadied the ladder, she lifted the nose and then the tail to release the loops. Clutching the toy around the middle, she stepped down. "Whew. This thing is heavier than it looks."

We bent over the airplane, Charlotte crouching to peer into the nose, which was the larger section. She made a sound of disgust. "Nothing." She scooted along to reach inside the tail. "Another clue." She showed me the slip of paper.

"'Bearing gifts.'" I groaned. "That's ridiculous. It could be anything. Everything in here is a potential gift."

Charlotte's gaze had fastened on something in the front window.

"What is it?" I asked, hoping she'd had a brainstorm. Without answering, she marched to the window and picked up the very large teddy bear sitting behind the dollhouse. "Come on, Griffin," she said. "We're going to check you out." She carried him to the counter, his Santa hat bobbing, and gently laid him down.

"You think something's inside him?" I asked.

"Maybe." Charlotte nodded toward the door. "Turn the sign, will you? I don't want to get interrupted." She began to probe his abdomen as intently as a doctor performing an exam. "I feel something." She stepped back. "You try."

I took her place, using my fingers to gingerly push on the bear. At first the stuffing readily gave way. Then, right in the middle of his trunk, I pressed something hard. Testing the previous spot again, I said, "It changes right here."

"That's what I thought." Charlotte pulled out a drawer and dug around. "These should work." She brandished a seam ripper.

"I take it we're going to operate," I said, tongue in cheek.

She gestured with the tool. "We are. Turn him over, will you?"

I flipped the teddy bear onto his back, where a long seam ran from neck to bum. The stitches, while neat, were far from perfect. "He's been under the knife before."

Charlotte took a close look. "I see that." With an expert touch, she inserted the pointed end and traced it down the seam. The stitches readily gave way. "Grandad and I refurbished a few stuffies in our day." She set the tool down and pulled apart the fur. Dense brown filling puffed up out of the cavity.

"What is that?" I asked.

"Horsehair." Charlotte moved the top layer aside.

"Here we go." She reached into the bear and pulled out a bundle of unbleached muslin.

Breathless, I watched as she unwrapped the cloth to reveal a beautiful blond doll wearing a fur coat, hat, and boots. She had a tiny dog with her, also wearing fur.

"You found her." I could barely talk. "She's gorgeous."

"Isn't she? Handmade by the designer." Charlotte began to blink rapidly and I realized she was crying. "Grandad." She grabbed a tissue and dabbed at her eyes. "He was so good to me."

I had to agree. The rare doll was quite a gift. Selling her would realize enough money to help capitalize the shop for years.

No wonder the rest of the family had been looking for it. "Charlotte, you've got to take her to the bank right now. Put her in a safety deposit box."

My urgency touched her and panic flared briefly in her eyes. "You're right. I should." She glanced at her phone and groaned. "They're closing soon."

"Go," I said. "I'll watch the shop for you until you get back. Show me your cash system and I'll take care of any sales."

She hesitated. "It might take me a while. You know how banks are."

"I don't care. I'll square it with Mum and Aunt Violet." I pointed to the bear. "Where should I put Griffin?"

"How about out back on the table? I'll stitch him up later." Charlotte rewrapped the doll before putting her into a tote. She shivered. "I'm going to be paranoid all the way to the bank."

I had an idea. "Want Kieran to go with you?" Maybe it was overkill but I'd feel better.

"Would you ask? It's just that . . ."

"You don't have to explain. I'd be nervous carrying something that valuable around town." I pulled out my phone and called him rather than texted, in case he didn't notice the message. He was amenable to acting as escort and promised to be right over. "He'll be here in five. Let me move the bear and then you can show me your sales portal." I also called Mum to tell her what was up. She said that they'd handle it and to take my time.

After Charlotte and Kieran left with the doll, I turned the shop sign to open, lingering in the window to look out into the lane. Foot traffic was light as the business day wound down.

I wandered over to the dollhouse, idly checking to see if it was the same as before. Why wouldn't it be?

My heart jumped into my throat. A bowl sat on the kitchen table, a dish that I was pretty sure hadn't been there before. A reference to Reece's poisoning? This was too freaky.

After I gathered my wits, I took a picture of the kitchen and the rest of the house, too. This was the third time the furnishings and dolls had been moved. At least we'd have something to compare to if it happened again.

Tori. It had to be her. She was the only person related to the cases who had been in here.

What a sick sense of humor. Or was it a confession?

I peered up the lane. No potential customers were coming along so, without thinking about it too much, I called Detective Inspector Sean Ryan.

By some miracle—or not, I would rather have left a message—he picked up. "Ryan here."

"S—DI Ryan, it's Molly Kimball." My insides shook. Was he going to listen to me? During the

interview at the bookshop, I'd gathered that Charlotte
was a strong suspect.

"Yes, Miss Kimball." His voice was terse. Then,
when I didn't respond immediately, his tone softened. "I
know you wouldn't have called unless it was important."

"It might be. I guess that's up to you to determine."
I swallowed, trying to moisten my dry throat. "I talked
to a student earlier today. Percy Bellows. Dorcas Winters brought a box of food, including packets of noodles, to Reece and Barnaby's rooms a couple of days
before Reece died. Percy said Dorcas and Barnaby
searched Reece's desk. He has no idea why."

After a moment, he said, "That's it?"

"More or less. I also found out that Andre Lewis,
from Mistletoe Farm, visited Reece the day he died. I
saw him driving away when I arrived at St. Aelred."

"You didn't obtain a full transcript of the conversation?" Sean asked dryly.

"Not yet. One more thing." The door opened, causing
bells to jingle. I turned my back, speaking fast. "Have to
go for a customer, but wanted you to know. We found the
doll. You know, the one people have been looking for."

I signed off hastily and pivoted to say hello, sliding
my phone into my pocket.

Dorcas Winters was standing right behind me.

CHAPTER 24

"Dorcas." I took a step back, my heart hammering. "Hi. How can I help you?" I racked my brain, trying to remember what I'd said. No names mentioned at the end, right?

Dorcas studied me, her eyes unblinking, not saying a word.

I forced myself to feign cheer. "Can you believe how fast Christmas is coming? Is there something special you're looking for? There's a great selection here." I laughed again. "But you probably know that already."

She continued to regard me with that strange expression, dazed almost. Lights on, nobody home.

Should I ask her—tell her—to leave? I couldn't just run out and leave her unattended in the shop. What if she was here to hurt Charlotte? Or to search for the doll? Maybe she'd heard me say it had been found and was now in shock that her plan had been foiled.

A tremor ran over Dorcas and her gloved hands twitched, as if she was waking up. "What are you doing here?" Her voice was raspy.

"Helping out for an hour or so, while Charlotte runs

an errand." I backed up and then headed toward the counter, where I could pretend to be busy.

Walking with a stiff-legged gait, she followed. "You seem to be everywhere I look, Molly. Right in the middle of our business."

"Really?" Where was my phone? Oh, yeah, in my pocket. Discreetly as possible, I slid it out and held it, ready to dial for help. "Not on purpose, I assure you. I mean, it's all a coincidence, I swear—"

The door jingled open again. I gave a gasp of relief. Charlotte was back—no, wait. *Barnaby* had arrived.

What were they going to do? Tag-team me and make me eat poison? And then attack Charlotte when she came back?

My hands shook as I began to tap at my phone. "You both need to leave. Right now." I opened the keypad, ready to summon the police.

Barnaby barely threw me a glance. "Mum." He approached his mother and put his arm around her shoulders. "What are you doing here?"

She hung her head, muttering something inaudible.

I saw Charlotte through the window. Finally. I skirted around mother and son and went to the door. "We have a situation," I whispered.

Her gaze went past me, taking them in. "Uh, hello," she said loudly. "What are you doing here?"

Barnaby looked around. "Charlotte. Sorry." He gently steered his mother by the shoulders, assisting her toward the door. "We won't bother you again."

"I hope not," Charlotte called. "Don't come back."

The door slammed shut behind them, the bells dancing.

◗◖

Thanks to the strange encounter with Dorcas, I was nervous when Kieran and I walked into rehearsal that evening. Was she going to be hostile? Or would she ask her mother-in-law to boot me off the cast? Although I'd been reluctant to join in the first place, it would be a disappointment to leave. Besides, we still hadn't found the killer.

Thankfully, Dorcas avoided making eye contact with me. As for Althea, she moved me around the stage like a prop. I was Lady Nightingale to her and that was fine with me.

The second rehearsal saw more changes to the play, which was now more of a farce than anything. Kieran and I were separated by misunderstandings, as were Dorcas and Andre. We sang in various formations about love and longing with cheerful numbers and antics from Barnaby, the heartbreaker in the court, and Sir Jon, Lord of Misrule, in between. George, as the Stranger from the North, was revealed as the queen's long-lost love, which almost made me throw up. His deer-in-the-headlights expression as she approached, eyes closed and lips pursed, was hilarious.

"Rehearsal every night until the performance," Althea announced at the end of the night. "Ten days to get it right." She riveted each of us with a searing stare. "You *will* get it right, won't you? We don't want to waste the BBC's time, do we?" *Or mine* was implied.

"I'm beginning to think you're right," George said, coming along beside me as we exited the hall. "If I'd known a kiss was required . . ."

"Yes, be careful," Kieran said, joking. "Lest some poison yet doth hang on her lips." A misquote of Shakespeare.

"Maybe literally," I said with a shudder.

George was taken aback. "What's all this?"

I realized I hadn't been keeping him and Sir Jon up to date. "Can I stand you a pint? We have a lot to discuss."

Joined by Sir Jon, we stopped at The Despairing Scribe, a nearby pub. The sign depicted a man with a noose around his neck and a quill and manuscript in hand.

"Often felt that way often at university," Kieran said as we settled in a warm booth near a crackling fire. "The pressure to get things done on time and to a very high standard."

"But you didn't pay people to help," I said. "Am I right?"

"What's this?" George asked.

The server was approaching. "Tell you after we order." Once the round of brown ale was delivered, I gave them a succinct yet thorough briefing. Since the dinner with Sir Jon and George at the bookshop, the police had tested the skin cream and found aconite, and Reece Harrison had also been poisoned.

"Bloody hell!" George exclaimed. "Arthur Pemberly was murdered?"

"Looks that way." I put a hand on his arm. "See why I was worried about you?"

He took a long swallow of beer. "I do, indeed." Then another. "Assuming she's the guilty party."

"It's a strong possibility," I said. "Although I've learned that Dorcas is deep in debt and owes money to the estate. Plus the others also had access to Arthur or the cream that killed him: Barnaby, Tori, Reece, and even Andre Lewis."

"And Charlotte," Sir Jon said softly. "This looks bad for her as well."

"Especially after framing her for the poisoned cakes," Kieran said crisply. "I'm with Molly on this one. Charlotte is innocent."

Sir Jon lifted his hand, summoning another round. "And I'm inclined to agree with you. Charlotte and Arthur were very close. He was like a father figure to her after her parents died."

"Should I quit?" George asked. "I'm a bit freaked out now." He shuddered. "Especially since she added that kiss to the play."

"Up to you," I said. "I'm hoping that over the next ten days, someone will crack and confess. Dorcas, for example." I told them about her visit to the toy shop. "Maybe she was going to ask Charlotte to forgive the loan? Or, more likely, knock her out and search for the doll. Me being there really messed her up."

"Any sign of the doll?" Sir Jon asked, his expression alert.

"We found it today, sewed inside a huge toy bear," I said. "The shop mascot, actually."

Kieran puffed up with pride. "And I escorted Charlotte and the doll to the bank. It's now safely locked up."

Sir Jon nodded in approval. "Good, very good. That's one issue taken care of."

The server brought the new round and after he left, I said, "At this point, I'm waiting desperately for something to break. All we have are a lot of balls in the air."

"It's always this way," Kieran said. "The calm before the storm."

"Speaking of which . . ." Sir Jon was looking out the window. Tiny flakes had begun to fall, spinning and dancing lazily on their way to the ground.

I jumped up with a squeal, trying to get a better view. "Snow? Maybe we'll have a white Christmas."

A dusting of white would only make Cambridge even more magical.

"Long as I don't have to shovel," George said gloomily. "It's not good for my back."

◆◆

Despite the long rehearsal and two beers, I was wired when I got back to the bookshop. Mum and Aunt Violet were already upstairs, so I puttered around the dimly lit shop by myself. I reshelved books, broke up cardboard boxes for recycling, and checked my display of dollhouse books. We'd already sold several and I found a few more to add, then rearranged the books to best effect.

Puck, who was waiting for me to go to bed, sat in the window, a safe distance from all the hubbub. Now and then I glanced out at the lane to check on the snow. Still drifting down, it was starting to accumulate. Not enough for a shovel, though, or even a broom. A light layer like glaze on a cake.

Bump. Bump. Bump. Puck was batting at the front window, which he'd been doing lately. "What is it?" I strode over to find out.

Bump. He did it one last time before sitting down with a look of satisfaction on his face. *Finally got your attention.*

With Santa and other holiday lights on, I couldn't see beyond a few feet. I went over to the door and cupped my face with my hands to peer outside.

Huddled in a long coat, Tori Winters was standing outside the shop, snowflakes swirling around her and landing on her bare head. She looked like she was all alone in the world like the little match girl.

I turned the locks and opened the door. "Tori. What are you doing out there? Come in." She didn't move until I made an impatient gesture. "Please. I'm letting all the heat out."

She scuttled toward the open door and slipped past me. "I wasn't sure if you were still up."

"Normally I'm not." I flipped the locks closed again. "Want a drink? Tea with brandy—or without?"

She unbuttoned her coat with a shiver. "With sounds good, thanks." Spotting Puck, she descended upon him with a cry. "Hello, cutie."

He endured her enthusiastic patting stoically, although normally he would have run. He made the decisions about being touched.

"I'll be right back," I said. "Make yourself comfortable." Rather than invite her back, I wanted a moment to compose myself for this unexpected visit. She probably wanted a report about my talk with Percy and I had no idea what to tell her. He'd implicated her family members more than anyone else.

In the kitchen, I put together a tray with milk and sugar, spoons, napkins, a small bottle of brandy, and a packet of gingersnaps. The tea I made in mugs, with tea bags.

When I returned to the shop, tray in hand, Tori was playing with Puck, trailing a length of ribbon for him to tackle. He was really going all-out kitten for her. She looked up with a smile. "I love your cat."

"He's a sweetie for sure." I put the tray down on the counter. "I'll let you add your own brandy." I pulled two chairs close while she did that, then fixed my own brew. Normally I don't take sugar in my tea, but it made the brandy taste even better. A reviving hot toddy.

We sat, mugs in hand. Tori blew on the hot liquid

before taking a sip. She sighed. "This is perfect, thanks. I walked for *miles* tonight. Just thinking. You know how it is."

"I do. Taking a long walk often helps me get my head on straight."

How is she going to get home? I wondered. I didn't feel right about releasing her back into the night alone.

We sipped in silence, the snow continuing to fall in the lane, Puck curled up and purring on a nearby chair. "Did you get a chance to talk to Percy?" she asked.

"I did." To stall, I took a bite of gingersnap. "I asked him if anyone in the study group was angry with Reece. He said, yeah, people got annoyed because he could, ah, be demanding at times. That's it."

She pressed her lips together. "Hmm. I was hoping he'd have a lead for you. For us. He's a lot closer to the other students than I am." She shook her head. "None of them will talk to me now. They've all run for cover, in case the administration gets wind of the ghostwriting."

"Don't blame them." Personally, I hoped they would find other, more ethical employment. The students who paid for papers must also be shivering in their boots.

"He didn't give you anything?" Tori's voice was pleading. "Not a single clue?"

I couldn't tell her that her adoptive mother had delivered noodles to the room or that she and Barnaby had searched Reece's desk. I just couldn't. Sean Ryan knew about the incident and I'd have to trust him to take it from here.

There was one development I could pass along. "Charlotte and I found the missing Madame Alexander doll today." Tori glanced in the direction of the toy shop. "She's in a safe place now. Not at the store. So people can stop looking for it." This last was a dig and I bit my tongue. Oops.

Tori didn't say anything for a moment and I wondered how she would choose to react. We all knew that they'd been searching for the doll. Why else break into the shop or Arthur's house? Maybe now they'd stop harassing Charlotte.

Then she pushed back in her chair, making the legs scrape against the wooden floor. "What are you saying, Molly?" She loomed over me, tiny fists clenched, her body shaking.

I leaned back. "Um, that we found the doll?"

To my relief, she whirled around and began searching for her things. Coat on, fingers fumbling at the buttons. "I can't believe it. Accusing us of trying to steal."

"Don't shoot the messenger, 'kay? I told you the news. That's all."

Her response was a harrumphing sound as she abandoned the buttoning and pulled on her gloves. She stomped toward the front door, only to be stalled by the fact it was locked.

"Let me get that." I hurried over and flipped open the locks. "You okay to walk? It's pretty late." I wasn't sure how far she had to go to get home.

"Like you care," she snarled. "I'll get a cab."

I remembered there were late-night taxi stands in Market Square, only a few blocks away.

"Listen, Tori." I took a breath. "For what it's worth, I don't think you killed Reece. Or tried to kill Barnaby or Charlotte." Her eyes flared when the point hit home. "I do have a question. Why didn't anyone come to your defense when the police accused you?" For some reason, she hadn't felt comfortable going to her family. Instead she'd asked me and Charlotte for help. That was very telling.

Without responding, she pushed past me and ran out the door. I watched as she hurried up the lane, her boots leaving black prints in the snow. They were soon filled in by falling flakes, and within a few minutes, there was no sign that anyone had been out there.

Just like our killer. He or she kept striking, only to vanish without a trace.

CHAPTER 25

It was *Madrigals and Mayhem*'s opening—and only—night.

Since the night Tori came to the shop, all had been calm. No arrests, no more murders, nothing. Rehearsals had gone well, and Althea and Dorcas had treated me with civility if not warmth.

The tension I felt was like a held breath before a scream.

Kieran and I milled around backstage with cast and crew, getting dressed, doing last-minute prep, eating and drinking from the buffet table—or, as in my case, trying to choke something down. All of us were very aware of the Beeb crew tweaking cameras and booms and checking the wires snaking all over the place.

We were going to be on *television*. I almost threw up at the thought.

"You okay, Molly?" Kieran peered closely at my face. "You've gone all pale."

"It's the face powder," I said, waving off his concern. If I voiced my fears, I might have a full-blown meltdown.

He took my hand, which lay like a cold and clammy thing in his warm grip. He leaned over, almost kissing my cheek before remembering the makeup. "I have a special treat planned for us on Christmas Eve."

I snatched at the distraction. "Really? What is it?"

"It's a secret. But I know you're going to love it."

"Ah." I stamped my foot, shod in a facsimile of a Renaissance-era slipper. "Don't do that to me."

His smile was teasing. "Don't want to spoil the surprise."

"The place is really filling up," someone reported after peeking through the curtains. "Gonna be a full house. They're all in costume, too. I wasn't expecting that."

"Really?" Mum and Aunt Violet had wrangled tickets and they hadn't said a word. I marched over to the curtains. "Let me look."

As the other actor had said, the audience was bedecked in colorful period garb: wimples and flat velvet hats, brocade gowns and doublets. Silver and gold trim and artificial jewels sparkled under the glittering chandeliers. A few even wore Venetian masks, perhaps to hide from the cameras when they panned the audience. A small orchestra played sprightly Renaissance dance music, which only added to the ambiance.

The effect of seeing the audience enter into our performance this way electrified me, burning away the stage fright. Instead of *us* and *them*, it would be *we*. I lifted my chin. We were dining tonight with the queen.

I swept back to Kieran's side with a flurry of skirts.

Kieran extended an arm. "Ready, milady?" he asked.

We got in line with the others as the orchestra began playing the introductory fanfare. Rather than go directly on stage, singing our first song, we exited a side door and circuited the room with a measured pace. The audience, now seated, observed us with wide grins and whispers. Sir Jon, with his shaking bells, capering dance, and audience interaction, was a huge hit.

Meeting the gaze of two women by chance, I stumbled, my foot tripping over nothing, and was forced to grip Kieran's arm to remain upright.

Charlotte and Tori, masked and costumed, were sitting in the front row. A warning bell rang in my brain. Why were they here? What were they planning? I hoped it was only to needle Althea with their presence, not anything more disruptive.

Under normal circumstances, the pair would have been included in this production, as Dorcas and Barnaby were. As murder suspects, they had been exiled from the family. Certainty hardened in my heart. To protect the real killer or killers.

We climbed the steps to the stage and took our places at the long table as we sang the last chorus. Before we could sit, a trumpeter announced, "All rise for the queen." The audience also stood.

Wearing a magnificent red-and-black gown with a fan collar and holding a scepter, Althea swept into the room through the entrance doors to a blare of trumpets. She was gorgeous, the focus of every eye, the undisputed star of the show.

Dorcas, her daughter-in-law, regarded her with hatred, this truth quickly covered by a set smile when Andre touched her arm.

Althea joined us onstage, seated in the middle of the long table on a chair elevated above the rest. Servants immediately began to dance attendance. "Welcome to my Court," Althea said in a regal voice. "May the festivities begin."

The back doors blew open again and now the Stranger from the North arrived: George, draped in sackcloth and holding a staff. They'd put a long, white beard on him as well as thick, beetling brows. He raised his staff. "Will you welcome a stranger to your feast, Your Majesty? I've heard tell of your legendary hospitality. This night is not fit for man nor beast." He shivered dramatically.

Althea stared at him for a long moment. Then she curled one hand. "Enter, stranger. Join us as we lift the wassail bowl."

As the play kicked into gear, servers with trays entered to serve the audience. Sir Jon pranced. Barnaby played his lute, lovelorn. Kieran and I fought, flirted, and lamented. In between were other vignettes and songs. The cameras watched steadily, their red lights like pinpoints.

I had finally relaxed my guard and my covert glances toward Charlotte and Tori when the debacle erupted.

"You must tell me," Althea was saying in a pleading voice to the Stranger from the North. "I must know the truth—"

A hard, round dinner roll whizzed through the air and hit Althea smack in the bodice. In the brief hush before the cast and audience could react, Tori stood. "I didn't mean to do it," she sang out. "The cakes were a gift."

Charlotte rose. "For who?" She was also singing the words.

Tori pointed. "For you." As Charlotte put both hands to her face in exaggerated shock, Tori left her seat, carrying the basket of rolls, and began to sashay along the aisle. "Dear brother, it was an accident. Please believe me, truly."

The audience settled back in their seats, figuring this

was part of the show. Althea sat frozen, her features fixed in a horrified stare.

Barnaby stepped forward, lute in hand. "I forgive you, sister," he sang before strumming a few chords. "We've been caught in the same trap."

Tori was onstage now. "Whatever do you mean, kind sir?" she said in a straight voice before curtsying, somehow keeping hold of the basket.

They turned to look at the head table. "I also brought a gift," Barnaby declaimed. "A gift that was tainted, but not by my hand." He lowered his voice to a deeper register. "It was poison, poison that killed a man."

The audience gasped and began murmuring among themselves. Still thinking it was part of the show, they were delighted by this sudden ramping up of the stakes.

A thrill ran down my spine. He was either talking about the cream that killed Arthur or the noodles that poisoned Reece.

"Was it you?" Barnaby asked Andre. "Or you?" His own mother.

Andre shook his head as Dorcas jumped to her feet, patting her chest. "I too am a fly in the spider's web." Her face crumpled and she began to cry. "Because of her, many men have died."

"'Tis true what they say?" George asked, stepping away from the throne. "Have I had a narrow escape?" He finally got it.

All hell broke loose. Althea grabbed George's staff and began to wave it, snarling. Tori fired the rolls at her, one after the other like missiles. Althea managed to bat most of them away. George ducked for cover.

"Food fight!" one of the other cast members called. He began to toss oranges and rolls, the others returning fire. The fake boar's head went flying, splintering apart with a crack when it hit the floor. Most of the food on our table was fake, fortunately. The orchestra lurched into a dance tune, adding a soundtrack to the melee. The red lights continued to beam.

Madrigals and Mayhem indeed. Kieran and I ran for the back, hovering where we could watch without injury.

The audience still thought it was all good fun, laughing and nudging each other, a few even getting up to dance. Except for one man in costume, who left his seat and charged toward the front of the room.

Detective Inspector Sean Ryan.

His first stop was the director, and at her request, the red lights winked out. No more filming. The orchestra squeaked to a halt, the dancers faltering when the music stopped.

Onstage, the fracas was still underway, and Ryan waded in, subduing the throng with sharp commands as he went. The last orange finally thudded to the ground and all was quiet. Althea crouched on her throne like the malevolent spider she resembled. Dorcas stood in Andre's arms. Tori and Charlotte watched from one side with Barnaby, who was still holding his lute.

Tableau with Oranges was my ridiculous thought.

"Show's over, folks," Ryan called out. He dug his identification out of his doublet pocket and flashed it. "DI Ryan. I'm with the Cambridge police."

Gita Adhikari revealed herself, taking off her mask and striding forward, her expression imperious under a peaked hennin. She looked fabulous. A couple of officers, including Constable Derby, who had great legs for tights, began to usher the audience out.

Some of the spectators didn't go easily, protesting

and complaining, even threatening to go over Ryan's head. The film crew was also reluctant but leave they did, their equipment still in place. Standing with a hand resting on his hip, Ryan looked unconcerned by the balky response. This was his stage now.

Mum and Aunt Violet, both pretty in their chemises and farthingales, lingered as long as they could, casting glances back when they finally straggled out.

The double doors shut behind the last guest and the officers moved to stand watch, one on each side like palace guards. We were down to the main players, including me, Kieran, Sir Jon, and George. Sir Jon winked at me, which told me that he'd been involved somehow. A set of ears for Ryan within the camp? Quite possibly. I also learned that Charlotte and Tori had bought raffle tickets from the winner of the contest headed up by Lady Asha Scott. That explained their attendance without anyone knowing in advance.

Ryan pointed at Tori. "We'll begin with you, Miss Winters. What did you mean by, 'I didn't mean to do it'?"

Althea scowled ferociously and Tori ducked her head, shoulders hunched. The bravado she'd shown earlier seemed to have vanished.

An uneasy silence fell as we waited.

Charlotte touched Tori's arm. "It's okay," she whispered. "Tell them. You'll be all right."

"You think?" Tori whispered back. At Charlotte's nod, Tori lifted her chin. "I brought the tea cakes to the toy shop. My grandmother—Althea—told me they were a gift for Charlotte from the family."

"How did you get in?" Ryan sounded casual, as if they were two friends having a chat.

Tori visibly relaxed. "We had keys. Arthur's keys.

I went over there after dark and let myself in. I put the box on the break room table and then locked up again." Her features crumpled. "I had no idea they were poisoned and that Barnaby would eat them."

"It's okay," Barnaby said. "I forgive you." He grimaced. "Serves me right for being so greedy."

"I'm not so forgiving," Charlotte said with a glare at Althea. "Hanging isn't good enough for her."

Althea's eyes crinkled in mirth. "There's the matter of proof, my dear."

Ryan made a brusque slicing motion. "Over to you, Mr. Winters. What did you mean by, 'I also brought a gift'?" The man must have been taking notes. Or he had a photographic memory.

Barnaby flushed. "I had no idea. You have to believe me. I would never—Arthur was good to me." He sent a look of pure rage toward Althea. "He wasn't my grandfather but I wish he had been. My real one died." He chewed at his lips as though wanting to say more.

"What happened, Barnaby?" Ryan asked. His voice was low, as if not wanting to spook a skittish horse.

The young man put both hands to his face, as if hiding from the truth. "Reece. Reece gave me a tube of cream from the farm. Said it was for Arthur's arthritis."

Reece? A shock went down my spine. Then I noticed Althea's sly smirk.

"Reece was a pawn," I called out. "You can bet on it."

Ryan didn't respond but I saw his eyes shift to Althea. He wasn't fooled or charmed by this queen bee.

"Speaking of Reece," Ryan said. "Mrs. Winters. You said you were 'a fly in the spider's web.' What did you mean by that?"

Dorcas pulled away from Andre and moved to face Althea. With a trembling hand, she pointed. "It's her. She's the spider. She trapped us all. Wrapped us in sticky silk with promises and money and when that didn't work, with threats. She doesn't like it that I'm trying to move on after my husband's death. She can't stand the thought of losing control." She put that shaky hand to her mouth. "She's been undermining me at the college. Dripping poison in the dean's ear about my stability, my fitness for promotion. She denies it, of course." Dorcas stamped her foot. "I know it's you."

Althea rubbed her nose with one dainty hand, looking amused.

In Greek mythology, aconite had been used to turn Arachne into a spider. In Althea's case, I was sure her venomous ways predated the use of the poison. Was she going to get away with her crimes? The deaths of her first two husbands hadn't even been investigated. Had she been emboldened to widen her web, so to speak?

"It's all very concerning, I'm sure," Ryan said soothingly. "Was there anything specific you were referring to tonight?"

Dorcas let out a breath. "Yes. The box of food I took to the rooms. There was a packet of noodles in there. The same kind Reece was eating when he died. Althea suggested we put together a care package."

"Did she help you gather the food?" Ryan asked.

Dorcas shook her head, despair pooling in her eyes. "No," she croaked. "I put the box together. I know what the boys like."

I could see it all clearly now. Althea had manipulated Tori, Barnaby, Reece, and Dorcas to do her dirty work for her. The problem was proof, as she had pointed out.

What connected her to any of these crimes besides their claims that she had asked them to help by delivering a "gift"?

The poison. Aconite was extracted from the monkshood plant. How could we establish a connection between Althea and the deadly flower?

CHAPTER 26

Charlotte and her family were hauled down to the station to make official statements. The rest of us adjourned to the bookshop for a drink. Mum and Aunt Violet already had the bar set up in the kitchen when we got there.

"Pick your poison," Aunt Violet said with a cackle, earning groans from us. "We have gin, whiskey, vodka, and tequila. Plus wine and beer."

"I'll take a shot," I said, pulling out glasses. "Anyone else?"

In the end, we stood in a circle, shots in hand. "You're all looking at me," Sir Jon said. "Should I make the toast?"

"Please," Aunt Violet said. "Then I want to hear every detail."

Sir Jon lifted his glass. "'Cry havoc and let slip the dogs of war.'" A quote from Shakespeare's *Julius Caesar*.

"'Cry havoc,'" we all echoed and drank. The whiskey burned a welcome trail down my gullet.

"Interesting choice," George said, placing his glass on the counter. "Hit me again, Violet."

"I thought we could use a rallying motto," Sir Jon said. "I was so sure she'd break down and confess."

"Not Althea." Aunt Violet snorted. "She's the queen of denial."

"Good one." I sloshed whiskey into my glass and Kieran's. "I'm not letting this go."

He picked up his shot. "What are you going to do?"

"I have no idea." I clinked my glass with his. "I'll think of something." I had a question. "Sir Jon, why were the police there? Did they know Tori and Charlotte were going to confront Althea?" I wondered if it had been an attempted sting.

Sir Jon leaned back in his chair. "Nothing so formal. It was my suggestion, as a way to get closer to Althea and the family. To observe. They got more than they bargained for. Alas, it wasn't enough." He inhaled. "We were also tracking Dorcas. Reece was the middleman to a crooked dealer of stolen collectibles and antiques as an outlet for the Madame Alexander doll. The dealer is now in custody, so her calls after Reece's death have been going to an officer."

I was grateful for this proof that Charlotte had been right to suspect her family of theft—and that we had thwarted them.

"I bet that's what Dorcas and Barnaby were looking for in Reece's desk!" I exclaimed. "The dealer's number. A student saw them search."

Sir Jon nodded. "That tallies with what I know."

"Back to Althea," George said, a worried look on his face. He was still rattled from his close call with the black widow. "They still need evidence that she is the actual poisoner. Right now it's all circumstantial."

"What happened after we left?" Mum asked.

"Yes, I'm still waiting to hear," Aunt Violet put in.

Between the four of us, we told the tale, quoting Ryan's questions and the answers provided by Althea's accusers.

"Good thing it wasn't a live performance," George said. "As it is, they're going to have trouble controlling any bootleg recordings made by the audience."

"It wasn't live?" I exclaimed. "I thought it was. That's why I was so nervous."

"They were recording for broadcast next week," Sir Jon said. "They'll be spending a lot of time in the editing bay, I reckon."

"Or else face lawsuits," George commented. "Damage to Althea's reputation and all that." He thought a moment. "She'll probably sue her family anyway. No doubt ringing up the attorneys as we speak. Bigwigs from St. Hildegard were there." Althea's employer.

"None so litigious as the guilty," Sir Jon said.

George left first, then Kieran, who I caught under the mistletoe on his way out. "Good night, Lady Nightingale," he said.

I curtseyed. "And to you, good sir."

After walking him out, I went up to my room right behind Mum, leaving Sir Jon and Aunt Violet in the kitchen.

In the bedroom, I went to stand by the window, staring down into the dark lane. A clock chimed midnight with a sonorous bong.

Puck jumped onto the bed, kneading his paws. *What are you doing?* his expression said. *This isn't our ritual.*

"Sorry," I told him. "I'm too worked up to sleep." Determination and whiskey sat in my gut like rocks. I could not let Althea literally get away with murder. *A matter of proof,* she'd said so smugly.

Okay. What did we need to prove? First, that Althea had access to the poison.

I pulled out my phone for a refresher. Aconite was derived from monkshood, a plant so poisonous that gloves were strongly recommended to handle it. Probably not a popular pick for the average flower patch. So, unless she'd found a source and purchased the extracted toxin, which would leave an evidence trail, she must have prepared it herself.

She probably also grew the plants. Stumbling upon monkshood in the wild seemed farfetched, although garden escapees did pop up in southern England, the website said.

A thought made me plop down on the foot of the bed, bouncing Puck, who complained with a soft moan. "Sorry, boy."

Arthur Pemberly's garden. Quite large, it contained a veritable riot of plants, bushes, and trees. The perfect place to covertly grow a poisonous plant.

We needed to check it out.

But it was December. How could we find the plant now, when the garden was dormant?

I started a new search, this time for pictures of monkshood in the winter.

After several tries, I was successful. Monkshood produced seedpods. Even if the seeds had dropped, the open pods would still be on the stalks.

A light came on upstairs in the toy shop. Charlotte was home—and awake. I checked my phone for a text from her. No updates yet.

The light winked out again. Remembering our conversation in her flat, I picked up the flashlight I kept by the bed in case of a power outage.

What was the SOS signal? I had to dredge my

memory banks to being a kid sleeping in a tent with my friends. Was it slow, fast, slow or the other way around?

Did it matter? I aimed the flashlight at Charlotte's window, hoping she would see it. If she didn't respond, well, I'd send a text. This was more fun, though.

I went with three fast blinks, followed by three slow, then three fast again. Puck lifted his head. *What are you doing now?* "Not sure, Puck. Not sure."

A moment later, there was return fire from across the lane, a copy of my signal.

She was still awake. I put down the flashlight and picked up my phone. *Up for a visit? Have something to run by you.*

I was still dressed, so, careful not to disturb anyone, I crept downstairs to the kitchen to snag my coat and the Cortina keys. "Oops. Sorry."

Aunt Violet and Sir Jon were snogging under the mistletoe.

Coat in hand, I backed out, closing the door softly. I wasn't even sure they'd noticed me; in fact, I hoped they hadn't. I didn't want to spoil the moment.

◆◆◆

Fifteen minutes later, I was easing the Cortina up the alley, Charlotte in the passenger seat. She'd jumped right on board when I proposed checking out Arthur's garden in the middle of the night.

"This is nuts," I muttered, laughing. "What are we thinking?"

Charlotte stared out the window at the empty sidewalk, watching the wind blow a stray piece of garland along. "We've got to do something. Ryan was this close"—she demonstrated with her hand—"to arresting Tori, Barnaby, and Dorcas. Not that he has proof they tampered with anything. Only that they delivered the poison."

"Tell me about the garden. Who usually took care of it?"

"Grandad. His ritual was to putter around out there between getting home from the toy shop and dinner. He said it was relaxing. That all stopped when he got sick."

"How about Althea?"

"Eh, not really. She liked to sit on the patio and relax. Have him wait on her hand and foot."

I could picture it. The imperious one giving orders. "He was a good man."

"When he did ask her to help, she'd always be worried about breaking a nail or getting her hands dirty." After a beat, she laughed. "Still doing that, isn't she?"

"She is. Except someone had to gather the monkshood and dry it or whatever to make the poison."

"What a witch," Charlotte muttered. Her voice was thick with tears when she said, "We have to catch her, Molly. She killed Grandad."

"We will," I said as firmly as I could. Inside, I was quivering with doubt. What if I was wrong about the garden?

Then we'd try another angle. Althea was guilty, no question. There had to be proof somewhere.

When we reached Arthur's street, Charlotte directed me to the alley behind the house. "We can park there and go in through the back gate." She dug around in her pocket. "I have the keys."

Going in that way would attract less attention, too.

Phronsie and her camera would pick us up if we went in through the front door. Not that we weren't allowed to be here. Charlotte still owned the house, as far as I knew.

"You haven't sold this place, have you?" I asked as we made our way to the gate.

"Nope." Charlotte positioned the key. "It's not even listed yet." She went to put the key in the lock only to have the gate swing inward. "What? It's not locked. I know I locked it."

"Who else has a key?" I followed her into the garden, a frosty expanse of grass hemmed by dark clumps of bushes and trees.

"I don't know." Again, she sounded close to tears. "I had the house locks changed but didn't even think about the gate."

"Understandable. Nothing valuable out here, right?"

"Just a shed full of old tools and patio furniture."

I wondered how to approach finding the dormant monkshood among the sticks and stalks in the perennial beds. Plant by plant? "Any thoughts on how she grew monkshood without it being noticed?"

Charlotte halted, hands on hips as she glanced around. "It's bluish-purple with spiky stems, right? Maybe near other flowers that are similar. Like delphiniums."

"Good thought. Why don't we start there?"

She led me across the grass toward a shed sided with plain boards. It sat among wide flower borders with slate stone walkways, and in the summer, must be stunning.

At the edge of the flower bed, she stopped and switched on a flashlight. "I don't remember exactly where they are."

I crunched through the frozen grass to join her.

"That's fine." Taking out my phone, I brought up a picture of the monkshood seedpods. "That's what we're looking for."

With Charlotte training the light on each plant in turn, I bent close to examine them. We were fortunate no one had cut back the debris this fall. Mum always had in Vermont, as part of putting the garden to bed.

It was tedious work and late and my eyes were dry with strain. I almost missed the telltale pods, little twins open at the top like cones.

"Move the light back," I told Charlotte, gesturing. As she complied, I enlarged the photo on my phone and held it next to the plant. "I'm pretty sure this is it." I reached for the light so I could hold it for her. "You look."

She took my phone and compared it. "By Jove, I think we've got it. What now?"

I swapped the light for my phone. "I'm going to take pictures and send them to Sean Ryan, along with a geo-marker. I have your permission to be here, right?" I knew I did. I was being funny.

"Of course." She pointed. "Those don't." While I took several pictures and composed the text, she swung the light around, checking out the garden. "It's great we found the plant. It's not enough, though. Anyone could have put it there."

Meaning the suspects. "True. We need evidence that Althea handled it." If there were any to be found. I looked at the outbuilding. "Have you been in the shed lately?"

Charlotte studied the building. "Not for a couple of years. Not since Grandad stopped working out here. When I visited, I would bring him a cold drink and watch him putter around."

I walked up the stone path toward the door. "We should look inside." I pressed the latch and pulled. The door creaked open, releasing a gust of earthy air. I turned on my flashlight and scanned the space. A long wood workbench. Shelves crammed with gardening supplies. A stack of lawn chairs and pillows. What was I expecting? A chemistry lab?

The countertop held a collection of tools and plant trays and pots. I could see Arthur standing there, starting seeds or repotting plants.

A pair of pink gloves sat to one side. Very small pink gloves. They wouldn't fit me.

"Come look at these gloves," I called to Charlotte. "Are they yours?"

"Not mine." She grabbed my arm, her eyes wide. "Maybe they're Althea's. She has small hands." She reached for one.

"Don't touch. There might be residue on them." If Althea had used them to handle the monkshood plant, then it was possible. They could also get DNA from inside the gloves, I thought.

A dog barked, shrill and high-pitched. "Phronsie's Wiggles," Charlotte said. "I wonder what he's doing out." Wiggles was a Yorkie, I recalled.

The barking got louder, as if the dog was coming into Arthur's backyard. "Maybe he smells us."

"I'll go take him home." With a sigh, Charlotte went toward the half-open door. Then she stepped back and closed it. "Someone's coming."

"Phronsie?"

"No. She wouldn't be carrying a flashlight." She waved a hand. "Turn yours off."

There was a dusty, cobweb-draped window overlooking the garden and I joined her there. A light was bobbing along the side of the house, the barking right behind it. The person holding the torch turned and waved it. The little dog ducked and darted in the glancing light.

"Get out of here, you mutt!" a woman shouted.

"Althea," Charlotte whispered.

Collecting more poison—or destroying the evidence? I guessed the latter. With the police now laser-focused on the family, she was trying to cover her tracks.

"What should we do if she comes in here?" Charlotte whispered.

"Prevent her from getting those gloves." My heart was pounding despite the fact that we had a right to be on the property and Althea did not. Plain and simple, she scared me. She had murdered two people at least and tried to kill Charlotte.

The bobbing beam went right over to where we'd found the monkshood. She set the flashlight on the ground, the light revealing that she was holding a small spade. Smart to bring her own tool, in case the shed was locked.

She held the spade upright and pressed it down with her foot, grunting. The soil was probably frozen, so good luck with that.

"What should we do?" Charlotte whispered. "We can't let her get away with this."

I took the phone out of my pocket. Contact Sean Ryan? I'd sent the text but of course he hadn't replied. It was the middle of the night.

"You should call the police," I suggested. "You're the homeowner and someone is prowling in your back garden. You've had recent break-ins, tell them."

"Great idea. But she'll hear me talking and run away."

I heard a jingling sound. The dog was back, trotting through the yard toward Althea. "I'll distract her. Soon as you hear my voice, call. Tell them it's urgent."

Charlotte took out her own phone and brought up the keypad. "Okay. I'm ready. Go."

I had no idea what I was doing.

Wiggles was now cavorting about Althea, nipping at her as if he knew she didn't belong there. Brave little fellow.

Glad of the distraction, I turned on my flashlight and stepped out of the shed. I beamed the light directly at Althea, who winced and put up a hand.

"What are you doing here?" I asked. "This is private property." I practically bellowed the words to give Charlotte cover.

"Move that light," Althea ordered. Eyes squeezed shut, she ducked back.

I decided to have mercy and lowered the light a degree. "Doing a little gardening? Isn't it kind of late for that? In December, I mean, not to mention at one A.M." I was speaking nonsense to keep her attention on me.

Her gaze flashed to the plant she'd been trying to dig up. "Arthur told me I could take whatever I wanted. It's a plant that has a lot of meaning for me." She was doing her best to sound pathetic, the grieving widow.

I'll say it had meaning. It was her weapon of choice—and her ticket to life in prison.

"Ah, that's so sweet," I said. "Why don't you go ahead, then? I'm sure Charlotte won't mind."

Her eyes shifted back and forth. "Where is she?"

"Somewhere around. I heard the dog barking so came out to check on it."

Wiggles was now sitting on the grass, tongue hanging out as if he were laughing.

Althea reached for the spade, which was lying on the ground. "If you're sure?"

"I am." While her attention was focused, I slipped my phone out and brought up the photo app. I had turned off the annoying shutter-click sound, right? I hoped so. How about video? That would be even better. I brought up the commands.

She bent over the spade, again trying to force the blade into the ground. Making sure she was fully in the frame, I pressed the button. We were rolling.

"Tough with the frozen ground, huh?" I said.

"Yes, it is," she said, pausing for breath. She brushed her forehead with a gloved hand. "If it wasn't such a special gift, I wouldn't be out here, believe me."

I choked back a response. *Really special for those who had died.*

She started digging again, this time making progress. What now? I couldn't let her actually dig up the monkshood or chop it up with the shovel.

Distraction. "You were right about Charlotte." I lowered my voice as if I didn't want to be heard.

She took the bait. "Oh?" A smile spread across her face. "I knew you were a bright girl, Molly. Some people are just so good at fooling others." She rested her hands on the spade. "Everyone thought she was a sweet girl, so thoughtful and kind. But I always saw behind the facade. She's selfish and greedy. It's all about Charlotte."

Textbook projection. I merely nodded, as if going along with her delusions.

"Greedy?" Charlotte burst out the shed door. "You're one to talk. You only married Grandad because he had money."

Startled, Althea took a step back. "What . . . what are you doing here?"

"I own the place, remember?" Charlotte ran toward Althea. "You are trespassing."

"Don't touch her," I warned. The last thing Charlotte needed was an assault charge.

Picking up on the idea, Althea shouted and fell over. "She pushed me." She grabbed her leg. "My leg is broken. I heard it snap."

"It's all on video, lady," I said, the app still recording. "Don't bother with the dramatics."

Wiggles was now all over Althea, licking her face and sniffing her. "Get him away," she cried. "You nasty little mutt."

"Wiggles? Wiggles, where are you?" Phronsie came trotting into the yard. "I'm sorry. I fell asleep. I didn't mean to leave him outside." She took in the scene. "Oh my. Let me help you." She reached for Althea's hand.

"Don't touch her," I snapped. "She's been handling a toxic plant." There might be residue on her gloves.

Phronsie pulled her hand back. "What? Why?"

"That's a very good question," I said. "Charlotte, are the police coming?"

"They said they'd be right over."

"The police?" Althea tried to scramble to her feet. So much for the broken bone.

We let her struggle—not to be rude. To be safe.

Blue lights flashed out front. "Shall I go meet them and send them back?" Phronsie offered. "Come on, Wiggles."

"Please," Charlotte said. "We'll be right here keeping an eye on this one."

Althea scowled. "No proof. You don't have any proof."

Yes, we did. Althea Winters was going down.

CHAPTER 27

Christmas Eve at last, and an air of expectation lay over the city. Except in the bookshop, where we were absolutely fried. Resting my head on one hand, I could barely lift my coffee cup. How was I going to make it until midnight, when Kieran and I were to attend a service? Caffeine was my only hope.

My phone dinged with a text from Charlotte. *Happy Christmas Eve, Molly.*

Happy Christmas Eve to you. I had a thought. *What are you doing tomorrow?*

Christmas dinner in my garret with Tori. It will be fun. First holiday without Althea. Dorcas and Barnaby have gone to France.

I pictured the pair, seated at a table set with a candle and a meager dinner. Like something out of Dickens.

"Mind if we add two guests tomorrow?" I asked. "Tori and Charlotte are alone."

"More the merrier," Aunt Violet said. "We'll throw a couple more potatoes in the pot."

Come here. We have plenty. Sir Jon and George will be here. Plus my gruesome aunt and her family. We can ignore her. Kieran was spending Christmas with his family, including his brother, Alan, who rarely came to town.

If you're sure? I wasn't hinting . . . I make a mean turkey roll . . .

We're sure. See you at one. Dinner is at two.

Overall, Tori and Charlotte were doing well, recovering from the havoc caused by Althea Winters and her crime spree. Althea was spending the holidays in jail after her high-powered lawyer's request for bail was denied. Apparently, the judge had decided that she was too dangerous. An accurate assessment in my view.

"We had one of our best holiday seasons yet," Aunt Violet said with satisfaction as she studied the figures Mum had tallied. She glanced around at the gaps in the shelves, the curls of ribbon and wrapping paper, the window display, and Santa, still glowing. The cats were curled together in the red velvet chair, a rare sign of detente. "Well done, ladies. Well done."

The shop door opened with a jingle and Sean Ryan walked in. "Good morning, ladies," he said jovially. "I come bearing gifts." He had a brown paper sack in his hand, which he delivered to Mum. "A little Christmas cheer."

Flustered, Mum pulled a bottle of Bailey's Irish Cream out of the bag. "Oh, how nice. Thank you . . . I didn't . . ."

Aunt Violet rose to the occasion with aplomb, picking up a book, a new collection of Agatha Christie short stories, and handing it to Sean. "Happy Christmas to our favorite detective." She slid a glance at me. "After Molly."

"*Midwinter Murder,*" he said, studying the cover. "Perfect."

"We'll try not to get involved in any," I joked. "I'm ready for a break." After a pause, I asked, "Is this an official visit?"

He shook his head. "Not today. We've got most of the loose ends wrapped up and now we wait for trial."

"No confession, huh?" Not that I really expected Althea to confess. She probably relished the drama of a court case, with all eyes on her. It would be a media sensation.

"Afraid not." His smile was wry. "It will be a fight to the finish. As is her right," he added.

A look of determination passed over Mum's face, and with a sudden move, she pushed back from the desk, a look of determination on her face. "Cup of tea, Sean?"

He brightened. "I'd love one." As he followed her to the kitchen, he said, "Actually, I have a question for you. Are you free New Year's Eve? I've got . . ."

Aunt Violet turned to me and winked. "I think that mistletoe might be about to get another workout."

A bittersweet moment for sure. My bereaved mother was finally moving on, it seemed. Before he died, Dad had made her promise to keep living, to be open to the possibility of a new relationship. If she wanted to date Sean Ryan, who was a very good guy, then I was all for it.

⁂

A simple stone chapel, plain wooden chairs, scores of candles, and the scent of evergreens and melting wax: the Leper Chapel was magical tonight.

Voices rose together in a carol, the sound amplified by the arched ceiling. "I love this," I whispered to Kieran after the song ended, the congregation shuffling in expectation of the service's start. He smiled at me. "Thought you might."

It was chilly, and I huddled close to his shoulder through the readings, more carols, and the dispensation of communion. There were better known, more elaborate celebrations around the city, namely in the larger churches with their incredible choirs, but this was perfect, the season of goodwill distilled to basic elements.

Uplifted and happy, I slid my arm through his as we filed out of the church. The night was overcast, clouds reflecting the city glow, and we could see our breath.

"What's next?" I asked, remembering he'd said there was a surprise. I'd pictured hot toddies at a pub while we exchanged gifts. Or maybe a late-night snack at his place.

"You'll see," he said, guiding us toward the sidewalk. He must have sensed me staring at him because he laughed. "You're not going to figure it out, so don't even try. Even if you are a great detective."

I pretended to pout. "Okay. I'll wait."

We set off in the Land Rover, retracing our route. Then, to my surprise, he turned down an obscure side street, rows of terraces on both sides. Now I was really puzzled.

At the end, facing the river, was a boathouse. An idea began to form. Seriously? At night in winter?

"This is our stop," Kieran said, pulling into a parking space. "Hop out."

He went around and opened the lift gate. "Here." He handed me a picnic basket, then gathered a pile of folded tartan blankets.

I was starting to get it now but I kept quiet as we walked around the boathouse and onto the dock. A figure standing there turned to greet us. "Hello. You made it."

As we drew closer, I realized I'd met him. "Fergus." The last piece fell into place.

"That's me." He took a closer look. "I recognize you. How've you been?"

"Great. Yourself?" I'd met Fergus in May, when he'd been my punt chauffeur.

"Can't complain." He turned to Kieran. "Ready?"

"We are." Kieran handed him the blankets and Fergus loaded them in a punt. He took the picnic basket from me and placed it inside, then helped me climb aboard.

"A punt ride on Christmas Eve?" I exclaimed. "I never would have guessed."

"Christmas Day, actually," Fergus said. He waited for Kieran to settle in beside me, blankets both around and over our laps before picking up the pole.

Black water rippled against the sides of the craft as we set off down the river. I was perfectly toasty in our nest despite the cool breeze caused by our movement.

"Toddy?" Kieran flipped open the basket and took out a thermos. With my help, he filled two cups. There was a charcuterie assortment in a container, with crackers and grapes on the side, and we nibbled between sips.

I gasped in disbelief. "You've got to be kidding." Snowflakes had started to fall as we approached the lacy stone Bridge of Sighs, one of Cambridge's most beautiful structures. "Did you arrange this?"

Kieran grinned. "Of course. You can order weather online, don't you know." He put his arm around me and squeezed. "Glad you like my surprise."

"I love it." This night would be one to remember.

We skimmed under the bridge and then past some of the most notable colleges, lights illuminating the towers and battlements. The paths along the banks were empty, those still in residence tucked in for the night. Or what was left of it.

When we reached Queens' College, Fergus turned the punt around for the journey back to our vehicle. "You still doing okay?" Kieran asked.

I moved my bum to a more comfortable spot, rearranging the blanket. "I'm great. I want to keep going forever." All of life, the good and the difficult, awaited us on shore. Out here, I could pretend that Kieran and I were in our own little world. With Fergus. "How are you doing, Fergus?"

He glanced over his shoulder. "Doing fine, doing fine. I enjoy punting at night. No crazy tourists and students to watch out for."

"I hear you," Kieran said. "Thanks again for taking us out."

"No problem." Fergus fell silent, concentrating on his task.

We were passing back under the Bridge of Sighs when Kieran kissed me, slow and deep and sweet. He pulled back a little and stared into my eyes.

My heart began to pound. Not that my pulse wasn't already racing. All he had to do was touch me and my insides melted, gooey and warm.

"I love you," he said. He shifted a little, his gaze slipping away. "I've been wanting to say that for a while. I know it's way too early . . . we've only been dating six months . . ."

I touched his cheek, late-night stubble grazing my fingers, and turned his face back to me. Looking him dead in the eye, I said, "I love you, too."

My stomach did a cartwheel when I heard the words out loud. I'd certainly thought it more than once, but actually voicing them was like stepping off a cliff. *Oops.* He'd said it first, I reminded myself.

He said I love you.

His arms went around me in a crushing hug and we stayed like that the rest of the way, glued together, our hearts beating fast, kissing now and then. As we glided along, black water gently rippling, the silent city glittered behind a veil of falling snow. It had never been more beautiful.

CHAPTER 28

Exhausted yet charged up after only a few hours of sleep, I staggered into the kitchen. "Merry Christmas."

"Merry Christmas," Mum and Aunt Violet chorused. Mum was wrist-deep in a turkey while Aunt Violet sat in her chair, cup of tea in hand. "What time did you get in?" Mum asked.

"Around four." I turned the kettle on. As I moved, the charm bracelet Kieran had given me slid on my wrist. He'd loved the miniature Burt Randle book of Kipling's poetry I'd given him, a nice collector's item. What do you get a guy who basically has everything? "Kieran and I went punting."

"In this weather?" Aunt Violet tutted. "You *are* brave."

"It was gorgeous." I scooped grounds into the French press. *He loves me.* "We had a late-night picnic on the water. It even snowed." I glanced out the window. A dusting of the white stuff lay on the ground, which meant it was still cold. "How are the roads, do you know?" Maybe my aunt and uncle wouldn't be able to get here.

"Fine, I'm sure," Aunt Violet said. "Can you refill the

teapot, please?" She noticed my bracelet. "What's that you're wearing?"

I came over to show her. "It's a charm bracelet. Only one charm so far." It was a bicycle that looked exactly like Belinda, my turquoise cruiser. "From Kieran."

"It's lovely." She yawned and as she covered her mouth, something sparkled on her hand.

"What is that?" I took her hand and studied the ring, a gorgeous, marquise-set diamond. "Aunt Violet. You've been holding out on us."

A smile broke across her face. "We're engaged." She laughed softly. "I know it's slightly ridiculous at our age . . ."

"No, it isn't." I looked at Mum. "Did you know?"

Mum spooned stuffing into the turkey. "Found out this morning. It's wonderful news."

"First Daisy and now you." The kettle was boiling so I dashed to turn off the gas. "It's a season for love." And murder. And awful relatives. Oh well. With Charlotte and Tori here, plus Sir Jon and George, we'd outnumber them.

Although my cousin Charlie was okay. It wasn't his fault he had an awful mother.

"After I get this in the oven, we'll do gifts," Mum said. She pointed to a basket holding a cloth. "Warm croissants from the French bakery."

Croissants were one of our family traditions. Mum made them herself when we couldn't buy good ones in Vermont. While my coffee steeped, I nibbled on one, so tasty it didn't need any additions.

The turkey went in, fresh tea was poured, my coffee got milk, and we sat to unwrap.

They made me do mine first. Aunt Violet had made me a soft, fluffy sweater that would look perfect with a skirt or dressy pants. "I never saw you working on this," I said, holding it up. "It's gorgeous."

"I knitted it up in my bedroom," she said, pleased. "Wouldn't be much of a surprise if I was sitting right here, would it?"

Mum had given me a pair of black Chelsea boots, ankle-high with thick soles. "I love them." I slipped my feet inside, admiring how they looked.

"I remember those," Aunt Violet said. "They were all the rage when I was at university."

"What's old is new again." Still wearing the boots, I retrieved packages from under the tree. Aunt Violet got a very large box and Mum the one containing Sasha. I couldn't wait for her to open it.

Aunt Violet loved the yarn. "Thank you, Molly. How did you know?" She winked.

Mum was taking her time opening the gift. "Tear it off," I jibed. She'd always been careful not to damage the paper. To prolong the reveal, more like. I was a ripper.

I'd used an innocuous shoebox so once unwrapped, she still had no clue. She removed the lid, then pushed aside layers of tissue. Then she stared. "Molly." Almost reverently, she lifted the doll from its nest. "She's beautiful."

If I'd had a tail, it would be wagging, I was so pleased at her response. "Charlotte helped me find her."

Mum turned the doll, tweaking the skirt, smoothing her hair. "She's exactly like mine."

"I hoped so." I went over and gave her a kiss. "So glad you like her."

She squeezed my hand. "You're so much like your father. Thoughtful and kind."

That almost made me cry, so naturally I had to

lighten the moment. "I don't want you playing with dolls when you should be doing your chores." That was also Dad.

We all laughed. "Speaking of chores, who is going to peel the potatoes?" Mum asked.

◆◆

"Ho, ho, ho, Merry Christmas," George said as he came through the back door, Sir Jon right behind him. Both were carrying paper sacks holding liquor and wine. George stamped his feet on the rug. "How is everyone?" Sir Jon slipped by to greet Aunt Violet with a kiss.

"We're doing well, kind sir. Yourself?" I was putting the finishing touches on the long table, which I'd set with red-and-green plaid placemats, good silver and crystal glasses, and centerpieces of holly and evergreens.

"Still relieved after my narrow escape." George shuddered a trifle dramatically. "Is the black widow still safely behind bars?"

"She sure is." I folded the last napkin and tucked it under a fork. "By the way, Charlotte and Tori will be joining us. They were both going to be alone."

"We can't have that," George grumbled. No doubt he would take them under his wing, as he had us. Day or night, he was there to help.

I heard someone knocking out in the bookshop. "I bet that's them now." They probably hadn't realized they could come through the alley and the back garden, as George and Sir Jon had.

Puck accompanied me as I hurried to unlock the door. Both cats had been hanging around the kitchen, eager for a taste of turkey. "Merry Christmas," I said, opening the door. "Quick, come in. It's frigid out there."

I took a closer look at Tori, who looked like she'd been crying. "What's wrong?"

Puck was winding around Tori's ankles and she bent to pat him. "I did something awful," she muttered.

"What?" I looked to Charlotte for a clue. And a cue.

"I told her it's okay," Charlotte said. "I'm not holding a grudge."

I spoke to Tori's hat, her face hidden as she focused on the cat. "You don't have to tell me. It's none of my business."

She looked up. "Yeah, I do." She gave Puck a last pat and stood. "I'm the one who rearranged things in the dollhouse. And blocked the flat door." Sadness flashed in her eyes. "Reece helped me move the cabinet."

"Why did you do that, Tori? It really freaked me out." A flash of shock washed over me. Had we been wrong about Althea? Or rather, had Tori been her accomplice?

Tori bit at her bottom lip. "I wanted to scare Charlotte. Althea had me convinced that she cheated the family out of the inheritance." Her gaze dropped. "I also wanted her to know that we were going inside the shop, that she couldn't keep us out."

"I agree, you made a few bad judgment calls," I finally said. "It's Charlotte's decision how this affects your relationship going forward."

Charlotte slung an arm around her cousin's shoulders. "I say we put it behind us. You would never have done any of that without Althea manipulating you."

Tears welled in Tori's eyes. "Are you sure? I wish I could just start over."

"You can," Charlotte said. "Right now."

Laughter and chatter drifted from the kitchen, and I guessed the others were enjoying a cup of good cheer.

"Let's go join the party," I said. "You can leave your coats in the back hall."

Charlotte handed me a gift bag. "Merry Christmas."

"Thank you." I peeked inside to see two boxes of chocolates from Charbonnel et Walker, chocolatiers to the queen. "Awesome. What a treat."

We entered the kitchen to find that Uncle Chris, Aunt Janice, and Charlie had just arrived. Charlie smiled at my friends, probably glad he wasn't the only young person in the room—besides me, of course.

As they edged toward him to say hello, my attention was caught by Janice, who was holding a package out to my mother. "This is for you." Her cheeks were beet red and her usually well-groomed hair was disheveled, as if she'd been running her hands through it.

Mum took the package with a frown. "You didn't have to bring a gift. I told Chris—"

Janice's hands twisted together. "It was my idea. Please, open it."

"All right." Mum glanced around to check if anyone minded, then began to tug at the paper. No neat un-wrapping this time, I noticed, smiling.

Under the paper was a shoebox. Mum gasped when she opened the lid. "My doll. Where did you get this?" Her eyes flashed with surprise and anger.

"I had it all along," Janice mumbled, her fingers clasped so tightly I thought she might break a bone. "I always wanted a Sasha and I couldn't . . . resist."

Mum stared at her sister-in-law and I could tell she was struggling not to lose her temper. Not only had my aunt nosed around in my mother's belongings, she'd helped herself to her most cherished possession. Why? Out of spite? Or maybe it was jealousy. My aunt was a strange one.

"I'm really sorry." Janice's expression was pleading.

In a sudden move, Mum thrust the box at me, then stepped forward and gave Janice a cautious hug. "Thank you. I know that wasn't easy and I appreciate it."

Janice's nod was abrupt. "You're welcome, Nina." She lifted her chin. "We brought the Pimm's, Christmas crackers, and mince pies as you requested."

"Wonderful." Mum turned to George and Sir Jon. "Can you please do the honors? I'd like to do a toast before we eat."

General chatter and laughter broke out as George mixed the drinks. Aunt Violet, assisted by Sir Jon, pulled the golden-brown turkey out of the oven and placed it aside to rest before carving. Brussels sprouts, roasted potatoes and carrots, gravy, and cranberry sauce completed the main course. I put the Sasha doll, which was an almost exact duplicate of the one I'd bought, under the tree with the other gifts.

Once everyone had a drink in hand, Sir Jon took the floor. "First, I'd like to announce something really wonderful. Violet Marlowe has finally agreed to marry me." He put an arm around my aunt and drew her close.

"Hear, hear," George said heartily while the rest of us cheered and called out congratulations.

"Such good news," Janice said effusively. "Is there a date set?"

Sir Jon looked to Aunt Violet for an answer. "We're getting married in June," she said.

We'd need to make sure they didn't pick the same date as Daisy and Tim. What fun, two weddings to look forward to. Daisy was with Tim's family for Christmas and I looked forward to her report later.

"I want a big party," Aunt Violet said. "We're going to rock Cambridge."

"Literally, with a reprise of my old band," Sir Jon added. We all cheered again. Then he lifted his glass and we all quieted. "'Be blest with health, and peace, and sweet content.' To quote Robert Burns."

"'Be blest with health, and peace, and sweet content,'" we echoed before drinking.

"Now let's eat!" Charlie cried, and we all laughed.